D0114194

NIGHT LIGHT

NIGHT LIGHT

Stories of Aging

Edited by Constance Rooke

Toronto
OXFORD UNIVERSITY PRESS
1986

In memory of
JUNE BARROWS

CANADIAN CATALOGUING IN PUBLICATION DATA
Main entry under title:
Night light : stories of aging
ISBN 0-19-540552-8
1. Aging - Fiction. 2. Old age - Fiction.
3. Short stories. I. Rooke, Constance, 1942-
PN6120.95.05N53 1986 823'.01'08354 C86-094191-4

© Oxford University Press 1986
OXFORD is a trademark of Oxford University Press
1 2 3 4 - 9 8 7 6
Printed in Canada by Webcom Limited

Contents

Acknowledgements

SAUL BELLOW. "Leaving the Yellow House" from *Mosby's Memoirs and Other Stories*, by Saul Bellow. Copyright © 1957 by Saul Bellow, renewed © 1985 by Saul Bellow. First published in *Esquire Magazine*. Reprinted by permission of Viking Penguin, Inc. PAUL BOWLES. "The Scorpion" copyright © 1950 by Paul Bowles. Reprinted from *The Collected Stories of Paul Bowles* with the permission of Black Sparrow Press. JOHN CHEEVER. "The World of Apples" copyright © 1966 by John Cheever. Reprinted from *The World of Apples*, by John Cheever, by permission of Alfred A. Knopf, Inc. MAVIS GALLANT. "Irina" from *From the Fifteenth District* by Mavis Gallant. Reprinted by permission of Georges Borchardt, Inc. and the author. Copyright © 1979 by Mavis Gallant. Originally appeared in *The New Yorker*. DORIS LESSING. "An Old Woman and Her Cat" from *The Story of a Non-Marrying Man* by Doris Lessing. Copyright © 1972 Doris Lessing. Reprinted by permission of Jonathan Clowes Ltd., London, on behalf of the Doris Lessing Trust. ALICE MUNRO. "Spelling" from *Who Do You Think You Are?* by Alice Munro. Reprinted by permission of Macmillan of Canada, A Division of Canada Publishing Corporation. TILLIE OLSEN. "Tell Me A Riddle" excerpted from the book *Tell Me a Riddle* by Tillie Olsen. Copyright © 1956, 1957, 1960, 1961 by Tillie Olsen. Reprinted by permission of Delacorte Press/Seymour Lawrence. MICHAEL ONDAATJE. "The Passions of Lalla" from *Running in the Family* by Michael Ondaatje. Used by permission of the author. ISAAC BASHEVIS SINGER. "Old Love" from *Passions* by Isaac Bashevis Singer. Copyright © 1975 by Isaac Bashevis Singer. Originally appeared in *The New Yorker*. Reprinted by permission of Farrar, Straus and Grioux, Inc. ELIZABETH TAYLOR. "Mice and Birds and Boy" by Elizabeth Taylor from *A Dedicated Man*. Copyright © 1965 by Elizabeth Taylor. Reprinted by permission of Brandt & Brandt Literary Agents Inc. GUY VANDERHAEGHE. "Dancing Bear" from *Man Descending* © 1982 by Guy Vanderhaeghe. Reprinted by permission of Macmillan of Canada, A Division of Canada Publishing Corporation. EUDORA WELTY. "A Worn Path". Copyright 1941, 1969 by Eudora Welty. Reprinted from her volume *A Curtain of Green and Other Stories* by permission of Harcourt Brace Jovanovich, Inc.

Introduction

Like most projects, this anthology has more than one beginning. The earliest is a question that I asked my grandmother when I was ten: "Do you feel like the same person, Grandmama, even though you're old?" Her answer was to throw back her head and laugh, as if she had been waiting for just that brazen inquiry, as if she were pleased that it had come at last from me. And she told a story about being in a courthouse, how she was six years old and dressed in plaid satin, waiting for her father. There were grand mirrors all around, reaching to the high, garlanded ceiling of the lobby. "I looked for a long time, at myself. Then I put my ten stretched-out fingers to the glass, and ten more sprouted from my fingertips. The traffic on that bridge has been steady ever since." As she pronounced that last sentence, Grandmama turned her celebrated hypnotic gaze on me. At six, she had the will to persevere, to create an extraordinary and indelible character; at sixty, when she directed part of her energy across the storyteller's bridge to me, my grandmother had thirty years still to go of solitary communion with that child in plaid.

I had asked her to tell me a riddle. The one she told had something to do with the mask of old age, with representation by a face on which the lines of growth are truly etched—and falsely, because by a consummate irony, they spell our decline. And it had to do with internal consistency, or continuity, despite all outer changes. But there was another dimension to my grandmother's riddle. She raised her bridge, she turned it, and she gave me access to herself in a shapely line: "The traffic on that bridge has been steady ever since." Surely I would not have been so affected by a lesser phrase? This encounter with my grandmother was in its own way a literary experience; literature itself is a riddle, since it requires us to think long and hard and roundabout, if we would tease its meaning out. Always, its secret concerns the human heart. Always, it joins us to another even as it admits the irreducible solitude in which we read and live.

"Tell me a riddle, Grandma": but in Tillie Olsen's story, Eva must at first decline. "*I know no riddles,*" she says. Eva has been "forced to live to the rhythms of others" for too long; now she must "live within," to accomplish the "journey to the self" before her life is over. As she dies, her children think: "Too late to ask: and what did you learn with your living, Mother, and what do we need to know?" Her answer has been partly given in the quotations, the flood of other people's stainless words, that Eva ("Mrs. Philosopher," "Mrs. Babbler") can no longer contain. John Cheever's old laureate in "The World of Apples" completes his pilgrimage in a similar manner, as he cries out, "God bless Walt Whitman. God bless Hart Crane. God bless Dylan Thomas. God bless William Faulkner, Scott Fitzgerald, and especially Ernest Hemingway." In Alice Munro's "Spelling," an ancient woman bends the last of "all her energy to master" the spelling of words supplied her; thus does she "c-e-l-e-b-r-a-t-e," through that most rudimentary power of language, "a parade of private visitors, not over yet."

The riddle told by Tillie Olsen's story is that each of us must take the journey alone—Eva cannot, therefore, supply her children with a neatly packaged answer; yet we can pass our impressions along, trusting in "the fossil memory" and the power of metamorphosis, believing that "knowledge was holy," that "life may be hated or wearied of, but never despised." Clearly we want something of what Eva's husband yearns to "package" for the children: "*that joyous certainty, that sense of mattering, of moving and being moved, of being one and indivisible with the great of the past, with all that freed and ennobled man*." We get something of that sense from literature. And we may bolster it through the recognition that others have found value in the work we care about most deeply. (Thus, it seems intolerable that Eva should have been deprived of the opportunity to celebrate Chekhov in a "reading circle.")

I can remember an interview in which Alice Munro was asked to name her favorite stories, those she would include in an ideal anthology—and the rush of pleasure I felt when she gave "Tell Me a Riddle" as the one indispensable entry. That was another of the beginnings of *Night Light*, for it coincided with the realization that many of the contemporary stories and poems and novels I was recommending to others were concerned with old age. I began to feel that a special radiance, an intensity resulting from the proximity to darkness, might characterize a good deal of the literature of old age. I thought, for instance, of certain luminous poems by Canadian women, especially P.K. Page; of Paul Scott's masterpiece, *Staying On*; of *The Stone Angel*, which is certainly Margaret Laurence's greatest book; of Yasunari Kawabata's *House of the Sleeping Beauties*; and of Australian novels like Patrick White's *The Eye of the Storm* and *Riders in the Chariot*, Jessica Anderson's *Tirra Lirra by the River*, and David Malouf's *An Imaginary Life*. And finally, I thought how many of the stories I would place in my own ideal anthology would also work for an anthology of stories on aging.

Simone de Beauvoir remarks with some bitterness in *The Coming of Age* that "if an old man is dealt with in his subjective aspect he is not a good hero for a novel; he is finished, set, with no hope, no development to be looked for . . . nothing that can happen to him is of any importance." In fact, the old person is an especially useful protagonist since he or she makes available to the writer nearly the whole span of a life history—as opposed to just that truncated, glibly predictive bit before the heroine decides whom to marry. The old person picks up the human story at a pivotal and richly dramatic point, when the evaluation of life seems most urgent, and when the question of what comes next is most poignant. Very often, a fiction writer dealing with an elderly protagonist will exploit both sides of that pivot, casting the narrative as a life review and using the character's death as a literary climax. Yet the writer also achieves immediacy by depicting a character's present life. And we as readers enter that present world of the elderly as we always enter fiction, to relish it or to pray for amelioration.

What happens to old people—in fiction and out of it—has an importance that is denied only by those who would discount the humanity of the old in order to exempt themselves from the aging process. Writers who take the fictional journey into old age, anticipating or reflecting their own life course, remind us of that importance; they remove an illusory border, which would separate old people from something called society, even as they show how stubbornly that border is defended. The need to assert human dignity, to discover what Simone de Beauvoir calls the "subjective aspect" behind the mask of old age, makes the literature of old age affirmative even when the circumstances that surround the elderly protagonist—including poverty, illness, and loneliness—are most dark.

This paradox of exclusion, when old age is an essential part of the human story, may be illuminated if we consider the life cycle as a circle. Significantly, the literature of old age often employs circular structures and images; in "Tell Me a Riddle," for instance, we find the "circular sea" upon which Eva rides her "steerage ship of memory." We enter the circle at birth, having come from a state of potentiality. Our purpose in life is to grow, to assume an individual shape. At the moment of death, the figure we have drawn completes itself. We return to the unknown, departing the particular for the universal, and in that sense may be said to leave the circle at our point of entry. This description of the life story assumes a continuous circle of narration in which old age is something more than an epilogue; it assumes that the process of self-actualization is the task of a lifetime.

Yet the circle may also be seen through a glass darkly, as an image of futility. Eva battles against this spectre of endless repetition, and against any segmentation of the human circle, with her most vital cry: "This to teach. To smash all ghettos that divide man—not to go back, not to go back—this to teach." At the same time, she must labor under the shadow of Sisyphus, that "ancient man who fought to heights a great rock that crashed back down eternally." A dark reading of the circle expresses our fear that humankind does not progress, but the design of a single life may also appear circular in this darker sense if we consider that old age returns us to the powerlessness of childhood. Thus do the old find themselves consigned to a ghetto once more. Thus do we mock our own implicit circularity.

Commonly, we regard the first phase of the life cycle (childhood and youth) as a preparation for life in society. The middle phase (the prime of life) allows participation in society and the exercise of our developed powers. The last phase (old age) involves leaving the social circle, or disengagement. This pattern, which in theory would deny to children and the elderly the right of participation in society, cannot be excused in practice. Nor can it be reconciled conceptually with a continuous circle of "narration," the pattern of self-actualization enacted over a lifetime, except by a radical shift.

The task of our first life phase is sometimes given as the development of ego; this notion is congruent with the progression from inchoate infancy to a carefully designed and self-assured maturity. The task of old age is sometimes given as the transcendence of ego, which may be translated as a willingness to let go of social power. It is easy enough to detect a vested interest in the allocation of these tasks. The process may be recommended as spiritually advantageous for the old, when its egotistical motive is simply to reduce clutter (or competition) in the circle. Yet it remains a possibility that disengagement will benefit the old. If we shift our gaze, to regard that singular achieved ego as a failure, as only a fractional representation of what the human being ought to be, then disengagement or the transcendence of ego will seem a vital task. Wholeness, indeed, may require a multiplicity of selves; and ego may be an impediment to growth. Less radically, we may say that some departure from accustomed behaviors will assist the completion of the human figure.

As might be supposed from their proximity on the circular model, stories about old people generally include an encounter with the Child. Often the child is within, standing at the threshold of a dream that the elderly protagonist requires in order to complete his course. In ''The World of Apples,'' for instance, Bascomb recalls suddenly his boyhood vision of an old man, naked and ''bellowing with joy'' as he plunges beneath an icy waterfall. Recognizing the old man as his father, the poet repeats in his own old age this extraordinary gesture of affirmation. And this plunge cleanses his body as it does his spirit, of the obscenities which had threatened to destroy his faith in life. The old woman of Paul Bowles' parable, ''The Scorpion,'' has a dream in which as a little girl she can kiss and consume the scorpion of death. In ''Tell Me a Riddle,'' Eva returns imaginatively on her last day to the road on which she ''first heard music.'' She is a little girl again, dancing in spite of poverty to the sound of joy. In Guy Vanderhaeghe's ''Dancing Bear,'' Dieter journeys in memory to a sort of crossroad where as a child he had learned that there is ''yes, well, sometimes cruelty too.'' His task as an old man will be to recover that child's lost innocence, and indeed to surpass the child, by asserting ''innocence'' once more despite long knowledge of life's cruelty.

In a lively marketplace, where all the possibilities of life seem to open out before him, Dieter sees a bear being led by the nose. Implicitly, the child foresees his adult fate in this tableau. Although the dancing bear performs wearily, its arms are ''opened in a wide, charitable manner''; society has scorned, mistreated, and constrained the bear, which would forgive and embrace it still. His performance winds down, and the crowd leaves. In his old age, Dieter has become that bear, that ''man in masquerade.'' And as the bear rebels, dancing in the face of those ''fleeing backs,'' so Dieter locks out his housekeeper. As the bear is beaten by his master, so Dieter's "master" exercises her cruelty once more; Mrs. Hax's anticipated blow to Dieter's head coincides through an authorial pun with the "stroke" that kills him. But in that last moment "appearances deceive," for he does *not* mistake Mrs. Hax for the dancing bear, "whose warm embrace he desired above all"; rather, he sees through the masquerade, embracing her in a "charitable manner" as his fellow bear, his fellow human creature. In this last gesture of his old age Dieter accomplishes all that he ran away from as a child.

In Elizabeth Taylor's "Mice and Birds and Boy," we observe the rise and fall of a lonely old woman's friendship with a child. Mrs. May exists in a kind of palimpsest, on which the memories of her childhood are written more vividly than those of either her "vague marriage" or her present reality. She needs William partly because she wants to live in the world; she wants him to tell her about it and is happy to exchange tales of her "different world" for the peculiarly fragmentary data that William offers. The child is at first sorry to see how badly the world treats his friend. He had supposed, for instance, that only children could be stared at so rudely. But soon he deserts her as well. As his father observes, William has "lost innocence," which is a kind of "simple vision."

With Mavis Gallant's "Irina," we come to what seems a very different perspective upon the relationship of youth and age. Irina is not lonely, and she is not pleased by the arrival of her grandson. Like Eva, she is irritated by the puerile assumption of her children that "what she craved now was a symbol of innocent, continuing life." Irina has her own urgent business, a quest on which she may embark only when husband and children are put aside. Nor is Irina especially impressed by the innocence of children. They are too likely to be harboring a Waffen-S.S. emblem in a pocket. Innocence, if it is not incipient guilt, is in another sense ignorance. "If people can be given numbers, like marks in school," Irina suggests, "then children are zero." The implication is not only that children are at the start of life, but that so far they are failing—in contrast to Mr. Aiken and herself, to whom we willingly grant top marks.

Yet Irina does enjoy her grandson's visit. They get on splendidly, since she is prepared to grant his essential independence. Taylor's Mrs. May, despite the intensity of her need for William, is also able to release the child: "He was like a most beloved caged bird that she has set at liberty. She felt regret and yet a sense of triumph, seeing him go.'' Riri too is ''flying'' on dream skis in Gallant's transcendent close. This fact is conveyed by a remote authorial voice, since Irina has scrupulously distanced herself from the content of the child's dream; but it seems very like a symbol of ''innocent, continuing life'' after all. In both William and Riri, innocence has begun to fade; the cruelty of labels—as Mrs. May becomes ''only an old witch I know''—and of ghettos overtakes it. It is the task of the elderly protagonist to see beyond that, to restore our simple vision. Thus, Irina's own quest for ''clarity'' is accomplished in the ''sunny icicle brightness'' of Riri's dream.

Gallant's heroine has an appeal for Riri that resembles in a muted way the attraction of Michael Ondaatje's Lalla for all of those children who ''flocked'' to her like birds, and were given stilts so that they could play up high. Like Irina, the extraordinary Lalla is ''far too busy with her own life'' and far too passionate about her belief in freedom to inhibit anyone else. Lalla, however, has all her life been a free spirit. The figure she describes in actuality is as continuous and as surreal as the flood that carries her away at the end of the story. ''The Passions of Lalla,'' it may be felt, is not strictly a story about old age; it is a fiction like Flaubert's ''Un Coeur Simple,'' in which the heroine's life span appears as a radiant and seamless whole. Yet old age is ''the phase when Lalla is remembered best,'' and the time when ''her freedom accelerated.''

Phoenix Jackson, in Eudora Welty's ''A Worn Path,'' has what Cheever's Bascomb covets as life's crowning glory; he calls it ''an organic peace of mind.'' The path old Phoenix takes, like her indomitable character, was completed long ago. She is herself, and she does not need to journey any further for that purpose; although she is ''bound to go on [her] way,'' she ''doesn't come for herself.'' Rather, she travels the circular path out of love for her grandson, who sounds strangely like Phoenix: ''We is the only two left in the world. He suffer and it don't seem to put him back at all. He got a sweet look. He going to last.'' Images of heaven suggest the nature of her spiritual achievement: ''a pearly cloud of mistletoe,'' a slice of marble cake brought to Phoenix in a dream by a heavenly Child, and in the office at the top of the stairs, ''nailed [like Christ] up on the wall the document that had been stamped with the gold seal and framed in the gold frame, which matched the dream that was hung up in her own head.'' Phoenix and her ''child'' and Christ appear as one and come together in the image of the windmill (a cross and a circle) that Phoenix will take home as a Christmas present for the child.

Doris Lessing says of Hetty in "An Old Woman and Her Cat" that "the older she got, this disreputable old tramp, the more there strengthened in her a quality of fierce, demanding childishness." "Part gypsy," she becomes more gypsy-like as she ages. She loves wild costumes and the clamor of street trading. As a kind of outlaw, she may remind us of Ondaatje's much more privileged, flower-stealing Lalla: both women enjoy the bustle of a social world, and neither will submit to being categorized or regimented by it. Hetty may also recall Taylor's Mrs. May, who was "really very dirty" and would mimic society's disdain to chide her parrot (". . . want must be your master, Bertha") in terms that are applicable to herself. Similarly, Hetty addresses her companion: "What do you think you are, a wild cat? Decent cats don't eat dirty birds. Only those old gypsies eat wild birds." And finally, Hetty's loyalty to her cat, together with our sense that deprivation and social injustice cannot touch the old woman's spirit, may cause us to link Hetty with Phoenix Jackson.

Hetty's cat takes care of her as well, in a form she values: the warmth of his body and pigeons he has caught himself. (Lessing handles this ironic paradigm with respect for both the old woman and her cat, and without a trace of sentimentality.) The alternative to such care would seem to be "the authorities," epitomized here by the "corpse removers" who roam through London's derelict buildings; these ghoulish figures recall others who take Hetty's friends off to die in an institution. Such women are regarded by the housing officer as "lucky to get a place in this 'Home,' even if it was—and he knew and deplored the fact—an institution in which the old were treated like naughty and dimwitted children until they had the good fortune to die." Lessing shows us that a *cat* could do a better job of it, better too than Hetty's "good daughter," whose last gesture was a Christmas card four years back.

The vital question of who shall care for the aged, when they can no longer manage for themselves, is of course addressed by many of the stories collected here. We see Munro's Rose imagining that she will take on the job of looking after Flo, and so prove her moral fiber; and we see how quickly that fancy dies. Flo herself, in any case, exhibits a "fierce unwillingness to be the object of anybody's rescue." It is apparent that with her "peculiar headgear"—a wig that looks like a dead squirrel, recalling the hair of old women in which "a nest of baby mouse skeletons" might be found—Flo is indeed "going off the track." But when the time comes for Flo to complete the circle, she concentrates on that like a woman going into labor: "death moving in her like a child." Rose wants badly to join Flo in a compatible mental space, and is delighted when Flo sees that the wig looks like a squirrel. They can laugh together in a shared reality. But that moment passes. And the story ends with Flo still in the Home, thinking of home and believing that all she has lost—the treasured "gall" of her life—is safe there, awaiting her return.

The financial circumstances of the characters assembled here vary radically. At one end of the spectrum we have the poverty of Phoenix Jackson or Lessing's heroine; at the other, the affluence of Cheever's Bascomb or of Harry Bendiner in I.B. Singer's "Old Love." Somewhere in the middle are characters like Hattie of Saul Bellow's "Leaving the Yellow House." We learn as we read these stories just how important money can be to the amelioration of the hardships of old age. Even in the case of Hattie, we see how her options are reduced by a shortage of cash: she can sign over her house in exchange for private help, or go to an institution, or resort to her brother's care—in return for which she will have to become "small-mouthed" and listen to the Bible before breakfast. (To spend one's last precious time in the company of people who are "not her kind" seems a special hardship to Hattie; it is an aspect of Dieter's humiliation in "Dancing Bear" as well.) But there are also hardships—the body's ills, the failure of memory, the loss of a beloved mate—that money cannot touch.

Implicit in many of these stories is an opposition between society as an "established" thing (which offers roles and an illusion of permanence) and nature as a condition of flux. The image of the house is interesting in this respect. Human beings require shelter from nature, as they require a stable place within society; and the house provides both. It is supported by money, and it is the outer shell of the body—which is a "house" that cannot shelter us forever from the exigencies of nature. Thus, it seems significant that Ondaatje's Lalla lacks a house of her own in the last part of her life, and that Lessing's Hetty dies in a building that is open to the weather—both of these women are gypsies at heart. Harry Bendiner has been insulating himself in a Miami Beach condominium, but at the end of "Old Love" he moves in imagination to a tent in British Columbia. Bellow's Hattie tries to reverse the usual pattern. Once she too had lived in a tent, on the open range with her cowboy lover; but now she is stubbornly holding on to her life, her newly acquired status, and her yellow house.

As the house is an image of society, so water signifies the flux and open form of nature. Again and again in these stories, water is associated with death and with the hope of spiritual renewal. Consider, for instance, the springs and the waterfall in "The World of Apples," the flood in "The Passions of Lalla," the lake in "Leaving the Yellow House," and the sea in "Tell Me a Riddle" or "Old Love." In Bellow and Singer, where the protagonist is attempting through a "house" to shield the body from "water," we are told that bathing in sea or icy lake has been discontinued. In Cheever we see how water finally cleanses us of social ills, and in Ondaatje how it cuts through the "house" to carry the traveller away. (Lalla dies "in the blue arms of a jacaranda tree"—in blue which is the color of imagination, in the arms of love and nature.)

The fear of death is often conveyed by nature's least pleasing animals—the sharks in Singer's story, the mice in Taylor's, the rats in Lessing's, and the scorpion in Paul Bowles' timeless study of a human being's preparation for death. In that story, a nameless old woman has retired to a cave which evokes both womb and tomb. In this chamber she recovers her independence and prepares for the death or birth that will allow her to complete the circle. A nameless old man waits on the rock outside, as if for his turn in the cave, and appears to congratulate her when at last she proceeds on the appointed path. The old woman is able to go because she has kissed in a dream of girlhood the scorpion-prince. And she is entered by him, so that her death is also a marriage.

Of course there is "procrastination" in these stories, an altogether natural fear of the unknown. There is the wheel-spinning of Hattie Waggoner, for instance, as she thinks "—a beginning. After that, there was the early middle, then middle middle, late middle middle, quite late middle. In fact the middle is all we know. The rest is just a rumor." But Hattie is also a "perennial survivor," a woman who for good or ill "will be in business till she's cleaned out." If there is fear in Hattie, there is also courage. And it is courage finally, along with zest for life, and an extraordinary grace under the pressure of darkness, that creates the light of these stories. I hope you like them.

Victoria, May 1986 CONSTANCE ROOKE

SAUL BELLOW

Leaving the Yellow House

The neighbors—there were in all six white people who lived at Sego Desert Lake—told one another that old Hattie could no longer make it alone. The desert life, even with a forced-air furnace in the house and butane gas brought from town in a truck, was still too difficult for her. There were women even older than Hattie in the county. Twenty miles away was Amy Walters, the gold miner's widow. But she was a hardier old girl. Every day of the year she took a bath in the icy lake. And Amy was crazy about money and knew how to manage it, as Hattie did not. Hattie was not exactly a drunkard, but she hit the bottle pretty hard, and now she was in trouble and there was a limit to the help she could expect from even the best of neighbors.

They were fond of her, though. You couldn't help being fond of Hattie. She was big and cheerful, puffy, comic, boastful, with a big round back and stiff, rather long legs. Before the century began she had graduated from finishing school and studied the organ in Paris. But now she didn't know a note from a skillet. She had tantrums when she played canasta. And all that remained of her fine fair hair was frizzled along her forehead in small gray curls. Her forehead was not much wrinkled, but the skin was bluish, the color of skim milk. She walked with long strides in spite of the heaviness of her hips, pushing on, round-backed, with her shoulders and showing the flat rubber bottoms of her shoes.

Once a week, in the same cheerful, plugging but absent way, she took off her short skirt and the dirty aviator's jacket with the wool collar and put on a girdle, a dress, and high-heeled shoes. When she stood on these heels her fat old body trembled. She wore a big brown Rembrandt-like tam with a ten-cent-store brooch, eye-like, carefully centered. She drew a straight line with lipstick on her mouth, leaving part of the upper lip pale. At the wheel of her old turret-shaped car, she drove, seemingly methodical but speeding dangerously, across forty miles of mountainous desert to buy frozen meat pies and whisky. She went to the Laundromat and the hairdresser, and then had lunch with two martinis at the Arlington. Afterward she would often visit Marian Nabot's Silvermine Hotel at Miller Street near skid row and pass the rest of the day gossiping and drinking with her cronies, old divorcees like herself who had settled in the West. Hattie never gambled any more and she didn't care for the movies. And at five o'clock she drove back at the same speed, calmly, partly blinded by the smoke of her cigarette. The fixed cigarette gave her a watering eye.

The Rolfes and the Paces were her only white neighbors at Sego Desert Lake. There was Sam Jervis too, but he was only an old gandy-walker who did odd jobs in her garden, and she did not count him. Nor did she count among her neighbors Darly, the dudes' cowboy who worked for the Paces, nor Swede, the telegrapher. Pace had a guest ranch, and Rolfe and his wife were rich and had retired. Thus there were three good houses at the lake, Hattie's yellow house, Pace's, and the Rolfes'. All the rest of the population—Sam, Swede, Watchtah the section foreman, and the Mexicans and Indians and Negroes—lived in shacks and boxcars. There were very few trees, cottonwoods and box elders. Everything else, down to the shores, was sagebrush and juniper. The lake was what remained of an old sea that had covered the volcanic mountains. To the north there were some tungsten mines; to the south, fifteen miles, was an Indian village—shacks built of plywood or railroad ties.

In this barren place Hattie had lived for more than twenty years. Her first summer was spent not in a house but in an Indian wickiup on the shore. She used to say that she had watched the stars from this almost roofless shelter. After her divorce she took up with a cowboy named Wicks. Neither of them had any money—it was the Depression—and they had lived on the range, trapping coyotes for a living. Once a month they would come into town, and rent a room and go on a bender. Hattie told this sadly, but also gloatingly, and with many trimmings. A thing no sooner happened to her than it was transformed into something else. "We were caught in a storm," she said, "and we rode hard, down to the lake and knocked on the door of the yellow house"—now her house. "Alice Parmenter took us in and let us sleep on the floor."

What had actually happened was that the wind was blowing—there had been no storm—and they were not far from the house anyway; and Alice Parmenter, who knew that Hattie and Wicks were not married, offered them separate beds; but Hattie, swaggering, had said in a loud voice, "Why get two sets of sheets dirty?" And her and her cowboy had slept in Alice's bed while Alice had taken the sofa.

Then Wicks went away. There was never anybody like him in the sack; he was brought up in a whorehouse and the girls had taught him everything, said Hattie. She didn't really understand what she was saying but believed that she was being Western. More than anything else she wanted to be thought of as a rough, experienced woman of the West. Still, she was a lady, too. She had good silver and good china and engraved stationery, but she kept canned beans and A-1 sauce and tuna fish and bottles of catsup and fruit salad on the library shelves of her living room. On her night table was the Bible her pious brother Angus— the other brother was a heller—had given her; but behind the little door of the commode was a bottle of bourbon. When she awoke in the night she tippled herself back to sleep. In the glove compartment of her old car she kept little sample bottles for emergencies on the road. Old Darly found them after her accident.

The accident did not happen far out in the desert as she had always feared, but very near home. She had had a few martinis with the Rolfes one evening, and as she was driving home over the railroad crossing she lost control of the car and veered off the crossing onto the tracks. The explanation she gave was that she had sneezed, and the sneeze had blinded her and made her twist the wheel. The motor was killed and all four wheels of the car sat smack on the rails. Hattie crept down from the door, high off the roadbed. A great fear took hold of her—for the car, for the future, and not only for the future but spreading back into the past—and she began to hurry on stiff legs through the sagebrush to Pace's ranch.

Now the Paces were away on a hunting trip and had left Darly in charge; he was tending bar in the old cabin that went back to the days of the pony express, when Hattie burst in. There were two customers, a tungsten miner and his girl.

"Darly, I'm in trouble. Help me. I've had an accident," said Hattie.

How the face of a man will alter when a woman has bad news

to tell him! It happened now to lean old Darly; his eyes went flat and looked unwilling, his jaw moved in and out, his wrinkled cheeks began to flush, and he said, "What's the matter—what's happened to you now?"

"I'm stuck on the tracks. I sneezed. I lost control of the car. Tow me off, Darly. With the pickup. Before the train comes."

Darly threw down his towel and stamped his high-heeled boots. "Now what have you gone and done?" he said. "I told you to stay home after dark."

"Where's Pace? Ring the fire bell and fetch Pace."

"There's nobody on the property except me," said the lean old man. "And I'm not supposed to close the bar and you know it as well as I do."

"Please, Darly. I can't leave my car on the tracks."

"Too bad!" he said. Nevertheless he moved from behind the bar. "How did you say it happened?"

"I told you, I sneezed," said Hattie.

Everyone, as she later told it, was as drunk as sixteen thousand dollars: Darly, the miner, and the miner's girl.

Darly was limping as he locked the door of the bar. A year before, a kick from one of Pace's mares had broken his ribs as he was loading her into the trailer, and he hadn't recovered from it. He was too old. But he dissembled the pain. The high-heeled narrow boots helped, and his painful bending looked like the ordinary stooping posture of a cowboy. However, Darly was not a genuine cowboy, like Pace who had grown up in the saddle. He was a late-comer from the East and until the age of forty had never been on horseback. In this respect he and Hattie were alike. They were not genuine Westerners.

Hattie hurried after him through the ranch yard.

"Damn you!" he said to her. "I got thirty bucks out of that sucker and I would have skinned him out of his whole pay check if you minded your business. Pace is going to be sore as hell."

"You've got to help me. We're neighbors," said Hattie.

"You're not fit to be living out here. You can't do it any more. Besides, you're swacked all the time."

Hattie couldn't afford to talk back. The thought of her car on the tracks made her frantic. If a freight came now and smashed it, her life at Sego Desert Lake would be finished. And where would she go then? She was not fit to live in this place. She had never made the grade at all, only seemed to have made it. And Darly—

why did he say such hurtful things to her? Because he himself was sixty-eight years old, and he had no other place to go, either; he took bad treatment from Pace besides. Darly stayed because his only alternative was to go to the soldiers' home. Moreover, the dude women would still crawl into his sack. They wanted a cowboy and they thought he was one. Why, he couldn't even raise himself out of his bunk in the morning. And where else would he get women? "After the dude season," she wanted to say to him, "you always have to go to the Veterans' Hospital to get fixed up again." But she didn't dare offend him now.

The moon was due to rise. It appeared as they drove over the ungraded dirt road toward the crossing where Hattie's turret-shaped car was sitting on the rails. Driving very fast, Darly wheeled the pickup around, spraying dirt on the miner and his girl, who had followed in their car.

"You get behind the wheel and steer," Darly told Hattie.

She climbed into the seat. Waiting at the wheel, she lifted up her face and said, "Please God, I didn't bend the axle or crack the oil pan."

When Darly crawled under the bumper of Hattie's car the pain in his ribs suddenly cut off his breath, so instead of doubling the tow chain he fastened it at full length. He rose and trotted back to the truck on the tight boots. Motion seemed the only remedy for the pain; not even booze did the trick any more. He put the pickup into towing gear and began to pull. One side of Hattie's car dropped into the roadbed with a heave of springs. She sat with a stormy, frightened, conscience-stricken face, racing the motor until she flooded it.

The tungsten miner yelled, "Your chain's too long."

Hattie was raised high in the air by the pitch of the wheels. She had to roll down the window to let herself out because the door handle had been jammed from inside for years. Hattie struggled out on the uplifted side crying, "I better call the Swede. I better have him signal. There's a train due."

"Go on, then," said Darly. "You're no good here."

"Darly, be careful with my car. Be careful."

The ancient seat bed at this place was flat and low, and the lights of her car and of the truck and of the tungsten miner's Chevrolet were bright and big at twenty miles. Hattie was too frightened to think of this. All she could think was that she was a procrastinating old woman, she had lived by delays; she had meant to stop drinking, she had put off the time, and now she had smashed her car—a terrible end, a terrible judgment on her. She got to the ground and, drawing up her skirt, she started to get over the tow chain. To prove that the chain didn't have to be shortened, and to get the whole thing over with, Darly threw the pickup forward again. The chain jerked up and struck Hattie in the knee and she fell forward and broke her arm.

She cried, "Darly, Darly, I'm hurt. I fell."

"The old lady tripped on the chain," said the miner. "Back up here and I'll double it for you. You're getting nowheres."

Drunkenly the miner lay down on his back in the dark, soft red cinders of the roadbed. Darly had backed up to slacken the chain.

Darly hurt the miner, too. He tore some skin from his fingers by racing ahead before the chain was secure. Without complaining, the miner wrapped his hand in his shirttail saying, "She'll do it now." The old car came down from the tracks and stood on the shoulder of the road.

"There's your goddamn car," said Darly to Hattie.

"Is it all right?" she said. Her left side was covered with dirt, but she managed to pick herself up and stand, round-backed and heavy, on her stiff legs. "I'm hurt, Darly." She tried to convince him of it.

"Hell if you are," he said. He believed she was putting on an act to escape blame. The pain in his ribs made him especially impatient with her. "Christ, if you can't look after yourself any more you've got no business out here."

"You're old yourself," she said. "Look what you did to me. You can't hold your liquor."

This offended him greatly. He said, "I'll take you to the Rolfes. They let you booze it up in the first place, so let them worry about you. I'm tired of your bunk, Hattie."

He raced uphill. Chains, spade, and crowbar clashed on the sides of the pickup. She was frightened and held her arm and cried. Rolfe's dogs jumped at her to lick her when she went through the gate. She shrank from them crying, "Down, down."

"Darly," she cried in the darkness, "take care of my car. Don't leave it standing there on the road. Darly, take care of it, please."

But Darly in his ten-gallon hat, his chin-bent face wrinkled, small and angry, a furious pain in his ribs, tore away at high speed.

"Oh, God, what will I do," she said.

The Rolfes were having a last drink before dinner, sitting at their fire of pitchy railroad ties, when Hattie opened the door. Her knee was bleeding, her eyes were tiny with shock, her face grey with dust.

"I'm hurt," she said desperately. "I had an accident. I sneezed and lost control of the wheel. Jerry, look after the car. It's on the road."

They bandaged her knee and took her home and put her to bed. Helen Rolfe wrapped a heating pad around her arm.

"I can't have the pad," Hattie complained. "The switch goes on and off, and every time it does it starts my generator and uses up the gas."

"Ah, now, Hattie," Rolfe said, "this is not the time to be stingy. We'll take you to town in the morning and have you looked over. Helen will phone Dr. Stroud."

Hattie wanted to say, "Stingy! Why you're the stingy ones. I just haven't got anything. You and Helen are ready to hit each other over two bits in canasta." But the Rolfes were good to her; they were her only real friends here. Darly would have let her lie in the yard all night, and Pace would have sold her to the bone man. He'd give her to the knacker for a buck.

So she didn't talk back to the Rolfes, but as soon as they left the yellow house and walked through the super-clear moonlight under the great skirt of box-elder shadows to their new station wagon, Hattie turned off the switch, and the heavy swirling and battering of the generator stopped. Presently she became aware of real pain, deeper pain, in her arm, and she sat rigid, warming the injured place with her hand. It seemed to her that she could feel the bone sticking out. Before leaving, Helen Rolfe had thrown over her a comforter that had belonged to Hattie's dead friend India, from whom she had inherited the small house and everything in it. Had the comforter lain on India's bed the night she died? Hattie tried to remember, but her thoughts were mixed up. She was fairly sure the deathbed pillow was in the loft, and she believed she had put the death bedding in a trunk. Then how had this comforter got out? She couldn't do anything about it now but draw it away from contact with her skin. It kept her legs warm. This she accepted, but she didn't want it any nearer.

More and more Hattie saw her own life as though, from birth to present, every moment had been filmed. Her fancy was that when she died she would see the film shown. Then she would know how she had appeared from the back, watering the plants, in the bathroom, asleep, playing the organ, embracing—everything, even tonight, in pain, almost the last pain, perhaps, for she couldn't take much more. How many twists and angles had life to show her yet? There couldn't be much film left. To lie awake and think such thoughts was the worst thing in the world. Better death than insomnia. Hattie not only loved sleep, she believed in it.

The first attempt to set the bone was not successful. "Look what they've done to me," said Hattie and showed visitors the discolored breast. After the second operation her mind wandered. The sides of her bed had to be raised, for in her delirium she roamed the wards. She cursed at the nurses when they shut her in. "You can't make people prisoners in a democracy without a trial, you bitches." She had learned from Wicks how to swear. "*He* was profane," she used to say. "I picked it up unconsciously."

For several weeks her mind was not clear. Asleep, her face was lifeless; her cheeks were puffed out and her mouth, no longer wide and grinning, was drawn round and small. Helen sighed when she saw her.

"Shall we get in touch with her family?" Helen asked the doctor. His skin was white and thick. He had chestnut hair, abundant but very dry. He sometimes explained to his patients, "I had a tropical disease during the war."

He asked, "Is there a family?"

"Old brothers. Cousins' children," said Helen. She tried to think who would be called to her own bedside (she was old enough for that). Rolfe would see that she was cared for. He would hire private nurses. Hattie could not afford that. She had already gone beyond her means. A trust company in Philadelphia paid her eighty dollars a month. She had a small savings account.

"I suppose it'll be up to us to get her out of hock," said Rolfe. "Unless the brother down in Mexico comes across. We may have to phone one of those old guys."

In the end, no relations had to be called. Hattie began to recover. At last she could recognize visitors, though her mind was still in disorder. Much that had happened she couldn't recall.

"How many quarts of blood did they have to give me?" she kept asking. "I seem to remember five, six, eight different transfusions. Daylight, electric light . . ." She tried to smile, but she couldn't make a pleasant face as yet. ''How am I going to pay?'' she said. ''At twenty-five bucks a quart. My little bit of money is just about wiped out.''

Blood became her constant topic, her preoccupation. She told everyone who came to see her, ''—have to replace all that blood. They poured gallons into me. Gallons. I hope it was all good.'' And, though very weak, she began to grin and laugh again. There was more hissing in her laughter than formerly; the illness had affected her chest.

''No cigarettes, no booze,'' the doctor told Helen.

''Doctor,'' Helen asked him, ''do you expect her to change?''

''All the same, I am obliged to say it.''

''Life sober may not be much of a temptation to her,'' said Helen.

Her husband laughed. When Rolfe's laughter was intense it blinded one of his eyes. His short Irish face turned red; on the bridge of his small, sharp nose the skin whitened. ''Hattie's like me,'' he said. ''She'll be in business till she's cleaned out. And if Sego Lake turned to whisky she'd use her last strength to knock her old yellow house down to build a raft of it. She'd float away on whisky. So why talk temperance?''

Hattie recognized the similarity between them. When he came to see her she said, ''Jerry, you're the only one I can really talk to about my troubles. What am I going to do for money? I have Hotchkiss Insurance. I paid eight dollars a month.''

''That won't do you much good, Hat. No Blue Cross?''

''I let it drop ten years ago. Maybe I could sell some of my valuables.''

''What valuables have you got?'' he said. His eye began to droop with laughter.

''Why,'' she said defiantly, ''there's plenty. First there's the beautiful, precious Persian rug that India left me.''

''Coals from the fireplace have been burning it for years, Hat!''

''The rug is in *perfect* condition,'' she said with an angry sway of the shoulders. ''A beautiful object like that never loses its value. And the oak table from the Spanish monastery is three hundred years old.''

''With luck you could get twenty bucks for it. It would cost fifty to haul it out of here. It's the house you ought to sell.''

''The house?'' she said. Yes, that had been in her mind. ''I'd have to get twenty thousand for it.''

''Eight is a fair price.''

''Fifteen. . . .'' She was offended, and her voice recovered its strength. ''India put eight into it in two years. And don't forget that Sego Lake is one of the most beautiful places in the world.''

''But where is it? Five hundred and some miles to San Francisco and two hundred to Salt Lake City. Who wants to live way out here but a few eccentrics like you and India? And me?''

''There are things you can't put a price tag on. Beautiful things.''

''Oh, bull, Hattie! You don't know squat about beautiful things. Any more than I do. I live here because it figures for me, and you because India left you the house. And just in the nick of time, too. Without it you wouldn't have had a pot of your own.''

His words offended Hattie; more than that, they frightened her. She was silent and then grew thoughtful, for she was fond of Jerry Rolfe and he of her. He had good sense and moreover he only expressed her own thoughts. He spoke no more than the truth about India's death and the house. But she told herself, He doesn't know everything. You'd have to pay a San Francisco architect ten thousand just to *think* of such a house. Before he drew a line.

''Jerry,'' the old woman said, ''what am I going to do about replacing the blood in the blood bank?''

''Do you want a quart from me, Hat?'' His eye began to fall shut.

''You won't do. You had that tumor, two years ago. I think Darly ought to give some.''

''The old man?'' Rolfe laughed at her. ''You want to kill him?''

''Why!'' said Hattie with anger, lifting up her massive face. Fever and perspiration had frayed the fringe of curls; at the back of the head the hair had knotted and matted so that it had to be shaved. ''Darly almost killed me. It's his fault that I'm in this condition. He must have *some* blood in him. He runs after all the chicks—all of them—young and old.''

''Come, you were drunk, too,'' said Rolfe.

''I've driven drunk for forty years. It was the sneeze. Oh, Jerry, I feel wrung out,'' said Hattie, haggard, sitting forward in bed. But her face was cleft by her nonsensically happy grin. She was not one to be miserable for long; she had the expression of a perennial survivor.

Every other day she went to the therapist. The young woman worked her arm for her; it was a pleasure and a comfort to Hattie, who would have been glad to leave the whole cure to her. However, she was given other exercises to do, and these were not so easy. They rigged a pulley for her and Hattie had to hold both ends of a rope and saw it back and forth through the scraping little wheel. She bent heavily from the hips and coughed over her cigarette. But the most important exercise of all she shirked. This required her to put the flat of her hand to the wall at the level of her hips and, by working her finger tips slowly, to make the hand ascend to the height of her shoulder. That was painful; she often forgot to do it, although the doctor warned her, ''Hattie, you don't want adhesions, do you?''

A light of despair crossed Hattie's eyes. Then she said, ''Oh, Dr. Stroud, buy my house from me.''

''I'm a bachelor. What would I do with a house?''

''I know just the girl for you—my cousin's daughter. Perfectly charming and very brainy. Just about got her Ph.D.''

''You must get quite a few proposals yourself,'' said the doctor.

''From crazy desert rats. They chase me. But,'' she said, ''after I pay my bills I'll be in pretty punk shape. If at least I could replace that blood in the blood bank I'd feel easier.''

''If you don't do as the therapist tells you, Hattie, you'll need another operation. Do you know what adhesions are?''

She knew. But Hattie thought, *How long must I go on taking care of myself*? It made her angry to hear him speak of another operation. She had a moment of panic, but she covered it up. With him, this young man whose skin was already as thick as buttermilk and whose chestnut hair was as dry as death, she always assumed the part of a child. In a small voice she said, ''Yes, doctor.'' But her heart was in a fury.

Night and day, however, she repeated, ''I was in the Valley of the Shadow. But I'm alive.'' She was weak, she was old, she couldn't follow a train of thought very easily, she felt faint in the head. But she was still here; here was her body, it filled space, a great body. And though she had worries and perplexities, and once in a while her arm felt as though it was about to give her the last stab of all; and though her hair was scrappy and old, like onion roots, and scattered like nothing under the comb, yet she sat and amused herself with visitors; her great grin split her face; her heart warmed with every kind word.

And she thought, People will help me out. It never did me any good to worry. At the last minute something turned up, when I wasn't looking for it. Marian loves me. Helen and Jerry love me. Half Pint loves me. They would never let me go to the ground. And I love them. If it were the other way around, I'd never let them go down.

Above the horizon, in a baggy vastness which Hattie by herself occasionally visited, the features of India, her *shade,* sometimes rose. India was indignant and scolding. Not mean. Not really mean. Few people had ever been really mean to Hattie. But India was annoyed with her. "The garden is going to hell, Hattie," she said. "Those lilac bushes are all shriveled."

"But what can I do? The hose is rotten. It broke. It won't reach."

"Then dig a trench," said the phantom of India. "Have old Sam dig a trench. But save the bushes."

Am I thy servant still? said Hattie to herself. *No,* she thought, *let the dead bury their dead.*

But she didn't defy India now any more than she had done when they lived together. Hattie was supposed to keep India off the bottle, but often both of them began to get drunk after breakfast. They forgot to dress, and in their slips the two of them wandered drunkenly around the house and blundered into each other, and they were in despair at having been so weak. Late in the afternoon they would be sitting in the living room, waiting for the sun to set. It shrank, burning itself out on the crumbling edges of the mountains. When the sun passed, the fury of the daylight ended and the mountain surfaces were more blue, broken, like cliffs of coal. They no longer suggested faces. The east began to look simple, and the lake less inhuman and haughty. At last India would say, "Hattie—it's time for the lights." And Hattie would pull the switch chains of the lamps, several of them, to give the generator a good shove. She would turn on some of the wobbling eighteenth-century-style lamps whose shades stood out from their slender bodies like dragonflies' wings. The little engine in the shed would shuffle, then spit, then charge and bang, and the first weak light would rise unevenly in the bulbs.

"Hettie!" cried India. After she drank she was penitent, but her penitence too was a hardship to Hattie, and the worse her temper the more British her accent became. *"Where the hell ah you Het-tie!"* After India's death Hattie found some poems she had written in which she, Hattie, was affectionately and even touchingly mentioned. That was a good thing—Literature. Education. Breeding. But Hattie's interest in ideas was very small, whereas

India had been all over the world. India was used to brilliant society. India wanted her to discuss Eastern religion, Bergson and Proust, and Hattie had no head for this, and so India blamed her drinking on Hattie. "I can't talk to you," she would say. "You don't understand religion or culture. And I'm here because I'm not fit to be anywhere else. I can't live in New York any more. It's too dangerous for a woman my age to be drunk in the street at night."

And Hattie, talking to her Western friends about India, would say, "She is a lady" (implying that they made a pair). "She is a creative person" (this was why they found each other so congenial). "But helpless? Completely. Why she can't even get her own girdle on."

"Hettie! Come here. Het-tie! Do you know what sloth is?"

Undressed, India sat on her bed and with the cigarette in her drunken, wrinkled, ringed hand she burned holes in the blankets. On Hattie's pride she left many small scars, too. She treated her like a servant.

Weeping, India begged her afterward to forgive her. *"Hattie, please don't condemn me in your heart. Forgive me, dear, I know I am bad. But I hurt myself more in my evil than I hurt you."*

Hattie would keep a stiff bearing. She would lift up her face with its incurved nose and puffy eyes and say, "I am a Christian person. I never bear a grudge." And by repeating this she actually brought herself to forgive India.

But of course Hattie had no husband, no child, no skill, no savings. And what she would have done if India had not died and left her the yellow house nobody knows.

Jerry Rolfe said privately to Marian, "Hattie can't do anything for herself. If I hadn't been around during the forty-four blizzard she and India both would have starved. She's always been careless and lazy and now she can't even chase a cow out of the yard. She's too feeble. The thing for her to do is to go East to her damn brother. Hattie would have ended at the poor farm if it hadn't been for India. But besides the damn house India should have left her some dough. She didn't use her goddamn head."

When Hattie returned to the lake she stayed with the Rolfes. "Well, old shellback," said Jerry, "there's a little more life in you now."

Indeed, with joyous eyes, the cigarette in her mouth and her hair newly frizzed and overhanging her forehead, she seemed to have triumphed again. She was pale, but she grinned, she chuckled, and she held a bourbon old-fashioned with a cherry and a slice of orange in it. She was on rations; the Rolfes allowed her two a day. Her back, Helen noted, was more bent than before. Her knees went outward a little weakly; her feet, however, came close together at the ankles.

"Oh, Helen dear and Jerry dear, I am so thankful, so glad to be back at the lake. I can look after my place again, and I'm here to see the spring. It's more gorgeous than ever."

Heavy rains had fallen while Hattie was away. The sego lilies, which bloomed only after a wet winter, came up from the loose dust, especially around the marl pit; but even on the burnt granite they seemed to grow. Desert peach was beginning to appear, and in Hattie's yard the rosebushes were filling out. The roses were yellow and abundant, and the odor they gave off was like that of damp tea leaves.

"Before it gets hot enough for the rattlesnakes," said Hattie to Helen, "we ought to drive up to Marky's ranch and gather watercress."

Hattie was going to attend to lots of things, but the heat came early that year and, as there was no television to keep her awake, she slept most of the day. She was now able to dress herself, though there was little more that she could do. Sam Jervis rigged the pulley for her on the porch and she remembered once in a while to use it. Mornings when she had her strength she rambled over to her own house, examining things, being important and giving orders to Sam Jervis and Wanda Gingham. At ninety, Wanda, a Shoshone, was still an excellent seamstress and housecleaner.

Hattie looked over the car, which was parked under a cottonwood tree. She tested the engine. Yes, the old pot would still go. Proudly, happily, she listened to the noise of tappets; the dry old pipe shook as the smoke went out at the rear. She tried to work the shift, turn the wheel. That, as yet, she couldn't do. But it would come soon, she was confident.

At the back of the house the soil had caved in a little over the cesspool and a few of the old railroad ties over the top had rotted. Otherwise things were in good shape. Sam had looked after the garden. He had fixed a new catch for the gate after Pace's horses—maybe because he could never afford to keep them in hay—had broken in and Sam found them grazing and drove them out. Luckily, they hadn't damaged many of her plants. Hattie felt a moment of wild rage against Pace. He had brought the horses into her garden for a free feed, she was sure. But her anger didn't last long. It was reabsorbed into the feeling of golden pleasure that enveloped her. She had little strength, but all that she had was a pleasure to her. So she forgave even Pace, who would have liked to do her out of the house, who had always used her, embarrassed her, cheated her at cards, swindled her. All that he did he did for the sake of his quarter horses. He was a fool about horses. They were ruining him. Racing horses was a millionaire's amusement.

She saw his animals in the distance, feeding. Unsaddled, the mares appeared undressed; they reminded her of naked women walking with their glossy flanks in the sego lilies which curled on the ground. The flowers were yellowish, like winter wool, but fragrant; the mares, naked and gentle, walked through them. Their strolling, their perfect beauty, the sound of their hoofs on stone touched a deep place in Hattie's nature. Her love for horses, birds, and dogs was well known. Dogs led the list. And now a piece cut from a green blanket reminded Hattie of her dog Richie. The blanket was one he had torn, and she had cut it into strips and placed them under the doors to keep out the drafts. In the house she found more traces of him: hair he had shed on the furniture. Hattie was going to borrow Helen's vacuum cleaner, but there wasn't really enough current to make it pull as it should. On the doorknob of India's room hung the dog collar.

Hattie had decided that she would have herself moved into India's bed when it was time to die. Why should there be two deathbeds? A perilous look came into her eyes, her lips were pressed together forbiddingly. *I follow*, she said, speaking to India with an inner voice, *so never mind*. Presently—before long—she would have to leave the yellow house in her turn. And as she went into the parlor, thinking of the will, she sighed. Pretty soon she would have to attend to it. India's lawyer, Claiborne, helped her with such things. She had phoned him in town, while she was staying with Marian, and talked matters over with him. He had promised to try to sell the house for her. Fifteen thousand was her bottom price, she said. If he couldn't find a buyer, perhaps he could find a tenant. Two hundred dollars a month was the rental she set. Rolfe laughed. Hattie turned toward him one of those proud, dulled looks she always took on when he angered her. Haughtily she said, ''For summer on Sego Lake? That's reasonable.''

''You're competing with Pace's ranch.''

''Why, the food is stinking down there. And he cheats the dudes,'' said Hattie. ''He really cheats them at cards. You'll never catch me playing blackjack with him again.''

And what would she do, thought Hattie, if Claiborne could neither rent nor sell the house? This question she shook off as regularly as it returned. *I don't have to be a burden on anybody*, thought Hattie. *It's looked bad many a time before, but when push came to shove, I made it. Somehow I got by*. But she argued with herself: *How many times? How long, O God—an old thing, feeble, no use to anyone*? Who said she had any right to own property?

She was sitting on her sofa, which was very old—India's sofa—eight feet long, kidney-shaped, puffy, and bald. An underlying pink shone through the green; the upholstered tufts were like the pads of dogs' paws; between them rose bunches of hair. Here Hattie slouched, resting, with knees wide apart and a cigarette in her mouth, eyes half-shut but farseeing. The mountains seemed not fifteen miles but fifteen hundred feet away, the lake a blue band; the tealike odor of the roses, though they were still unopened, was already in the air, for Sam was watering them in the heat. Gratefully Hattie yelled, ''Sam!''

Sam was very old, and all shanks. His feet looked big. His old railroad jacket was made tight across the back by his stoop. A crooked finger with its great broad nail over the mouth of the hose made the water spray and sparkle. Happy to see Hattie, he turned his long jaw, empty of teeth, and his long blue eyes, which seemed to bend back to penetrate into his temples (it was his face that turned, not his body), and he said, ''Oh, there, Hattie. You've made it home today? Welcome, Hattie.''

''Have a beer, Sam. Come around the kitchen door and I'll give you a beer.''

She never had Sam in the house, owing to his skin disease. There were raw patches on his chin and behind his ears. Hattie feared infection from his touch, having decided that he had impetigo. She gave him the beer can, never a glass, and she put on gloves before she used the garden tools. Since he would take no money from her—Wanda Gingham charged a dollar a day—she got Marian to find old clothes for him in town and she left food for him at the door of the damp-wood-smelling boxcar where he lived.

"How's the old wing, Hat?" he said.

"It's coming. I'll be driving the car again before you know it," she told him. "By the first of May I'll be driving again." Every week she moved the date forward. "By Decoration Day I expect to be on my own again," she said.

In mid-June, however, she was still unable to drive. Helen Rolfe said to her, "Hattie, Jerry and I are due in Seattle the first week of July."

"Why, you never told me that," said Hattie.

"You don't mean to tell me this is the first you heard of it," said Helen. "You've known about it from the first—since Christmas."

It wasn't easy for Hattie to meet her eyes. She presently put her head down. Her face became very dry, especially the lips. "Well, don't you worry about me. I'll be all right here," she said.

"Who's going to look after you?" said Jerry. He evaded nothing himself and tolerated no evasion in others. Except that, as Hattie knew, he made every possible allowance for her. But who would help her? She couldn't count on her friend Half Pint, she couldn't really count on Marian either. She had had only the Rolfes to turn to. Helen, trying to be steady, gazed at her and made sad, involuntary movements with her head, sometimes nodding, sometimes seeming as if she disagreed. Hattie, with her inner voice, swore at her: *Bitch-eyes. I can't make it the way she does because I'm old. Is that fair*? And yet she admired Helen's eyes. Even the skin about them, slightly wrinkled, heavy underneath, was touching, beautiful. There was a heaviness in her bust that went, as if by attachment, with the heaviness of her eyes. Her head, her hands and feet should have taken a more slender body. Helen, said Hattie, was the nearest thing she had on earth to a sister. But there was no reason to go to Seattle—no genuine business. Why the hell Seattle? It was only idleness, only a holiday. The only reason was Hattie herself; this was their way of telling her that there was a limit to what she could expect them to do for her. Helen's nervous head wavered, but her thoughts were steady. She knew what was passing through Hattie's mind. Like Hattie, she was an idle woman. Why was her right to idleness better?

Because of money? thought Hattie. Because of age? Because she has a husband? Because she had a daughter in Swarthmore College? But an interesting thing occurred to her. Helen disliked being idle, whereas Hattie herself had never made any bones about it: an idle life was all she was good for. But for her it had been uphill all the way, because when Waggoner divorced her she didn't have a cent. She even had to support Wicks for seven or eight years. Except with horses, Wicks had no sense. And then she had had to take tons of dirt from India. *I am the one,* Hattie asserted to herself. *I would know what to do with Helen's advantages. She only suffers from them. And if she wants to stop being an idle woman why can't she start with me, her neighbor?* Hattie's skin, for all its puffiness, burned with anger. She said to Rolfe and Helen. "Don't worry. I'll make out. But if I have to leave the lake you'll be ten times more lonely than before. Now I'm going back to my house."

She lifted up her broad old face, and her lips were childlike with suffering. She would never take back what she had said.

But the trouble was no ordinary trouble. Hattie was herself aware that she rambled, forgot names, and answered when no one spoke.

"We can't just take charge of her," Rolfe said. "What's more, she ought to be near a doctor. She keeps her shotgun loaded so she can fire it if anything happens to her in the house. But who knows what she'll shoot? I don't believe it was Jacamares who killed that Doberman of hers."

Rolfe drove into the yard the day after she moved back to the yellow house and said, "I'm going into town. I can bring you some chow if you like."

She couldn't afford to refuse his offer, angry though she was, and she said, "Yes, bring me some stuff from the Mountain Street Market. Charge it." She had only some frozen shrimp and a few cans of beer in the icebox. When Rolfe had gone she put out the package of shrimp to thaw.

People really used to stick by one another in the West. Hattie now saw herself as one of the pioneers. The modern breed had come later. After all, she had lived on the range like an old-timer. Wicks had had to shoot their Christmas dinner and she had cooked it—venison. He killed it on the reservation, and if the Indians had caught them, there would have been hell to pay.

The weather was hot, the clouds were heavy and calm in a large sky. The horizon was so huge that in it the lake must have seemed like a saucer of milk. *Some milk!* Hattie thought. Two thousand feet down in the middle, so deep no corpse could ever be recovered. A body, they said, went around with the currents. And there were rocks like eyeteeth, and hot springs, and colorless fish at the bottom which were never caught. Now that the white pelicans were nesting they patrolled the rocks for snakes and other egg thieves. They were so big and flew so slow you might imagine they were angels. Hattie no longer visited the lake shore; the walk exhausted her. She saved her strength to go to Pace's bar in the afternoon.

She took off her shoes and stockings and walked on bare feet from one end of her house to the other. On the land side she saw Wanda Gingham sitting near the tracks while her great-grandson played in the soft red gravel. Wanda wore a large purple shawl and her black head was bare. All about her was—was nothing, Hattie thought; for she had taken a drink, breaking her rule. Nothing but mountains, thrust out like men's bodies; the sagebrush was the hair on their chests.

The warm wind blew dust from the marl pit. This white powder made her sky less blue. On the water side were the pelicans, pure as spirits, slow as angels, blessing the air as they flew with great wings.

Should she or should she not have Sam do something about the vine on the chimney? Sparrows nested in it, and she was glad of that. But all summer long the king snakes were after them and she was afraid to walk in the garden. When the sparrows scratched the ground for seed they took a funny bound; they held their legs stiff and flung back the dust with both feet. Hattie sat down at her old Spanish monastery table, watching them in the cloudy warmth of the day, clasping her hands, chuckling and sad. The bushes were crowded with yellow roses, half of them now rotted. The lizards scrambled from shadow to shadow. The water was smooth as air, gaudy as silk. The mountains succumbed, falling asleep in the heat. Drowsy, Hattie lay down on her sofa. Its pads were like dogs' paws. She gave in to sleep and when she woke it was midnight; she did not want to alarm the Rolfes by putting on her lights so took advantage of the moon to eat a few thawed shrimps and go to the bathroom. She undressed and lifted herself into bed and lay there feeling her sore arm. Now she knew how much she missed her dog. The whole matter of the dog weighed heavily on her soul. She came close to tears, thinking about him, and she went to sleep oppressed by her secret.

I suppose I had better try to pull myself together a little, thought Hattie nervously in the morning. *I can't just sleep my way through.* She knew what her difficulty was. Before any serious question her mind gave way. It scattered or diffused. She said to herself, *I can see bright, but I feel dim. I guess I'm not so lively any more. Maybe I'm becoming a little touched in the head, as Mother was.* But she was not so old as her mother was when she did those strange things. At eighty-five, her mother had to be kept from going naked in the street. *I'm not as bad as that yet. Thank God! Yes, I walked into the men's wards, but that was when I had a fever, and my nightie was on.*

She drank a cup of Nescafé and it strengthened her determination to do something for herself. In all the world she had only her brother Angus to go to. Her brother Will had led a rough life; he was an old heller, and now he drove everyone away. He was too crabby, thought Hattie. Besides he was angry because she had lived so long with Wicks. Angus would forgive her. But then he and his wife were not her kind. With them she couldn't drink, she couldn't smoke, she had to make herself small-mouthed, and she would have to wait while they read a chapter of the Bible before breakfast. Hattie could not bear to sit at table waiting for meals. Besides, she had a house of her own at last. Why should she have to leave it? She had never owned a thing before. And now she was not allowed to enjoy her yellow house. *But I'll keep it,* she said to herself rebelliously. *I swear to God I'll keep it. Why, I barely just got it. I haven't had time.* And she went out on the porch to work the pulley and do something about the adhesions in her arm. She was sure now that they were there. *And what will I do?* she cried to herself. *What will I do? Why did I ever go to Rolfe's that night—and why did I lose control on the crossing*? She couldn't say, now, "I sneezed." She couldn't even remember what had happened, except that she saw the boulders and the twisting blue rails and Darly. It was Darly's fault. He was sick and old himself. *He* couldn't make it. He envied her the house, and her woman's peaceful life. Since she returned from the hospital he hadn't even come to visit her. He only said, "Hell, I'm sorry for her, but it was her fault." What hurt him most was that she had said he couldn't hold his liquor.

Fierceness, swearing to God did no good. She was still the same procrastinating old woman. She had a letter to answer from Hotchkiss Insurance and it drifted out of sight. She was going to phone Claiborne the lawyer, but it slipped her mind. One morning she announced to Helen that she believed she would apply to an institution in Los Angeles that took over the property of old people and managed it for them. They gave you an apartment right on the ocean, and your meals and medical care. You had to sign over half of your estate. ''It's fair enough,'' said Hattie. ''They take a gamble. I may live to be a hundred.''

''I wouldn't be surprised,'' said Helen.

However, Hattie never got around to sending to Los Angeles for the brochure. But Jerry Rolfe took it on himself to write a letter to her brother Angus about her condition. And he drove over also to have a talk with Amy Walters, the gold miner's widow at Fort Walters—as the ancient woman called it. The Fort was an old tar-paper building over the mine. The shaft made a cesspool unnecessary. Since the death of her second husband no one had dug for gold. On a heap of stones near the road a crimson sign FORT WALTERS was placed. Behind it was a flagpole. The American flag was raised every day.

Amy was working in the garden in one of dead Bill's shirts. Bill had brought water down from the mountains for her in a homemade aqueduct so she could raise her own peaches and vegetables.

''Amy,'' Rolfe said, ''Hattie's back from the hospital and living all alone. You have no folks and neither has she. Not to beat around the bush about it, why don't you live together?''

Amy's face had great delicacy. Her winter baths in the lake, her vegetable soups, the waltzes she played for herself alone on the grand piano that stood beside her wood stove, the murder stories she read till darkness obliged her to close the book—this life of hers had made her remote. She looked delicate, yet there was no way to affect her composure, she couldn't be touched. It was very strange.

''Hattie and me have different habits, Jerry,'' said Amy. ''And Hattie wouldn't like my company. I can't drink with her. I'm a teetotaller.''

''That's true,'' said Rolfe, recalling that Hattie referred to Amy as if she were a ghost. He couldn't speak to Amy of the solitary death in store for her. There was not a cloud in the arid sky today, and there was no shadow of death on Amy. She was tranquil, she seemed to be supplied with a sort of pure fluid that would feed her life slowly for years to come.

He said, ''All kinds of things could happen to a woman like Hattie in that yellow house, and nobody would know.''

''That's a fact. She doesn't know how to take care of herself.''

''She can't. Her arm hasn't healed.''

Amy didn't say that she was sorry to hear it. In the place of those words came a silence which might have meant that. Then she said, "I might go over there a few hours a day, but she would have to pay me."

"Now, Amy, you must know as well as I do that Hattie has no money—not much more than her pension. Just the house."

At once Amy said, no pause coming between his words and hers, "I would take care of her if she'd agree to leave the house to me."

"Leave it in your hands, you mean?" said Rolfe. "To manage?"

"In her will. To belong to me."

"Why, Amy, what would you do with Hattie's house?" he said.

"It would be my property, that's all. I'd have it."

"Maybe you would leave Fort Walters to her in your will," he said.

"Oh, no," she said. "Why should I? I'm not asking Hattie for her help. I don't need it. Hattie is a city woman."

Rolfe could not carry this proposal back to Hattie. He was too wise ever to mention her will to her.

But Pace was not so careful of her feelings. By mid-June Hattie had begun to visit his bar regularly. She had so many things to think about she couldn't stay at home. When Pace came in from the yard one day—he had been packing the wheels of his horse-trailer and was wiping grease from his fingers—he said with his usual bluntness, "How would you like it if I paid you fifty bucks a month for the rest of your life, Hat?"

Hattie was holding her second old-fashioned of the day. At the bar she made it appear that she observed the limit; but she had started drinking at home. One before lunch, one during, one after lunch. She began to grin, expecting Pace to make one of his jokes. But he was wearing his scoop-shaped Western hat as level as a Quaker, and he had drawn down his chin, a sign that he was not fooling. She said, "That would be nice, but what's the catch?"

"No catch," he said. "This is what we'd do. I'd give you five hundred dollars cash, and fifty bucks a month for life, and you let me sleep some dudes in the yellow house, and you'd leave the house to me in your will."

"What kind of a deal is that?" said Hattie, her look changing. "I thought we were friends."

"It's the best deal you'll ever get," he said.

The weather was sultry, but Hattie till now had thought that it was nice. She had been dreamy but comfortable, about to begin to enjoy the cool of the day; but now she felt that such cruelty and injustice had been waiting to attack her, that it would have been better to die in the hospital than be so disillusioned.

She cried, "Everybody wants to push me out. You're a cheater, Pace. God! I know you. Pick on somebody else. Why do you have to pick on me? Just because I happen to be around?"

"Why, no, Hattie," he said, trying now to be careful. "It was just a business offer."

"Why don't you give me some blood for the bank if you're such a friend of mine?"

"Well, Hattie, you drink too much and you oughtn't to have been driving anyway."

"I sneezed, and you know it. The whole thing happened because I sneezed. Everybody knows that. I wouldn't sell you my house. I'd give it away to the lepers first. You'd let me go away and never send me a cent. You never pay anybody. You can't even buy wholesale in town any more because nobody trusts you. I'm stuck, that's all, just stuck. I keep on saying that this is my only home in all the world, this is where my friends are, and the weather is always perfect and the lake is beautiful. But I wish the whole damn empty old place were in Hell. It's not human and neither are you. But I'll be here the day the sheriff takes away your horses—you never mind! I'll be clapping and applauding!"

He told her then that she was drunk again, and so she was, but she was more than that, and though her head was spinning she decided to go back to the house at once and take care of some things she had been putting off. This very day she was going to write to the lawyer, Claiborne, and make sure that Pace never got her property. She wouldn't put it past him to swear in court that India had promised him the yellow house.

She sat at the table with pen and paper, trying to think how to put it.

"I want this on record," she wrote. "I could kick myself in the head when I think of how he's led me on. I have been his patsy ten thousand times. As when that drunk crashed his Cub plane on the lake shore. At the coroner's jury he let me take the whole blame. He said he had instructed me when I was working for him never to take in any drunks. And this flier was drunk. He had nothing on but a T shirt and Bermuda shorts and he was flying from Sacramento to Salt Lake City. At the inquest Pace said I had disobeyed his instructions. The same was true when the cook went haywire. She was a tramp. He never hires decent help. He cheated her on the bar bill and blamed me and she went after me with a meat cleaver. She disliked me because I criticized her for drinking at the bar in her one-piece white bathing suit with the dude guests. But he turned her loose on me. He hints that he did certain services for India. She would never have let him touch one single finger. He was too common for her. It can never be said about India that she was not a lady in every way. He thinks he is the greatest sack-artist in the world. He only loves horses, as a fact. He has no claims at all, oral or written, on this yellow house. I want you to have this over my signature. He was cruel to Pickle-Tits who was his first wife, and he's no better to the charming woman who is his present one. I don't know why she takes it. It must be despair.'' Hattie said to herself, *I don't suppose I'd better send that.*

She was still angry. Her heart was knocking within; the deep pulses, as after a hot bath, beat at the back of her thighs. The air outside was dotted with transparent particles. The mountains were as red as furnace clinkers. The iris leaves were fan sticks—they stuck out like Jiggs's hair.

She always ended by looking out of the window at the desert and lake. *They drew you from yourself. But after they had drawn you, what did they do with you? It was too late to find out. I'll never know. I wasn't meant to. I'm not the type,* Hattie reflected. *Maybe something too cruel for women, young or old.*

So she stood up and, rising, she had the sensation that she had gradually become a container for herself. You get old, your heart, your liver, your lungs seem to expand in size, and the walls of the body give way outward, swelling, she thought, and you take the shape of an old jug, wider and wider toward the top. You swell up with tears and fat. She no longer even smelled to herself like a woman. Her face with its much-slept-upon skin was only faintly like her own—like a cloud that has changed. It was a face. It became a ball of yarn. It had drifted open. It had scattered.

I was never one single thing anyway, she thought. *Never my own. I was only loaned to myself.*

But the thing wasn't over yet. And in fact she didn't know for certain that it was ever going to be over. You only had other people's word for it that death was such-and-such. How do I know?

she asked herself challengingly. Her anger had sobered her for a little while. Now she was again drunk . . . *It was strange. It is strange. It may continue being strange.* She further thought, *I used to wish for death more than I do now. Because I didn't have anything at all. I changed when I got a roof of my own over me. And now? Do I have to go? I thought Marian loved me, but she already has a sister. And I thought Helen and Jerry would never desert me, but they've beat it. And now Pace has insulted me. They think I'm not going to make it.*

She went to the cupboard—she kept the bourbon bottle there; she drank less if each time she had to rise and open the cupboard door. And, as if she were being watched, she poured a drink and swallowed it.

The notion that in this emptiness someone saw her was connected with the other notion that she was being filmed from birth to death. That this was done for everyone. And afterward you could view your life. A hereafter movie.

Hattie wanted to see some of it now, and she sat down on the dogs'-paw cushions of her sofa and, with her knees far apart and a smile of yearning and of fright, she bent her round back, burned a cigarette at the corner of her mouth and saw—the Church of Saint Sulpice in Paris where her organ teacher used to bring her. It looked like country walls of stone, but rising high and leaning outward were towers. She was very young. She knew music. How she could ever have been so clever was beyond her. But she did know it. She could read all those notes. The sky was gray. After this she saw some entertaining things she liked to tell people about. She was a young wife. She was in Aix-les-Bains with her mother-in-law, and they played bridge in a mud bath with a British general and his aide. There were artificial waves in the swimming pool. She lost her bathing suit because it was a size too big. How did she get out? Ah, you got out of everything.

She saw her husband, James John Waggoner IV. They were snow-bound together in New Hampshire. "Jimmy, Jimmy, how can you fling a wife away?" she asked him. "Have you forgotten love? Did I drink too much—did I bore you?" He had married again and had two children. He had gotten tired of her. And though he was a vain man with nothing to be vain about—no looks, not too much intelligence, nothing but an old Philadelphia family—she had loved him. She too had been a snob about her Philadelphia connections. Give up the name of Waggoner? How could she? For this reason she had never married Wicks. "How dare you," she had said to Wicks, "come without a shave in a dirty shirt and muck on you, come and ask me to marry! If you want to propose, go and clean up first." But his dirt was only a pretext.

Trade Waggoner for Wicks? she asked herself again with a swing of her shoulders. She wouldn't think of it. Wicks was an excellent man. But he was a cowboy. Socially nothing. He couldn't even read. But she saw this on her film. They were in Athens Canyon, in a cratelike house, and she was reading aloud to him from *The Count of Monte Cristo*. He wouldn't let her stop. While walking to stretch her legs, she read, and he followed her about to catch each word. After all, he was very dear to her. Such a man! Now she saw him jump from his horse. They were living on the range, trapping coyotes. It was just the second gray of evening, cloudy, moments after the sun had gone down. There was an animal in the trap, and he went toward it to kill it. He wouldn't waste a bullet on the creatures but killed them with a kick, with his boot. And then Hattie saw that this coyote was all white—snarling teeth, white scruff. "Wicks, he's white! White as a polar bear. You're not going to kill him, are you?" The animal flattened to the ground. He snarled and cried. He couldn't pull away because of the heavy trap. And Wicks killed him. What else could he have done? The white beast lay dead. The dust of Wicks's boots hardly showed on its head and jaws. Blood ran from the muzzle.

And now came something on Hattie's film she tried to shun. It was she herself who had killed her dog, Richie. Just as Rolfe and Pace had warned her, he was vicious, his brain was turned. She, because she was on the side of all dumb creatures, defended him when he bit the trashy woman Jacamares was living with. Perhaps if she had had Richie from a puppy he wouldn't have turned on her. When she got him he was already a year and a half old and she couldn't break him of his habits. But she thought that only she understood him. And Rolfe had warned her, "You'll be sued, do you know that? The dog will take out after somebody smarter than that Jacamares's woman, and you'll be in for it."

Hattie saw herself as she swayed her shoulders and said, "Nonsense."

But what fear she had felt when the dog went for her on the porch. Suddenly she could see, by his skull, by his eyes that he was evil. She screamed at him, "Richie!" And what had she done to him? He had lain under the gas range all day growling and wouldn't come out. She tried to urge him out with the broom, and he snatched it in his teeth. She pulled him out, and he left the stick and tore at her. Now, as the spectator of this, her eyes opened, beyond the pregnant curtain and the air-wave of marl dust, summer's snow, drifting over the water. "Oh, my God! Richie!" Her thigh was snatched by his jaws. His teeth went through her skirt. She felt she would fall. Would she go down? Then the dog would rush at her throat—then black night, bad-odored mouth, the blood pouring from her neck, from torn veins. Her heart shriveled as the teeth went into her thigh, and she couldn't delay another second but took her kindling hatchet from the nail, strengthened her grip on the smooth wood, and hit the dog. She saw the blow. She saw him die at once. And then in fear and shame she hid the body. And at night she buried him in the yard. Next day she accused Jacamares. On him she laid the blame for the disappearance of her dog.

She stood up; she spoke to herself in silence, as was her habit. *God, what shall I do? I have taken life. I have lied. I have borne false witness. I have stalled. And now what shall I do? Nobody will help me.*

And suddenly she made up her mind that she should go and do what she had been putting off for weeks, namely, test herself with the car, and she slipped on her shoes and went outside. Lizards ran before her in the thirsty dust. She opened the hot, broad door of the car. She lifted her lame hand onto the wheel. Her right hand she reached far to the left and turned the wheel with all her might. Then she started the motor and tried to drive out of the yard. But she could not release the emergency brake with its rasplike rod. She reached with her good hand, the right, under the steering wheel and pressed her bosom on it and strained. No, she could not shift the gears and steer. She couldn't even reach down to the hand brake. The sweat broke out on her skin. Her efforts were too much. She was deeply wounded by the pain in her arm. The door of the car fell open again and she turned from the wheel and with her stiff legs hanging from the door she wept. What could she do now? And when she had wept over the ruin of her life she got out of the old car and went back to the house. She took the bourbon from the cupboard and picked up the ink bottle and a pad of paper and sat down to write her will.

"My Will," she wrote, and sobbed to herself.

Since the death of India she had numberless times asked the

question, To Whom? Who will get this when I die? She had unconsciously put people to the test to find out whether they were worthy. It made her more severe than before.

Now she wrote, "I Harriet Simmons Waggoner, being of sound mind and not knowing what may be in store for me at the age of seventy-two (born 1885), living alone at Sego Desert Lake, instruct my lawyer, Harold Claiborne, Paiute County Court Building, to draw my last will and testament upon the following terms."

She sat perfectly still now to hear from within who would be the lucky one, who would inherit the yellow house. For which she had waited. Yes, waited for India's death, choking on her bread because she was a rich woman's servant and whipping girl. But who had done for her, Hattie, what she had done for India? And who, apart from India, had ever held out a hand to her? Kindness, yes. Here and there people had been kind. But the word in her head was not kindness, it was succor. And who had given her that? *Succor?* Only India. If at least, next best after succor, someone had given her a shake and said, "Stop stalling. Don't be such a slow, old, procrastinating sit-stiller." Again, it was only India who had done her good. She had offered her succor. "Het-tie!" said that drunken mask. "Do you know what sloth is? Demn you! poky old demned thing!"

But I was waiting, Hattie realized. *I was waiting, thinking, "Youth is terrible, frightening. I will wait it out. And men? Men are cruel and strong. They want things I haven't got to give." There were no kids in me,* thought Hattie. *Not that I wouldn't have loved them, but such my nature was. And who can blame me for having it? My nature?*

She drank from an old-fashioned glass. There was no orange in it, no ice, no bitters or sugar, only the stinging, clear bourbon.

So then, she continued, looking at the dry sun-stamped dust and the last freckled flowers of red wild peach, *to live with Angus and his wife? And to have to hear a chapter from the Bible before breakfast? Once more in the house—not of a stranger, perhaps, but not far from it either?* In other houses, in someone else's house, to wait for mealtimes was her lifelong punishment. She always felt it in the throat and stomach. And so she would again, and to the very end. However, she must think of someone to leave the house to.

And first of all she wanted to do right by her family. None of them had ever dreamed that she, Hattie, would ever have something to bequeath. Until a few years ago it had certainly looked as if she would die a pauper. So now she could keep her head up with the proudest of them. And, as this occurred to her, she actually lifted up her face with its broad nose and victorious eyes; if her hair had become shabby as onion roots, if, at the back, her head was round and bald as a newel post, what did that matter? Her heart experienced a childish glory, not yet tired of it after seventy-two years. She, too, had amounted to something. *I'll do some good by going,* she thought. *Now I believe I should leave it to, to* . . . She returned to the old point of struggle. She had decided many times and many times changed her mind. She tried to think, *Who would get the most out of this yellow house?* It was a tearing thing to go through. If it had not been the house but, instead, some brittle thing she could hold in her hand, then her last action would be to throw and smash it, and so the thing and she herself would be demolished together. But it was vain to think such thoughts. To whom should she leave it? Her brothers? Not they. Nephews? One was a submarine commander. The other was a bachelor in the State Department. Then began the roll call of cousins. Merton? He owned an estate in Connecticut. Anna? She had a face like a hot-water bottle. That left Joyce, the orphaned daughter of her cousin Wilfred. Joyce was the most likely heiress. Hattie had already written to her and had her out to the lake at Thanksgiving, two years ago. But this Joyce was another odd one; over thirty, good, yes, but placid, running to fat, a scholar—ten years in Eugene, Oregon, working for her degree. In Hattie's opinion this was only another form of sloth. Nevertheless, Joyce yet hoped to marry. Whom? Not Dr. Stroud. He wouldn't. And still Joyce had vague hope. Hattie knew how that could be. At least have a man she could argue with.

She was now more drunk than at any time since her accident. Again she filled her glass. *Have ye eyes and see not? Sleepers awake*!

Knees wide apart she sat in the twilight, thinking. Marian? Marian didn't need another house. Half Pint? She wouldn't know what to do with it. Brother Louis came up for consideration next. He was an old actor who had a church for the Indians at Athens Canyon. Hollywood stars of the silent days sent him their negligees; he altered them and wore them in the pulpit. The Indians loved his show. But when Billy Shawah blew his brains out after his two-week bender, they still tore his shack down and turned the boards inside out to get rid of his ghost. They had their old religion. No, not Brother Louis. He'd show movies in the yellow house to the tribe or make a nursery out of it for the Indian brats.

And now she began to consider Wicks. When last heard from he was south of Bishop, California, a handy man in a saloon off toward Death Valley. It wasn't she who heard from him but Pace. Herself, she hadn't actually seen Wicks since—how low she had sunk then!—she had kept the hamburger stand on Route 158. The little lunchroom had supported them both. Wicks hung around on the end stool, rolling cigarettes (she saw it on the film). Then there was a quarrel. Things had been going from bad to worse. He'd begun to grouse now about this and now about that. He beefed about the food, at last. She saw and heard him. "Hat," he said, "I'm good and tired of hamburger." "Well, what do you think I eat?" she said with that round, defiant movement of her shoulders which she herself recognized as characteristic (*me all over*, she thought). But he opened the cash register and took out thirty cents and crossed the street to the butcher's and brought back a steak. He threw it on the griddle. "Fry it," he said. She did, and watched him eat.

And when he was through she could bear her rage no longer. "Now," she said, "you've had your meat. Get out. Never come back." She kept a pistol under the counter. She picked it up, cocked it, pointed it at his heart. "If you ever come in that door again, I'll kill you," she said.

She saw it all. *I couldn't bear to fall so low*, she thought, *to be slave to a shiftless cowboy*.

Wicks said, "Don't do that, Hat. Guess I went too far. You're right."

"You'll never have a chance to make it up," she cried. "Get out!"

On that cry he disappeared, and since then she had never seen him.

"Wicks, dear," she said. "Please! I'm sorry. Don't condemn me in your heart. Forgive me. I hurt myself in my evil. I always had a thick idiot head. I was born with a thick head."

Again she wept, for Wicks. She was too proud. A snob. Now they might have lived together in this house, old friends, simple and plain.

She thought, *He really was my good friend*.

But what would Wicks do with a house like this, alone, if he was alive and survived her? He was too wiry for soft beds or easy chairs.

And she was the one who had said stiffly to India, "I'm a Christian person. I do not bear a grudge.''

Ah yes, she said to herself. *I have caught myself out too often. How long can this go on?* And she began to think, or try to think, of Joyce, her cousin's daughter. Joyce was like herself, a woman alone, getting on in years, clumsy. Probably never been laid. Too bad. She would have given much, now, to succor Joyce.

But it seemed to her now that that too, the succor, had been a story. First you heard the pure story. Then you heard the impure story. Both stories. She had paid out years, now to one shadow, now to another shadow.

Joyce would come here to the house. She had a little income and could manage. She would live as Hattie had lived, alone. Here she would rot, start to drink, maybe, and day after day read, day after day sleep. See how beautiful it was here? It burned you out. How empty! It turned you into ash.

How can I doom a younger person to the same life? asked Hattie. It's for somebody like me. When I was younger it wasn't right. But now it is, exactly. Only I fit in here. It was made for my old age, to spend my last years peacefully. If I hadn't let Jerry make me drunk that night—if I hadn't sneezed! Because of this arm, I'll have to live with Angus. My heart will break there away from my only home.

She was now very drunk, and she said to herself, *Take what God brings. He gives no gifts unmixed. He makes loans.*

She resumed her letter of instructions to lawyer Claiborne: ''Upon the following terms,'' she wrote a second time. ''Because I have suffered much. Because I only lately received what I have to give away, I can't bear it.'' The drunken blood was soaring to her head. But her hand was clear enough. She wrote, ''It is too soon! Too soon! Because I do not find it in my heart to care for anyone as I would wish. Being cast off and lonely, and doing no harm where I am. Why should it be? This breaks my heart. In addition to everything else, why must I worry about this, which I must leave? I am tormented out of my mind. Even though by my own fault I have put myself into this position. And I am not ready to give up on this. No, not yet. And so I'll tell you what, I leave this property, land, house, garden, and water rights, to Hattie Simmons Waggoner. Me! I realize this is bad and wrong. Not possible. Yet it is the only thing I really wish to do, so may God have mercy on my soul.''

How could that happen? She studied what she had written and

finally she acknowledged that she was drunk. "I'm drunk," she said, "and don't know what I'm doing. I'll die, and end. Like India. Dead as that lilac bush."

Then she thought that there was a beginning, and a middle. She shrank from the last term. She began once more—a beginning. After that, there was the early middle, then middle middle, late middle middle, quite late middle. In fact the middle is all I know. The rest is just a rumor.

Only tonight I can't give the house away. I'm drunk and so I need it. And tomorrow, she promised herself, I'll think again. I'll work it out, for sure.

PAUL BOWLES

The Scorpion

An old woman lived in a cave which her sons had hollowed out of a clay cliff near a spring before they went away to the town where many people live. She was neither happy nor unhappy to be there, because she knew that the end of life was near and that her sons would not be likely to return no matter what the season. In the town there are always many things to do, and they would be doing them, not caring to remember the time when they had lived in the hills looking after the old woman.

At the entrance to the cave at certain times of the year there was a curtain of water-drops through which the old woman had to pass to get inside. The water rolled down the bank from the plants above and dripped onto the clay below. So the old woman accustomed herself to sitting crouched in the cave for long periods of time in order to keep as dry as possible. Outside through the moving beads of water she saw the bare earth lighted by the gray sky, and sometimes large dry leaves went past, pushed by the wind that came from higher parts of the land. Inside where she was the light was pleasant and of a pink color from the clay all around.

A few people used to pass from time to time along the path not far away, and because there was a spring nearby, those travelers who knew that it existed but not just where it was would sometimes come near to the cave before they discovered that the spring was not there. The old woman would never call to them. She would merely watch them as they came near and suddenly saw her. Then she would go on watching as they turned back and went in other directions looking for the water to drink.

There were many things about this life that the old woman liked. She was no longer obliged to argue and fight with her sons to make them carry wood to the charcoal oven. She was free to move about at night and look for food. She could eat everything she found without having to share it. And she owed no one any debt of thanks for the things she had in her life.

One old man used to come from the village on his way down to the valley, and sit on a rock just distant enough from the cave for her to recognize him. She knew he was aware of her presence in the cave there, and although she probably did not know this, she disliked him for not giving some sign that he knew she was there. It seemed to her that he had an unfair advantage over her and was using it in an unpleasant way. She thought up many ideas for annoying him if he should ever come near enough, but he always passed by in the distance, pausing to sit down on the rock for some time, when he would often gaze straight at the cave. Then he would continue slowly on his way, and it always seemed to the old woman that he went more slowly after his rest than before it.

There were scorpions in the cave all year round, but above all during the days just before the plants began to let water drip through. The old woman had a huge bundle of rags, and with this she would brush the walls and ceiling clear of them, stamping quickly on them with her hard bare heel. Occasionally a small wild bird or animal strayed inside the entrance, but she was never quick enough to kill it, and she had given up trying.

One dark day she looked up to see one of her sons standing in the doorway. She could not remember which one it was, but she thought it was the one who had ridden the horse down the dry river bed and nearly been killed. She looked at his hand to see if it was out of shape. It was not that son.

He began to speak: "Is it you?"

"Yes."

"Are you well?"

"Yes."

"Is everything well?"

"Everything."

"You stayed here?"

"You can see."

"Yes."

There was a silence. The old woman looked around the cave and was displeased to see that the man in the doorway made it practically dark in there. She busied herself with trying to distinguish various objects: her stick, her gourd, her tin can, her length of rope. She was frowning with the effort.

The man was speaking again.

"Shall I come in?"

She did not reply.

He backed away from the entrance, brushing the water drops from his garments. He was on the point of saying something profane, thought the old woman, who, even though she did not know which one this was, remembered what he would do.

She decided to speak.

"What?" she said.

He leaned forward through the curtain of water and repeated his question.

"Shall I come in?"

"No."

"What's the matter with you?"

"Nothing."

Then she added: "There's no room."

He backed out again, wiping his head. The old woman thought he would probably go away, and she was not sure she wanted him to. However, there was nothing else he could do, she thought. She heard him sit down outside the cave, and then she smelled tobacco smoke. There was no sound but the dripping of water upon the clay.

A short while later she heard him get up. He stood outside the entrance again.

"I'm coming in," he said.

She did not reply.

He bent over and pushed inside. The cave was too low for him to stand up in it. He looked about and spat on the floor.

"Come on," he said.

"Where?"

"With me."

"Why?"

"Because you have to come."

She waited a little while, and then said suspiciously: "Where are you going?"

He pointed indifferently toward the valley, and said: "Down that way."

"In the town?"

"Farther."

"I won't go."

"You have to come."

"No."

He picked up her stick and held it out to her.

"Tomorrow," she said.

"Now."

"I must sleep," she said, settling back into her pile of rags.

"Good. I'll wait outside," he answered, and went out.

The old woman went to sleep immediately. She dreamed that the town was very large. It went on forever and its streets were filled with people in new clothes. The church had a high tower with several bells that rang all the time. She was in the streets all one day, surrounded by people. She was not sure whether they were all her sons or not. She asked some of them: "Are you my sons?" They could not answer, but she thought that if they had been able to, they would have said: "Yes." Then when it was night she found a house with its door open. Inside there was a light and some women were seated in a corner. They rose when she went in, and said: "You have a room here." She did not want to see it, but they pushed her along until she was in it, and closed the door. She was a little girl and she was crying. The bells of the church were very loud outside, and she imagined they filled the sky. There was an open space in the wall high above her. She could see the stars through it, and they gave light to her room. From the reeds which formed the ceiling a scorpion came crawling. He came slowly down the wall toward her. She stopped crying and watched him. His tail curved up over his back and moved a little from side to side as he crawled. She looked quickly about for something to brush him down with. Since there was nothing in the room she used her hand. But her motions were slow, and the scorpion seized her finger with his pinchers, clinging there tightly although she waved her hand wildly about. Then she realized that he was not going to sting her. A great feeling of happiness went through her. She raised her finger to her lips to kiss the scorpion. The bells stopped ringing. Slowly in the peace which was beginning, the scorpion moved into her mouth. She felt his hard shell and his little clinging legs going across her lips and her tongue. He crawled slowly down her throat and was hers. She woke up and called out.

Her son answered: "What is it?"

"I'm ready."

"So soon?"

He stood outside as she came through the curtain of water, leaning on her stick. Then he began walking a few paces ahead of her toward the path.

"It will rain," said her son.

"Is it far?"

"Three days," he said, looking at her old legs.

She nodded. Then she noticed the old man sitting on the stone. He had an expression of deep surprise on his face, as if a miracle had just occurred. His mouth was open as he stared at the old woman. When they came opposite the rock he peered more intently than ever into her face. She pretended not to notice him. As they picked their way carefully downhill along the stony path, they heard the old man's thin voice behind them, carried by the wind.

"Good-bye."

"Who is that?" said her son.

"I don't know."

Her son looked back at her darkly.

"You're lying," he said.

JOHN CHEEVER

The World of Apples

Asa Bascomb, the old laureate, wandered around his work house or study—he had never been able to settle on a name for a house where one wrote poetry—swatting hornets with a copy of *La Stampa* and wondering why he had never been given the Nobel Prize. He had received nearly every other sign of renown. In a trunk in the corner there were medals, citations, wreaths, sheaves, ribbons, and badges. The stove that heated his study had been given to him by the Oslo P.E.N. Club, his desk was a gift from the Kiev Writer's Union, and the study itself had been built by an international association of his admirers. The presidents of both Italy and the United States had wired their congratulations on the day he was presented with the key to the place. Why no Nobel Prize? Swat, swat. The study was a barny, raftered building with a large northern window that looked off to the Abruzzi. He would sooner have had a much smaller place with smaller windows but he had not been consulted. There seemed to be some clash between the altitude of the mountains and the disciplines of verse. At the time of which I'm writing he was eighty-two years old and lived in a villa below the hill town of Monte Carbone, south of Rome.

He had strong, thick white hair that hung in a lock over his forehead. Two or more cowlicks at the crown were usually disorderly and erect. He wet them down with soap for formal receptions, but they were never supine for more than an hour or two and were usually up in the air again by the time champagne was poured. It was very much a part of the impression he left. As one remembers a man for a long nose, a smile, birthmark, or scar, one remembered Bascomb for his unruly cowlicks. He was known vaguely as the Cézanne of poets. There was some linear preciseness to his work that might be thought to resemble Cézanne but the vision that underlies Cézanne's paintings was not his. This mistaken comparison might have arisen because the title of his most popular work was *The World of Apples*—poetry in which his admirers found the pungency, diversity, color, and nostalgia of the apples of the northern New England he had not seen for forty years.

Why had he—provincial and famous for his simplicity—chosen to leave Vermont for Italy? Had it been the choice of his beloved Amelia, dead these ten years? She had made many of their decisions. Was he, the son of a farmer, so naïve that he thought living abroad might bring some color to his stern beginnings? Or had it been simply a practical matter, an evasion of the publicity that would, in his own country, have been an annoyance? Admirers found him in Monte Carbone, they came almost daily, but they came in modest numbers. He was photographed once or twice a year for *Match* or *Epoca*—usually on his birthday—but he was in general able to lead a quieter life than would have been possible in the United States. Walking down Fifth Avenue on his last visit home he had been stopped by strangers and asked to autograph scraps of paper. On the streets of Rome no one knew or cared who he was and this was as he wanted it.

Monte Carbone was a Saracen town, built on the summit of a loaf-shaped butte of sullen granite. At the top of the town were three pure and voluminous springs whose water fell in pools or conduits down the sides of the mountain. His villa was below the town and he had in his garden many fountains, fed by the springs on the summit. The noise of falling water was loud and unmusical—a clapping or clattering sound. The water was stinging cold, even in midsummer, and he kept his gin, wine, and vermouth in a pool on the terrace. He worked in his study in the mornings, took a siesta after lunch, and then climbed the stairs to the village.

The tufa and pepperoni and the bitter colors of the lichen that takes root in the walls and roofs are no part of the consciousness of an American, even if he had lived for years, as Bascomb had, surrounded by this bitterness. The climb up the stairs winded him. He stopped again and again to catch his breath. Everyone spoke to him. *Salve, maestro, salve!* When he saw the bricked-up transept of the twelfth-century church he always mumbled the date to himself as if he were explaining the beauties of the place to some companion. The beauties of the place were various and gloomy. He would always be a stranger there, but his strangeness seemed to him to be some metaphor involving time as if, climbing the strange stairs past the strange walls, he climbed through hours, months, years, and decades. In the piazza he had a glass of wine and got his mail. On any day he received more mail than the entire population of the village. There were letters from admirers, propositions to lecture, read, or simply show his face, and he seemed to be on the invitation list of every honorary society in the Western world excepting, of course, that society formed by the past winners of the Nobel Prize. His mail was kept in a sack, and if it was too heavy for him to carry, Antonio, the *postina's* son, would walk back with him to the villa. He worked over his mail until five or six. Two or three times a week some pilgrims would find their way to the villa and if he liked their looks he would give them a drink while he autographed their copy of *The World of Apples*. They almost never brought his other books, although he had published a dozen. Two or three evenings a week he played backgammon with Carbone, the local padrone. They both thought that the other cheated and neither of them would leave the board during a game, even if their bladders were killing them. He slept soundly.

Of the four poets with whom Bascomb was customarily grouped one had shot himself, one had drowned himself, one had hanged himself, and the fourth had died of delirium tremens. Bascomb had known them all, loved most of them, and had nursed two of them when they were ill, but the broad implication that he had, by choosing to write poetry, chosen to destroy himself was something he rebelled against vigorously. He knew the temptations of suicide as he knew the temptations of every other form of sinfulness and he carefully kept out of the villa all firearms, suitable lengths of rope, poisons, and sleeping pills. He had seen in Z—the closest of the four—some inalienable link between his prodigious imagination and his prodigious gifts for self-destruction, but Bascomb in his stubborn, countrified way was determined to break or ignore this link—to overthrow Marsyas and Orpheus. Poetry was a lasting glory and he was determined that the final act of a poet's life should not—as had been the case with Z—be played out in a dirty room with twenty-three empty gin bottles. Since he could not deny the connection between brilliance and tragedy he seemed determined to bludgeon it.

Bascomb believed, as Cocteau once said, that the writing of poetry was the exploitation of a substrata of memory that was imperfectly understood. His work seemed to be an act of recollection. He did not, as he worked, charge his memory with any practical tasks but it was definitely his memory that was called into play—his memory of sensation, landscapes, faces, and the immense vocabulary of his own language. He could spend a month or longer on a short poem but discipline and industry were not the words to describe his work. He did not seem to choose his words at all but to recall them from the billions of sounds that he had heard since he first understood speech. Depending on his memory, then, as he did, to give his life usefulness he sometimes wondered if his memory were not failing. Talking with friends and admirers he took great pains not to repeat himself. Waking at two or three in the morning to hear the unmusical clatter of his fountains he would grill himself for an hour on names and dates. Who was Lord Cardigan's adversary at Balaklava? It took a minute for the name of Lord Lucan to struggle up through the murk but it finally appeared. He conjugated the remote past of the verb *esse*, counted to fifty in Russian, recited poems by Donne, Eliot, Thomas, and Wordsworth, described the events of the Risorgimento beginning with the riots in Milan in 1812 up through the coronation of Vittorio Emanuele, listed the ages of prehistory, the number of kilometers in a mile, the planets of the solar system, and the speed of light. There was a definite retard in the responsiveness of his memory but he remained adequate, he thought. The only impairment was anxiety. He had seen time destroy so much that he wondered if an old man's memory could have more strength and longevity than an oak; but the pin oak he had planted on the terrace thirty years ago was dying and he could still remember in detail the cut and color of the dress his beloved Amelia had been wearing when they first met. He taxed his memory to find its way through cities. He imagined walking from the railroad station in Indianapolis to the memorial fountain, from the Hotel Europe in Leningrad to the Winter Palace, from the Eden-Roma up through Trastevere to San Pietro in Montori. Frail, doubting his faculties, it was the solitariness of this inquisition that made it a struggle.

His memory seemed to wake him one night or morning, asking him to produce the first name of Lord Byron. He could not. He decided to disassociate himself momentarily from his memory and surprise it in possession of Lord Byron's name but when he returned, warily, to this receptacle it was still empty. Sidney?

Percy? James? He got out of bed—it was cold—put on some shoes and an overcoat and climbed up the stairs through the garden to his study. He seized a copy of *Manfred* but the author was listed simply as Lord Byron. The same was true of *Childe Harold*. He finally discovered, in the encyclopedia, that his lordship was named George. He granted himself a partial excuse for this lapse of memory and returned to his warm bed. Like most old men he had begun a furtive glossary of food that seemed to put lead in his pencil. Fresh trout. Black olives. Young lamb roasted with thyme. Wild mushrooms, bear, venison, and rabbit. On the other side of the ledger were all frozen foods, cultivated greens, overcooked pasta, and canned soups.

In the spring a Scandinavian admirer wrote, asking if he might have the honor of taking Bascomb for a day's trip among the hill towns. Bascomb, who had no car of his own at the time, was delighted to accept. The Scandinavian was a pleasant young man and they set off happily for Monte Felici. In the fourteenth and fifteenth centuries the springs that supplied the town with water had gone dry and the population had moved halfway down the mountain. All that remained of the abandoned town on the summit were two churches or cathedrals of uncommon splendor. Bascomb loved these. They stood in fields of flowering weeds, their wall paintings still brilliant, their façades decorated with griffins, swans, and lions with the faces and parts of men and women, skewered dragons, winged serpents, and other marvels of metamorphoses. These vast and fanciful houses of God reminded Bascomb of the boundlessness of the human imagination and he felt lighthearted and enthusiastic. From Monte Felici they went on to San Georgio, where there were some painted tombs and a little Roman theater. They stopped in a grove below the town to have a picnic. Bascomb went into the woods to relieve himself and stumbled on a couple who were making love. They had not bothered to undress and the only flesh visible was the stranger's hairy backside. *Tanti, scusi,* mumbled Bascomb and he retreated to another part of the forest but when he rejoined the Scandinavian he was uneasy. The struggling couple seemed to have dimmed his memories of the cathedrals. When he returned to his villa some nuns from a Roman convent were waiting for him to autograph their copies of *The World of Apples*. He did this and asked his housekeeper, Maria, to give them some wine. They paid him the usual compliments—he had created a universe that seemed to welcome man; he had divined the voice of moral beauty in a rain wind—but all that he could think of was the stranger's back. It seemed to have more zeal and meaning than his celebrated search for truth. It seemed to dominate all that he had seen that day—the castles, clouds, cathedrals, mountains, and fields of flowers. When the nuns left he looked up to the mountains to raise his spirits but the mountains looked then like the breasts of women. His mind had become unclean. He seemed to step aside from its recalcitrance and watch the course it took. In the distance he heard a train whistle and what would his wayward mind make of this? The excitements of travel, the *prix fixe* in the dining car, the sort of wine they served on trains? It all seemed innocent enough until he caught his mind sneaking away from the dining car to the venereal stalls of the Wagon-Lit and thence into gross obscenity. He thought he knew what he needed and he spoke to Maria after dinner. She was always happy to accommodate him, although he always insisted that she take a bath. This, with the dishes, involved some delays but when she left him he definitely felt better but he definitely was not cured.

In the night his dreams were obscene and he woke several times trying to shake off this venereal pall or torpor. Things were no better in the light of morning. Obscenity—gross obscenity—seemed to be the only fact in life that possessed color and cheer. After breakfast he climbed up to his study and sat at his desk. The welcoming universe, the rain wind that sounded through the world of apples had vanished. Filth was his destiny, his best self, and he began with relish a long ballad called The Fart That Saved Athens. He finished the ballad that morning and burned it in the stove that had been given to him by the Oslo P.E.N. The ballad was, or had been until he burned it, an exhaustive and revolting exercise in scatology, and going down the stairs to his terrace he felt genuinely remorseful. He spent the afternoon writing a disgusting confession called The Favorite of Tiberio. Two admirers—a young married couple—came at five to praise him. They had met on a train, each of them carrying a copy of his *Apples*. They had fallen in love along the lines of the pure and ardent love he described. Thinking of his day's work, Bascomb hung his head.

On the next day he wrote The Confessions of a Public School Headmaster. He burned the manuscript at noon. As he came sadly down the stairs onto his terrace he found there fourteen students from the University of Rome who, as soon as he appeared, began to chant "The Orchards of Heaven"—the opening sonnet in *The World of Apples*. He shivered. His eyes filled with tears. He asked Maria to bring them some wine while he autographed their copies. They then lined up to shake his impure hand and returned to a bus in the field that had brought them out from Rome. He glanced at the mountains that had no cheering power—looked up at the meaningless blue sky. Where was the strength of decency? Had it any reality at all? Was the gross bestiality that obsessed him a sovereign truth? The most harrowing aspect of obscenity, he was to discover before the end of the week, was its boorishness. While he tackled his indecent projects with ardor he finished them with boredom and shame. The pornographer's course seems inflexible and he found himself repeating that tedious body of work that is circulated by the immature and the obsessed. He wrote The Confessions of a Lady's Maid, The Baseball Player's Honeymoon, and A Night in the Park. At the end of ten days he was at the bottom of the pornographer's barrel; he was writing dirty limericks. He wrote sixty of these and burned them. The next morning he took a bus to Rome.

He checked in at the Minerva where he always stayed and telephoned a long list of friends, but he knew that to arrive unannounced in a large city is to be friendless, and no one was home. He wandered around the streets and, stepping into a public toilet, found himself face to face with a male whore, displaying his wares. He stared at the man with the naïveté or the retard of someone very old. The man's face was idiotic—doped, drugged, and ugly—and yet, standing in his unsavory orisons, he seemed to old Bascomb angelic, armed with a flaming sword that might conquer banality and smash the glass of custom. He hurried away. It was getting dark and that hellish eruption of traffic noise that rings off the walls of Rome at dusk was rising to its climax. He wandered into an art gallery on the Via Sistina where the painter or photographer—he was both—seemed to be suffering from the same infection as Bascomb, only in a more acute form. Back in the streets he wondered if there was a universality to this venereal dusk that had settled over his spirit. Had the world, as well as he, lost its way? He passed a concert hall where a program of songs was advertised and thinking that music might cleanse the thoughts of his heart he bought a ticket and went in. The concert was poorly attended. When the accompanist appeared, only a third of the seats were taken. Then the soprano came on, a splendid ash blonde in a crimson dress, and while she sang *Die Liebhaber der Brücken* old Bascomb began the disgusting and unfortunate habit of imagining that he was disrobing her. Hooks and eyes, he wondered? A zipper? While she sang *Die Feldspar* and went on to *Le temps des lilas et le temps des roses ne reviendra plus* he settled for a zipper and imagined unfastening her dress at the back and lifting it gently off her shoulders. He got her slip over her head while she sang *L'Amore Nascondere* and undid the hooks and eyes of her brassiere during *Les Rêves de Pierrot*. His reverie was suspended when she stepped into the wings to gargle but as soon as she returned to the piano he got to work on her garter belt and all that it contained. When she took her bow at the intermission he applauded uproariously but not for her knowledge of music or the gifts of her voice. Then shame, limpid and pitiless as any passion, seemed to encompass him and he left the concert hall for the Minerva but his seizure was not over. He sat at his desk in the hotel and wrote a sonnet to the legendary Pope Joan. Technically it was an improvement over the limericks he had been writing but there was no moral improvement. In the morning he took the bus back to Monte Carbone and received some grateful admirers on his terrace. The next day he climbed to his study, wrote a few limericks and then took some Petronius and Juvenal from the shelves to see what had been accomplished before him in this field of endeavor.

Here were candid and innocent accounts of sexual merriment. There was nowhere that sense of wickedness he experienced when he burned his work in the stove each afternoon. Was it simply that his world was that much older, its social responsibilities that much more grueling, and that lewdness was the only answer to an increase of anxiety? What was it that he had lost? It seemed then to be a sense of pride, an aureole of lightness and valor, a kind of crown. He seemed to hold the crown up to scrutiny and what did he find? Was it merely some ancient fear of Daddy's razor strap and Mummy's scowl, some childish subservience to the bullying world? He well knew his instincts to be rowdy, abundant, and indiscreet and had he allowed the world and all its tongues to impose upon him some structure of transparent values for the convenience of a conservative economy, an established church, and a bellicose army and navy? He seemed to hold the crown, hold it up into the light, it seemed made of light and what it seemed to mean was the genuine and tonic taste of exaltation and grief. The limericks he had just completed were innocent, factual, and merry. They were also obscene, but when had the facts of life become obscene and what were the realities of this virtue he so painfully stripped from himself each morning? They seemed to be the realities of anxiety and love: Amelia standing in the diagonal beam of light, the stormy night his son was born, the day his daughter married. One could disparage them as homely but they were the best he knew of life—anxiety and love—and worlds away from the limerick on his desk that began: "There was a young consul named Caesar/Who had an enormous fissure." He burned his limerick in the stove and went down the stairs.

The next day was the worst. He simply wrote F - - k again and again covering six or seven sheets of paper. He put this into the stove at noon. At lunch Maria burned her finger, swore lengthily, and then said: "I should visit the sacred angel of Monte Giordano." "What is the sacred angel?" he asked. "The angel can cleanse the thoughts of a man's heart," said Maria. "He is in the old church at Monte Giordano. He is made of olive wood from the Mount of Olives and was carved by one of the saints himself. If you make a pilgrimage he will cleanse your thoughts." All Bascomb knew of pilgrimages was that you walked and for some reason carried a seashell. When Maria went up to take a siesta he looked among Amelia's relics and found a seashell. The angel would expect a present, he guessed, and from the box in his study he chose the gold medal the Soviet Government had given him on Lermontov's Jubilee. He did not wake Maria or leave her a note. This seemed to be a conspicuous piece of senility. He had never before been, as the old often are, mischievously elusive, and he should have told Maria where he was going but he didn't. He started down through the vineyards to the main road at the bottom of the valley.

As he approached the river a little Fiat drew off the main road and parked among some trees. A man, his wife, and three carefully dressed daughters got out of the car and Bascomb stopped to watch them when he saw that the man carried a shotgun. What was he going to do? Commit murder? Suicide? Was Bascomb about to see some human sacrifice? He sat down, concealed by the deep grass, and watched. The mother and the three girls were very excited. The father seemed to be enjoying complete sovereignty. They spoke a dialect and Bascomb understood almost nothing they said. The man took the shotgun from its case and put a single shell in the chamber. Then he arranged his wife and three daughters in a line and put their hands over their ears. They were squealing. When this was all arranged he stood with his back to them, aimed his gun at the sky, and fired. The three children applauded and exclaimed over the loudness of the noise and the bravery of their dear father. The father returned the gun to its case, they all got back into the Fiat and drove, Bascomb supposed, back to their apartment in Rome.

Bascomb stretched out in the grass and fell asleep. He dreamed that he was back in his own country. What he saw was an old Ford truck with four flat tires, standing in a field of buttercups. A child wearing a paper crown and a bath towel for a mantle hurried around the corner of a white house. An old man took a bone from a paper bag and handed it to a stray dog. Autumn leaves smoldered in a bathtub with lion's feet. Thunder woke him, distant, shaped, he thought, like a gourd. He got down to the main road where he was joined by a dog. The dog was trembling and he wondered if it was sick, rabid, dangerous, and then he saw that the dog was afraid of thunder. Each peal put the beast into a paroxysm of trembling and Bascomb stroked his head. He had never known an animal to be afraid of nature. Then the wind picked up the branches of the trees and he lifted his old nose to smell the rain, minutes before it fell. It was the smell of damp country churches, the spare rooms of old houses, earth closets, bathing suits put out to dry—so keen an odor of joy that he sniffed noisily. He did not, in spite of these transports, lose sight of his practical need for shelter. Beside the road was a little hut for bus travelers and he and the frightened dog stepped into this. The walls were covered with that sort of uncleanliness from which he hoped to flee and he stepped out again. Up the road was a farmhouse—one of those schizophrenic improvisations one sees so often in Italy. It seemed to have been bombed, spatch-cocked, and put together, not at random but as a deliberate assault on logic. On one side there was a wooden lean-to where an old man sat. Bascomb asked him for the kindness of his shelter and the old man invited him in.

The old man seemed to be about Bascomb's age but he seemed to Bascomb enviably untroubled. His smile was gentle and his face was clear. He had obviously never been harried by the wish to write a dirty limerick. He would never be forced to make a pilgrimage with a seashell in his pocket. He held a book in his lap—a stamp album—and the lean-to was filled with potted plants. He did not ask his soul to clap hands and sing, and yet he seemed to have reached an organic peace of mind that Bascomb coveted. Should Bascomb have collected stamps and potted plants? Anyhow, it was too late. Then the rain came, thunder shook the earth, the dog whined and trembled, and Bascomb caressed him. The storm passed in a few minutes and Bascomb thanked his host and started up the road.

He had a nice stride for someone so old and he walked, like all the rest of us, in some memory of prowess—love or football, Amelia or a good dropkick—but after a mile or two he realized that he would not reach Monte Giordano until long after dark and when a car stopped and offered him a ride to the village he accepted it, hoping that this would not put a crimp in his cure. It was still light when he reached Monte Giordano. The village was about the same size as his own with the same tufa walls and bitter lichen. The old church stood in the center of the square but the door was locked. He asked for the priest and found him in a vineyard, burning prunings. He explained that he wanted to make an offering to the sainted angel and showed the priest his golden medal. The priest wanted to know if it was true gold and Bascomb then regretted his choice. Why hadn't he chosen the medal given him by the French Government or the medal from Oxford? The Russians had not hall-marked the gold and he had no way of proving its worth. Then the priest noticed that the citation was written in the Russian alphabet. Not only was it false gold; it was Communist gold and not a fitting present for the sacred angel. At that moment the clouds parted and a single ray of light came into the vineyard, lighting the medal. It was a sign. The priest drew a cross in the air and they started back to the church.

It was an old, small, poor country church. The angel was in a chapel on the left, which the priest lighted. The image, buried in jewelry, stood in an iron cage with a padlocked door. The priest opened this and Bascomb placed his Lermontov medal at the angel's feet. Then he got to his knees and said loudly: "God bless Walt Whitman. God bless Hart Crane. God bless Dylan Thomas. God bless William Faulkner, Scott Fitzgerald, and especially Ernest Hemingway." The priest locked up the sacred relic and they left the church together. There was a café on the square where he got some supper and rented a bed. This was a strange engine of brass with brass angels at the four corners, but they seemed to possess some brassy blessedness since he dreamed of peace and woke in the middle of the night finding in himself that radiance he had known when he was younger. Something seemed to shine in his mind and limbs and lights and vitals and he fell asleep again and slept until morning.

On the next day, walking down from Monte Giordano to the main road, he heard the trumpeting of a waterfall. He went into the woods to find this. It was a natural fall, a shelf of rock and a curtain of green water, and it reminded him of a fall at the edge of the farm in Vermont where he had been raised. He had gone there one Sunday afternoon when he was a boy and sat on a hill above the pool. While he was there he saw an old man, with hair as thick and white as his was now, come through the woods. He had watched the old man unlace his shoes and undress himself with the haste of a lover. First he had wet his hands and arms and shoulders and then he had stepped into the torrent, bellowing with joy. He had then dried himself with his underpants, dressed, and gone back into the woods and it was not until he disappeared that Bascomb had realized that the old man was his father.

Now he did what his father had done—unlaced his shoes, tore at the buttons of his shirt and knowing that a mossy stone or the force of the water could be the end of him he stepped naked into the torrent, bellowing like his father. He could stand the cold for only a minute but when he stepped away from the water he seemed at last to be himself. He went on down to the main road where he was picked up by some mounted police, since Maria had sounded the alarm and the whole province was looking for the maestro. His return to Monte Carbone was triumphant and in the morning he began a long poem on the inalienable dignity of light and air that, while it would not get him the Nobel Prize, would grace the last months of his life.

MAVIS GALLANT

Irina

One of Irina's grandsons, nicknamed Riri, was sent to her at Christmas. His mother was going into hospital, but nobody told him that. The real cause of his visit was that since Irina had become a widow her children worried about her being alone. The children, as Irina would call them forever, were married and in their thirties and forties. They did not think they were like other people, because their father had been a powerful old man. He was a Swiss writer, Richard Notte. They carried his reputation and the memory of his puritan equity like an immense jar filled with water of which they had been told not to spill a drop. They loved their mother, but they had never needed to think about her until now. They had never fretted about which way her shadow might fall, and whether to stay in the shade or get out by being eccentric and bold. There were two sons and three daughters, with fourteen children among them. Only Riri was an only child. The girls had married an industrial designer, a Lutheran minister (perhaps an insolent move, after all, for the daughter of a militant atheist), and an art historian in Paris. One boy had become a banker and the other a lecturer on Germanic musical tradition. These were the crushed sons and loyal daughters to whom Irina had been faithful, whose pictures had travelled with her and lived beside her bed.

Few of Notte's obituaries had even mentioned a family. Some of his literary acquaintances were surprised to learn there had been any children at all, though everyone paid homage to the soft, quiet wife to whom he had dedicated his books, the subject of his first rapturous poems. These poems, conventional verse for the most part, seldom translated out of German except by unpoetical research scholars, were thought to be the work of his youth. Actually, Notte was forty when he finally married, and Irina barely nineteen. The obituaries called Notte the last of a breed, the end of a Tolstoyan line of moral lightning rods—an extinction which was probably hard on those writers who came after him, and still harder on his children. However, even to his family the old man had appeared to be the very archetype of a respected European novelist—prophet, dissuader, despairingly opposed to evil, cracked-voiced after having made so many pronouncements. Otherwise, he was not all that typical as a Swiss or as a Western, liberal, Protestant European, for he neither saved, nor invested, nor hid, nor disguised his material returns.

"What good is money, except to give away?" he often said. He had a wife, five children, and an old secretary who had turned into a dependent. It was true that he claimed next to nothing for himself. He rented shabby, ramshackle houses impossible to heat or even to clean. Owning was against his convictions, and he did not want to be tied to a gate called home. His room was furnished with a cot, a lamp, a desk, two chairs, a map of the world, a small bookshelf—no more, not even carpets or curtains. Like his family, he wore thick sweaters indoors as out, and crouched over inadequate electric fires. He seldom ate meat—though he did not deprive his children—and drank water with his meals. He had married once—once and for all. He could on occasion enjoy wine and praise and restaurants and good-looking women, but these festive outbreaks were on the rim of his real life, as remote from his children—as strange and as distorted to them—as some other country's colonial wars. He grew old early, as if he expected old age to suit him. By sixty, his eyes were sunk in pockets of lizard skin. His hair became bleached and lustrous, like the scrap of wedding dress Irina kept in a jeweller's box. He was photographed wearing a dark suit and a woman's plaid shawl—he was always cold by then, even in summer—and with a rakish felt hat shading half his face. His wife still let a few photographers in, at the end—but not many. Her murmured "He is working" had for decades been a double lock. He was as strong as Rasputin, his enemies said; he went on writing and talking and travelling until he positively could not focus his eyes or be helped aboard a train. Nearly to the last, he and Irina swung off on their seasonal cycle of journeys to Venice, to Rome, to cities where their married children lived, to Liège and Oxford for awards and honors. His place in a hotel dining room was recognizable from the door because of the pills, drops, and powders lined up to the width of a dinner plate. Notte's hypochondria had been known and gently caricatured for years. His sons, between them, had now bought up most of the original drawings: Notte, in infant's clothing, downing his medicine like a man (he had missed the Nobel); Notte quarrelling with Aragon and throwing up Surrealism; a grim female figure called "Existentialsim" taking his pulse; Notte catching Asian flu on a cultural trip to Peking. During the final months of his life his children noticed that their mother had begun acquiring medicines of her own, as if hoping by means of mirror-magic to draw his ailments into herself.

If illness became him, it was only because he was fond of ritual, the children thought—even the hideous ceremonial of pain. But Irina had not been intended for sickness and suffering; she was meant to be burned dry and consumed by the ritual of him. The children believed that the end of his life would surely be the death of their mother. They did not really expect Irina to turn her face to the wall and die, but an exclusive, even a selfish, alliance with Notte had seemed her reason for being. As their father grew old, then truly old, then old in mind, and querulous, and unjust, they observed the patient tenderness with which she heeded his sulks and caprices, his almost insane commands. They supposed this ardent submission of hers had to do with love, but it was not a sort of love they had ever experienced or tried to provoke. One of his sons saw Notte crying because Irina had buttered toast for him when he wanted it dry. She stroked the old man's silky hair, smiling. The son hated this. Irina was diminishing a strong, proud man, making a senile child of him, just as Notte was enslaving and debasing her. At the same time the son felt a secret between the two, a mystery. He wondered then, but at no other time, if the secret might not be Irina's invention and property.

Notte left a careful will for such an unworldly person. His wife was to be secure in her lifetime. Upon her death the residue of income from his work would be shared among the sons and daughters. There were no gifts or bequests. The will was accompanied by a testament which the children had photocopied for the beauty of the handwriting and the charm of the text. Irina, it began, belonged to a generation of women shielded from decisions, allowed to grow in the sun and shade of male protection. This flower, his flower, he wrote, was to be cherished now as if she were her children's child.

"In plain words," said Irina, at the first reading, in a Zurich lawyer's office, "I am the heir." She was wearing dark glasses because her eyes were tired, and a tight hat. She looked tense and foreign.

Well, yest, that was it, although Notte had put it more gracefully. His favorite daughter was his literary executor, entrusted with the unfinished manuscripts and the journals he had kept for sixty-five years. But it soon became evident that Irina had no intention of giving these up. The children adored their mother, but even without love as a factor would not have made a case of it; Notte's lawyer had already told them about disputes ending in mazelike litigation, families sundered; contents of a desk sequestered, diaries rotting in bank vaults while the inheritors thrashed it out. Besides, editing Notte's papers would keep Irina busy and an occupation was essential now. In loving and unloving families alike, the same problem arises after a death: What to do about the widow?

Irina settled some of it by purchasing an apartment in a small Alpine town. She chose a tall, glassy, urban-looking building of the kind that made conservationist groups send round-robin letters, accompanied by incriminating photographs, to newspapers in Lausanne. The apartment had a hall, an up-to-date kitchen, a bedroom for Irina, a spare room with a narrow bed in it, one bathroom, and a living room containing a couch. There was a glassed-in cube of a balcony where in a pinch an extra cot might have fitted, but Irina used the space for a table and chairs. She ordered red lampshades and thick curtains and the pale furniture that is usually sold to young couples. She seemed to come into her own in that tight, neutral flat, the children thought. They read some of the interviews she gave, and approved: she said, in English and Italian, in German and French, that she would not be a literary widow, detested by critics, resented by Notte's readers. Her firm diffidence made the children smile, and they were proud to read about her dignified beauty. But as for her intelligence—well, they supposed that the interviewers had confused fluency with wit. Irina's views and her way of expressing them were all camouflage, simply part of a ladylike undereducation, long on languages and bearing, short on history and arithmetic. Her origins were Russian and Swiss and probably pious; the children had not been drawn to that side of the family. Their father's legendary peasant childhood, his isolated valley-village had filled their imaginations and their collective past. There was a sudden April lightness in her letters now that relieved and yet troubled them. They knew it was a sham happiness, Nature's way of protecting the survivor from immediate grief. The crisis would come later, when her most secret instincts had built a seawall. They took turns invading her at Easter and in the summer, one couple at a time, bringing a child apiece—there was no room for more. Winter was a problem, however, for the skiing was not good just there, and none of them liked to break up their familes at Christmastime. Not only was Irina's apartment lacking in beds but there was absolutely no space for a tree. Finally, she offered to visit them, in regular order. That was how they settled it. She went to Bern, to Munich, to Zurich, and then came the inevitable Christmas when it was not that no one wanted her but just that they were all doing different things.

She had written in November of that year that a friend, whom she described, with some quaintness, as "a person," had come for a long stay. They liked that. A visit meant winter company, lamps on at four, China tea, conversation, the peppery smell of carnations (her favorite flower) in a warm room. For a week or two of the visit her letters were blithe, but presently they noticed that "the person" seemed to be having a depressing effect on their mother. She wrote that she had been working on Notte's journals for three years now. Who would want to read them except old men and women? His moral and political patterns were fossils of liberalism. He had seen the cracks in the Weimar Republic. He had understood from the beginning what Hitler meant. If at first he had been wrong about Mussolini, he had changed his mind even before Croce changed his, and had been safely back on the side of democracy in time to denounce Pirandello. He had given all he could, short of his life, to the Spanish Republicans. His measure of Stalin had been so wise and unshakably just that he had never been put on the Communist index—something rare for a Western Socialist. No one could say, ever, that Notte had hedged or retreated or kept silent when a voice was needed. Well, said Irina, what of it? He had written, pledged, warned, signed, declared. And what had he changed, diverted, or stopped? She suddenly sent the same letter to all five children: "This Christmas I don't want to go anywhere. I intend to stay here, in my own home."

They knew this was the crisis and that they must not leave her to face it alone, but that was the very winter when all their plans ran down, when one daughter was going into hospital, another moving to a different city, the third probably divorcing. The elder son was committed to a Christmas with his wife's parents, the younger lecturing in South Africa—a country where Irina, as Notte's constant reflection, would certainly not wish to set foot. They wrote and called and cabled one another: What shall we do? Can you? Will you? I can't.

Irina had no favorites among her children, except possibly one son who had been ill with rheumatic fever as a child and required long nursing. To him she now confided that she longed for her own childhood sometimes, in order to avoid having to judge herself. She was homesick for a time when nothing had crystallized and mistakes were allowed. Now, in old age, she had no excuse for errors. Every thought had a long meaning; every motive had angles and corners, and could be measured. And yet whatever she saw and thought and attempted was still fluid and vague. The shape of a table against afternoon light still held a mystery, awaited a final explanation. You looked for clarity, she wrote, and the answer you had was paleness, the flat white cast that a snowy sky throws across a room.

Part of this son knew about death and dying, but the rest of him was a banker and thoroughly active. He believed that, given an ideal situation, one should be able to walk through a table, which would save time and roundabout decisions. However, like all of Notte's children he had been raised with every awareness of solid matter too. His mother's youthful, yearning, and probably religious letter made him feel bland and old. He told his wife what he thought it contained, and she told a sister-in-law what she thought he had said. Irina was tired. Her eyesight was poor, perhaps as a result of prolonged work on those diaries. Irina did not need adult company, which might lead to morbid conversation; what she craved now was a symbol of innocent, continuing life. An animal might do it. Better still, a child.

Riri did not know that his mother would be in hospital the minute his back was turned. Balanced against a tame Christmas with a grandmother was a midterm holiday, later, of high-altitude skiing with his father. There was also some further blackmail involving his holiday homework, and then the vague state of behavior called "being reasonable"—that was all anyone asked. They celebrated a token Christmas on the twenty-third, and the next day he packed his presents (a watch and a tape recorder) and was put on a plane at Orly West. He flew from Paris to Geneva, where he spent the real Christmas Eve in a strange, bare apartment into which an aunt and a large family of cousins had just moved. In the morning he was wakened when it was dark and taken to a six-o'clock train. He said goodbye to his aunt at the station, and added, "If you ask the conductor or anyone to look after me, I'll—" Whatever threat was in his mind he seemed ready to carry out. He wore an R.A.F. badge on his jacket and carried a Waffen-S.S. emblem in his pocket. He knew better than to keep it in sight. At home they had already taken one away but he had acquired another at school. He had Astérix comic books for reading, chocolate-covered hazelnuts for support, and his personal belongings in a fairly large knapsack. He made a second train on his own and got down at the right station.

He had been told that he knew this place, but his memory, if it was a memory, had to do with fields and a picnic. No one met him. He shared a taxi through soft snow with two women, and paid his share—actually more than his share, which annoyed the women; they could not give less than a child in the way of a tip. The taxi let him off at a dark, shiny tower on stilts with granite steps. In the lobby a marble panel, looking like the list of names of war dead in his school, gave him his grandmother on the eighth floor. The lift, like the façade of the building, was made of dark mirrors into which he gazed seriously. A dense, thoughtful person looked back. He took off his glasses and the blurred face became even more remarkable. His grandmother had both a bell and a knocker at her door. He tried both. For quite a long time nothing happened. He knocked and rang again. It was not nervousness that he felt but a new sensation that had to do with a shut, foreign door.

His grandmother opened the door a crack. She had short white hair and a pale face and blue eyes. She held a dressing gown gripped at the collar. She flung the door back and cried, "Darling Richard, I thought you were arriving much later. Oh," she said, "I must look dreadful to you. Imagine finding me like this, in my dressing gown!" She tipped her head away and talked between her fingers, as he had been told never to do, because only liars cover their mouths. He saw a dark hall and a bright kitchen that was in some disorder, and a large dark, curtained room opposite the kitchen. This room smelled stuffy, of old cigarettes and of adults. But then his grandmother pushed the draperies apart and wound up the slatted shutters, and what had been dark, mound-like objects turned into a couch and a bamboo screen and a round table and a number of chairs. On a bookshelf stood a painting of three tulips that must have fallen out of their vase. Behind them was a sky that was all black except for a rainbow. He unpacked a portion of the things in his knapsack—wrapped presents for his grandmother, his new tape recorder, two school textbooks, a notebook, a Bic pen. The start of this Christmas lay hours behind him and his breakfast had died long ago.

"Are you hungry?" said his grandmother. He heard a telephone ringing as she brought him a cup of hot milk with a little coffee in it and two fresh croissants on a plate. She was obviously someone who never rushed to answer any bell. "My friend, who is an early riser, even on Christmas Day, went out and got these croissants. Very bravely, I thought." He ate his new breakfast, dipping the croissants in the milk, and heard his grandmother saying, "Well, I must have misunderstood. But he managed. . . . He didn't bring his skis. Why not? . . . I see." By the time she came back he had a book open. She watched him for a second and said, "Do you read at meals at home?"

"Sometimes."

"That's not the way I brought up your mother."

He put his nose nearer the page without replying. He read aloud from the page in a soft schoolroom plainchant: " 'Go, went, gone. Stand, stood, stood. Take, took, taken.' "

"Richard," said his grandmother. When he did not look up at once, she said, "I know what they call you at home, but what are you called at school?"

"Riri."

"I have three Richard grandsons," she said, "and not one is called Richard exactly."

"I have an Uncle Richard." he said.

"Yes, well, he happens to be a son of mine. I never allowed nicknames. Have you finished your breakfast?"

"Yes."

"Yes who? Yes what? What is your best language, by the way?"

"I am French," he said, with a sharp, sudden, hard hostility, the first tense bud of it, that made her murmur, "So soon?" She was about to tell him that he was not French—at least, not really—when an old man came into the room. He was thin and walked with a cane.

"Alec, this is my grandson," she said. "Riri, say how do you do to Mr. Aiken, who was kind enough to go out in this morning's snow to buy croissants for us all."

"I knew he would be here early," said the old man, in a stiff French that sounded extremely comical to the boy. "Irina has an odd ear for times and trains." He sat down next to Riri and clasped his hands on his cane; his hands at once began to tremble violently. "What does that interesting-looking book tell you?" he asked.

" 'The swallow flew away.' " answered Irina, reading over the child's head. " 'The swallow flew away with my hopes.' "

"Good God, let me look at that!" said the old man in his funny French. Sure enough, those were the words, and there was a swallow of a very strange blue, or at least a sapphire-and-turquoise creature with a swallow's tail. Riri's grandmother took her spectacles out of her dressing-gown pocket and brought the book up close and said in a loud, solemn way, " 'The swallows will have flown away.' " Then she picked up the tape recorder, which was the size of a glasses case, and after snapping the wrong button on and off, causing agonizing confusion and wastage, she said with her mouth against it, " 'When shall the swallows have flown away?' "

"No," said Riri, reaching, snatching almost. As if she had always given in to men, even to male children, she put the book down and the recorder too, saying "Mr. Aiken can help you with your English. He has the best possible accent. When he says 'the girl' you will think he is saying 'de Gaulle.' "

"Irina has an odd ear for English," said the old man calmly. He got up slowly and went to the kitchen, and she did too, and Riri could hear them whispering and laughing at something. Mr. Aiken came back alone carrying a small glass of clear liquid. "The morning heart-starter," he said. "Try it." Riri took a sip. It lay in his stomach like a warm stone. "No more effect on you than a gulp of milk," said the old man, marvelling, sitting down close to Riri again. "You could probably do with pints of this stuff. I can tell by looking at you you'll be a drinking man." His hands on the walking stick began to tremble anew. "I'm not the man I was," he said. "Not by any means." Because he did not speak English with a French or any foreign accent, Riri could not really understand him. He went on, "Fell down the staircase at the Trouville casino. Trouville, or that other place. Shock gave me amnesia. Hole in the stair carpet—must have been. I went there for years." he said. "Never saw a damned hole in anything. Now my hands shake."

"When you lift your glass to drink they don't shake." called Riri's grandmother from the kitchen. She repeated this in French, for good measure.

"She's got an ear like a radar unit," said Mr. Aiken.

Riri took up his tape recorder. In a measured chant, as if demonstrating to his grandmother how these things should be done, he said. " 'The swallows would not fly away if the season is fine.' "

"Do you know what any of it means?" said Mr. Aiken.

"He doesn't need to know what it means." Riri's grandmother answered for him. "He just needs to know it by heart."

They were glassed in on the balcony. The only sound they could hear was of their own voices. The sun on them was so hot that Riri wanted to take off his sweater. Looking down, he saw a chalet crushed in the shadows of two white blocks, not so tall as their own. A large, spared spruce tree suddenly seemed to retract its branches and allow a great weight of snow to slip off. Cars went by, dogs barked, children called—all in total silence. His grandmother talked English to the old man. Riri, when he was not actually eating, read "Astérix in Brittany" without attracting her disapproval.

"If people can be given numbers, like marks in school," she said, "Then children are zero." She was enveloped in a fur cloak, out of which her hands and arms emerged as if the fur had dissolved in certain places. She was pink with wine and sun. The old man's blue eyes were paler than hers. "Zero." She held up her thumb and forefinger in an O. "I was there with my five darling zeros while he . . . You are probably wondering if I was *ever* happy. At the beginning, in the first days, when I thought he would give me interesting books to read, books that would change all my life. Riri," she said, shading her eyes, "the cake and the ice cream were, I am afraid, the end of things for the moment. Could I ask you to clear the table for me?"

"I don't at home." Nevertheless he made a wobbly pile of dishes and took them away and did not come back. They heard him, indoors, starting all over: " 'Go, went, gone.' "

"I have only half a memory for dates." she said. "I forget my chidlren's birthdays until the last minute and have to send them telegrams. But I know *that* day. . . . "

"The twenty-sixth of May," he said. "What I forget is the year."

"I know that I felt young."

"You were. You *are* young." he said.

"Except that I was forty if a day." She glanced at the hands and wrists emerging from her cloak as if pleased at their whiteness. "The river was so sluggish, I remember. And the willows trailed in the river."

"Actually, there was a swift current after the spring rains."

"But no wind. The clouds were heavy."

"It was late in the afternoon." he said. "We sat on the grass."

"On a raincoat. You had thought in the morning those clouds meant rain."

"A young man drowned," he said. "Fell out of a boat. Funny, he didn't try to swim. So people kept saying."

"We saw three firemen in gleaming metal helmets. They fished for him so languidly—the whole day was like that. They had a grappling hook. None of them knew what to do with it. They kept pulling it up and taking the rope from each other."

"They might have been after water lilies, from the look of them."

"One of them bailed out the boat with a blue saucepan. I remember that. They'd got that saucepan from the restaurant."

"Where we had lunch," he said. "Trout, and a coffee cream pudding. You left yours."

"It was soggy cake. But the trout was perfection. So was the wine. The bridge over the river filled up slowly with holiday people. The three firemen rowed to shore."

"Yes, and one of them went off on a shaky bicycle and came back with a coil of frayed rope on his shoulder."

"The railway station was just behind us. All those people on the bridge were waiting for a train. When the firemen's boat slipped off down the river, they moved without speaking from one side of the bridge to the other, just to watch the boat. The silence of it."

"Like the silence here."

"This is planned silence," she said.

Riri played back his own voice. A tinny, squeaky Riri said, " 'Go, went, gone. Eat, ate, eaten. See, saw, sen.' "

" 'Seen!' " called his grandmother from the balcony. " 'Seen, not 'sen.' His mother made exactly that mistake," she said to the old man. "Oh, stop that," she said. He was crying. "Please, please, stop that. How could I have left five children?"

"Three were grown," he gasped, wiping his eyes.

"But they didn't know it. They didn't know they were grown." They still don't know it. And it made six children, counting him."

"The secretary mothered him," he said. "All he needed."

"I know, but you see she wasn't his wife, and he liked saying to strangers 'my wife,' 'my wife this' 'my wife that.' What is it Riri? Have you come to finish doing the thing I asked?"

He moved close to the table. His round glasses made him look desperate and stern. He said, "Which room is mine!" Darkness had gathered round him in spite of the sparkling sky and a row of icicles gleaming and melting in the most dazzling possible light. Outrage, a feeling that consideration had been wanting—that was how homesickness had overtaken him. She held his hand (he did not resist—another sign of his misery) and together they explored the apartment. He saw it all—every picture and cupboard and doorway—and in the end it was he who decided that Mr. Aiken must keep the spare room and he, Riri, would be happy on the living-room couch.

The old man passed them in the hall; he was obviously about to rest on the very bed he had just been within an inch of losing. He carried a plastic bottle of Evian. "Do you like the bland taste of water?" he said.

Riri looked boldly at his grandmother and said, "Yes," bursting into unexplained and endless-seeming laughter. He seemed to feel a relief at this substitute for impertinence. The old man laughed too, but broke off, coughing.

At half past four, when the windows were as black as the sky in the painting of tulips and began to reflect the lamps in a disturbing sort of way, they drew the curtains and had tea around the table. They pushed Riri's books and belongings to one side and spread a cross-stitched tablecloth. Riri had hot chocolate, a croissant left from breakfast and warmed in the oven, which made it deliciously greasy and soft, a slice of lemon sponge cake, and a banana. This time he helped clear away and even remained in the kitchen, talking, while his grandmother rinsed the cups and plates and stacked them in the machine.

The old man sat on a chair in the hall struggling with snow boots. He was going out alone in the dark to post some letters and to buy a newspaper and to bring back whatever provisions he thought were required for the evening meal.

"Riri, do you want to go with Mr. Aiken? Perhaps you should have a walk."

"At home I don't have to."

His grandmother looked cross; no, she looked worried. She was biting something back. The old man had finished the contention with his boots and now he put on a scarf, a fur-lined coat, a fur hat with earflaps, woollen gloves, and he took a list and a shopping bag and a different walking stick, which looked something like a ski pole. His grandmother stood still, as if dreaming, and then (addressing Riri) decided to wash all her amber necklaces. She fetched a wicker basket from her bedroom. It was lined with orange silk and filled with strings of beads. Riri followed her to the bathroom and sat on the end of the tub. She rolled up her soft sleeves and scrubbed the amber with laundry soap and a stiff brush. She scrubbed and rinsed and then began all over again.

"I am good at things like this," she said. "Now, unless you hate to discuss it, tell me something about your school."

At first he had nothing to say, but then he told her how stupid the younger boys were and what they were allowed to get away with.

"The younger boys would be seven, eight?" Yes, about that. "A hopeless generation?"

He wasn't sure; he knew that his class had been better.

She reached down and fetched a bottle of something from behind the bathtub and they went back to the sitting room together. They put a lamp between them, and Irina began to polish the amber with cotton soaked in turpentine. After a time the amber began to shine. The smell made him homesick, but not unpleasantly. He carefully selected a necklace when she told him he might take one for his mother, and he rubbed it with a soft cloth. She showed him how to make the beads magnetic by rolling them in his palms.

"You can do that even with plastic," he said.

"Can you? How very sad. It is dead matter."

"Amber is too," he said politely.

"What do you want to be later on? A scientist?"

"A ski instructor." He looked all round the room, at the shelves and curtains and at the bamboo folding screen, and said, "If you didn't live here, who would?"

She replied, "If you see anything that pleases you, you may keep it. I want you to choose your own present. If you don't seen anything, we'll go out tomorrow and look in the shops. Does that suit you?" He did not reply. She held the necklace he had picked and said, "Your mother will remember seeing this as I bent down to kiss her good night. Do you like old coins? One of my sons was a collector." In the wicker basket was a lacquered box that contained his uncle's coin collection. He took a coin but it meant nothing to him; he let it fall. It clinked, and he said. "We have a dog now." The dog wore a metal tag that rang when the dog drank out of a china bowl. Through a sudden rainy blur of new homesickness he saw that she had something else, another lacquered box, full of old cancelled stamps. She showed him a stamp with Hitler and one with an Italian king. "I've kept funny things," she said. "Like this beautiful Russian box. It belonged to my grandmother, but after I have died I expect it will be thrown out. I gave whatever jewelry I had left to my daughters. We never had furniture, so I became attached to strange little baskets and boxes of useless things. My poor daughters—I had precious little to give. But they won't be able to wear rings any more than I could. We all come into our inherited arthritis, these knotted-up hands. Our true heritage. When I was your age, about, my mother was dying of . . . I wasn't told. She took a ring from under her pillow and folded my hand on it. She said that I could always sell it if I had to, and no one need know. You see, in those days women had nothing of their own. They were like brown paper parcels tied with string. They were handed like parcels from their fathers to their husbands. To make the parcel look attractive it was decked with curls and piano lessons, and rings and gold coins and banknotes and shares. After appraising all the decoration, the new owner would undo the knots."

"Where is that ring?" he said. The blur of tears was forgotten.

"I tried to sell it when I needed money. The decoration on the brown paper parcel was disposed of by then. Everything thrown, given away. Not by me. My pearl necklace was sold for Spanish refugees. Victims, flotsam, the injured, the weak—they were important. I wasn't. The children weren't. I had my ring. I took it to a municipal pawnshop. It is a place where you take things and they give you money. I wore dark glasses and turned up my coat collar, like a spy." He looked as though he understood that. "The man behind the counter said that I was a married woman and I needed my husband's written consent. I said the ring was mine. He said nothing could be mine, or something to that effect. Then he said he might have given me something for the gold in the band of the ring but the stones were worthless. He said this happened in the finest of families. Someone had pried the real stones out of their setting."

"Who did that?"

"A husband. Who else would? Someone's husband—mine, or my mother's, or my mother's mother's, when it comes to that."

"With a knife?" said Riri. He said, "The man might have been pretending. Maybe he took out the stones and put in glass."

"There wasn't time. And they were perfect imitations—the right shapes and sizes."

"He might have had glass stones all different sizes."

"The women in the family never wondered if men were lying," she said. "They never questioned being dispossessed. They were taught to think that lies were a joke on the liar. That was why they lost out. He gave me the price of the gold in the band, as a favour, and I left the ring there. I never went back."

He put the lid on the box of stamps, and it fitted; he removed it, put it back, and said, "What time do you turn on your TV?"

"Sometimes never. Why?"

"At home I have it from six o'clock."

The old man came in with a pink-and-white face, bearing about him a smell of cold and of snow. He put down his shopping bag and took things out—chocolate and bottles and newspapers. He said, "I had to go all the way to the station for the papers. There is only one shop open, and even then I had to go round to the back door."

"I warned you that today was Christmas," Irina said.

Mr. Aiken said to Riri, "When I was still a drinking man this was the best hour of the day. If I had a glass now, I could put ice in it. Then I might add water. Then if I had water I could add whiskey. I know it is all the wrong way around, but at least I've started with a glass."

"You had wine with your lunch and gin instead of tea and I

believe you had straight gin before lunch,'' she said, gathering up the beads and coins and the turpentine and making the table Riri's domain again.

''Riri drank that,'' he said. It was so obviously a joke that she turned her head and put the basket down and covered her laugh with her fingers, as she had when she'd opened the door to him—oh, a long time ago now.

''I haven't a drop of anything left in the house,'' she said. That didn't matter, the old man said, for he had found what he needed. Riri watched and saw that when he lifted his glass his hand did not tremble at all. What his grandmother had said about that was true.

They had early supper and then Riri, after a courageous try at keeping awake, gave up even on television and let her make his bed of scented sheets, deep pillows, a feather quilt. The two others sat for a long time at the table, with just one lamp, talking in low voices. She had a pile of notebooks from which she read aloud and sometimes she showed Mr. Aiken things. He could see them through the chinks in the bamboo screen. He watched the lamp shadows for a while and then it was as if the lamp had gone out and he slept deeply.

The room was full of mound shapes, as it had been that morning when he arrived. He had not heard them leave the room. His Christmas watch had hands that glowed in the dark. He put on his glasses. It was half past ten. His grandmother was being just a bit loud at the telephone; that was what had woken him up. He rose, put on his slippers, and stumbled out to the bathroom.

''Just answer yes or no,'' she was saying. ''No, he can't. He has been asleep for an hour, two hours, at least. . . . Don't lie to me—I am bound to find the truth out. Was it a tumor? An extrauterine pregnancy? . . . Well, look. . . . Was she or was she not pregnant? What can you mean by 'not exactly'? If you don't know, who will?'' She happened to turn her head, and saw him and said without a change of tone, ''Your son is here, in his pajamas; he wants to say good night to you.''

She gave up the telephone and immediately went away so that the child could talk privately. She heard him say, ''I drank some kind of alcohol.''

So that was the important part of the day: not the journey, not the necklace, not even the strange old guest with the comic accent. She could tell from the sound of the child's voice that he was smiling. She picked up his bathrobe, went back to the hall, and put it over his shoulders. He scarcely saw her: he was concentrated on the distant voice. He said, in a matter-of-fact way, "All right, goodbye," and hung up.

"What a lot of things you have pulled out of that knapsack," she said.

"It's a large one. My father had it for military service."

Now, why should that make him suddenly homesick when his father's voice had not? "You are good at looking after yourself," she said. "Independent. No one has to tell you what to do. Of course, your mother had sound training. Once when I was looking for a nurse for your mother and her sisters, a great peasant woman came to see me, wearing a black apron and black buttoned boots. I said, 'What can you teach children?' And she said, 'To be clean and polite.' Your grandfather said, 'Hire her,' and stamped out of the room."

His mother interested, his grandfather bored him. He had the Christian name of a dead old man.

"You will sleep well," his grandmother promised, pulling the feather quilt over him. "You will dream short dreams at first, and by morning they will be longer and longer. The last one of all just before you wake up will be like a film. You will wake up wondering where you are, and then you will hear Mr. Aiken. First he will go round shutting all the windows, then you will hear his bath. He will start the coffee in an electric machine that makes a noise like a door rattling. He will pull on his snow boots with a lot of cursing and swearing and go out to fetch our croissants and the morning papers. Do you know what day it will be? The day after Christmas." He was almost asleep. Next to his watch and his glasses on a table close to the couch was an Astérix book and Irina's Russian box with old stamps in it. "Have you decided you want the stamps?"

"The box. Not the stamps."

He had taken, by instinct, the only object she wanted to keep. "For a special reason?" she said. "Of course, the box is yours. I am only wondering."

"The cover fits," he said.

She knew that the next morning he would have been here forever and that at parting time, four days later, she would have to remind him that leaving was the other half of arriving. She smiled, knowing how sorry he would be to go and how soon he would leave her behind. "This time yesterday . . . " he might say, but no more than once. He was asleep. His mouth opened slightly and the hair on his forehead became dark and damp. A doubled-up arm looked uncomfortable but Irina did not interfere; his sunken mind, his unconscious movements, had to be independent, of her or anyone, particularly of her. She did not love him more or less than any of her grandchildren. You see, it all worked out, she was telling him. You, and your mother, and the children being so worried, and my old friend. Anything can be settled for a few days at a time, though not for longer. She put out the light, for which his body was grateful. His mind, at that moment, in a sunny icicle brightness, was not only skiing but flying.

DORIS LESSING

An Old Woman and Her Cat

Her name was Hetty, and she was born with the twentieth century. She was seventy when she died of cold and malnutrition. She had been alone for a long time, since her husband had died of pneumonia in a bad winter soon after the Second World War. He had not been more than middleaged. Her four children were now middleaged, with grown children. Of these descendants one daughter sent her Christmas cards, but otherwise she did not exist for them. For they were all respectable people, with homes and good jobs and cars. And Hetty was not respectable. She had always been a bit strange, these people said, when mentioning her at all.

When Fred Pennefather, her husband, was alive and the children just growing up, they all lived much too close and uncomfortable in a Council flat in that part of London which is like an estuary, with tides of people flooding in and out: they were not half a mile from the great stations of Euston, St. Pancras, and King's Cross. The blocks of flats were pioneers in that area, standing up grim, grey, hideous, among many acres of little houses and gardens, all soon to be demolished so that they could be replaced by more tall grey blocks. The Pennefathers were good tenants, paying their rent, keeping out of debt; he was a building worker, "steady," and proud of it. There was no evidence then of Hetty's future dislocation from the normal, unless it was that she very often slipped down for an hour or so to the platforms where the locomotives drew in and ground out again. She liked the smell of it all, she said. She liked to see people moving about, "coming and going from all those foreign places." She meant Scotland, Ireland, the North of England. These visits into the din, the smoke, the massed swirling people were for her a drug, like other people's drinking or gambling. Her husband teased her, calling her a gypsy. She was in fact part gypsy, for her mother had been one, but had chosen to leave her people and marry a man who lived in a house. Fred Pennefather liked his wife for being different from the run of the women he knew, and had married her because of it, but her children were fearful that her gypsy blood might show itself in worse ways than haunting railway stations. She was a tall woman with a lot of glossy black hair, a skin that tanned easily, and dark strong eyes. She wore bright colors, and enjoyed quick tempers and sudden reconciliations. In her prime she attracted attention, was proud and handsome. All this made it inevitable that the people in those streets should refer to her as "that gypsy woman." When she heard them, she shouted back that she was none the worse for that.

After her husband died and the children married and left, the Council moved her to a small flat in the same building. She got a job selling food in a local store, but found it boring. There seem to be traditional occupations for middleaged women living alone, the busy and responsible part of their lives being over. Drink. Gambling. Looking for another husband. A wistful affair or two. That's about it. Hetty went through a period of, as it were, testing out all these, like hobbies, but tired of them. While still earning her small wage as a saleswoman, she began a trade in buying and selling secondhand clothes. She did not have a shop of her own, but bought clothes from householders, and sold these to stalls and the secondhand shops. She adored doing this. It was a passion. She gave up her respectable job and forgot all about her love of trains and travellers. Her room was always full of bright bits of cloth, a dress that had a pattern she fancied and did not want to sell, strips of beading, old furs, embroidery, lace. There were street traders among the people in the flats, but there was something in the way Hetty went about it that lost her friends. Neighbors of twenty or thirty years' standing said she had gone queer, and wished to know her no longer. But she did not mind. She was enjoying herself too much, particularly the moving about the streets with her old perambulator, in which she crammed what she was buying or selling. She liked the gossiping, the bargaining, the wheedling from householders. It was this last which—and she knew this quite well, of course—the neighbors objected to. It was the thin edge of the wedge. It was begging. Decent people did not beg. She was no longer decent.

Lonely in her tiny flat, she was there as little as possible, always preferring the lively streets. But she had after all to spend some time in her room, and one day she saw a kitten lost and trembling in a dirty corner, and brought it home to the block of flats. She was on a fifth floor. While the kitten was growing into a large strong tom, he ranged about that conglomeration of staircases and lifts and many dozens of flats, as if the building were a town. Pets were not actively persecuted by the authorities, only forbidden and then tolerated. Hetty's life from the coming of the cat became more sociable, for the beast was always making friends with somebody in the cliff that was the block of flats across the court, or not coming home for nights at a time, so that she had to go and look for him and knock on doors and ask, or returning home kicked and limping, or bleeding after a fight with his kind. She made scenes with the kickers, or the owners of the enemy cats, exchanged cat lore with cat lovers, was always having to bandage and nurse her poor Tibby. The cat was soon a scarred warrior with fleas, a torn ear, and a ragged look to him. He was a multicolored cat and his eyes were small and yellow. He was a long way down the scale from the delicately colored, elegantly shaped pedigree cats. But he was independent, and often caught himself pigeons when he could no longer stand the tinned cat food, or the bread and packet gravy Hetty fed him, and he purred and nestled when she grabbed him to her bosom at those times she suffered loneliness. This happened less and less. Once she had realized that her children were hoping that she would leave them alone because the old rag trader was an embarrassment to them she accepted it, and a bitterness that always had wild humor in it only welled up at times like Christmas. She sang or chanted to the cat: "You nasty old beast, filthy old cat, nobody wants you, do they Tibby, no, you're just an alley tom, just an old stealing cat, hey Tibs, Tibs, Tibs."

The building teemed with cats. There were even a couple of dogs. They all fought up and down the grey cement corridors. There were sometimes dog and cat messes which someone had to clear up, but which might be left for days and weeks as part of neighborly wars and feuds. There were many complaints. Finally an official came from the Council to say that the ruling about keeping animals was going to be enforced. Hetty, like others, would have to have her cat destroyed. This crisis coincided with a time of bad luck for her. She had had flu, had not been able to earn money, had found it hard to get out for her pension, had run into debt. She owed a lot of back rent, too. A television set she had hired and was not paying for attracted the visits of a television representative. The neighbors were gossiping that Hetty had "gone savage." This was because the cat had brought up the stairs and along the passageways a pigeon he had caught, shedding feathers and blood all the way; a woman coming in to complain found Hetty plucking the pigeon to stew it, as she had done with others, sharing the meal with Tibby.

"You're filthy," she would say to him, setting the stew down to cool in his dish. "Filthy old thing. Eating that dirty old pigeon. What do you think you are, a wild cat? Decent cats don't eat dirty birds. Only those old gypsies eat wild birds."

One night she begged help from a neighbor who had a car, and put into the car herself, the television set, the cat, bundles of clothes, and the pram. She was driven across London to a room in a street that was a slum because it was waiting to be done up. The neighbor made a second trip to bring her bed and her mattress, which were tied to the roof of the car, a chest of drawers, an old trunk, saucepans. It was in this way that she left the street in which she had lived for thirty years, nearly half her life.

She set up house again in one room. She was frightened to go near "them" to re-establish pension rights and her identity, because of the arrears of rent she had left behind, and because of the stolen television set. She started trading again, and the little room was soon spread, like her last, with a rainbow of colors and textures and lace and sequins. She cooked on a single gas ring and washed in the sink. There was no hot water unless it was boiled in saucepans. There were several old ladies and a family of five children in the house, which was condemned.

She was in the ground floor back, with a window which opened onto a derelict garden, and her cat was happy in a hunting ground that was a mile around this house where his mistress was so splendidly living. A canal ran close by, and in the dirty city-water were islands which a cat could reach by leaping from moored boat to boat. On the islands were rats and birds. There were pavements full of fat London pigeons. The cat was a fine hunter. He soon had his place in the hierarchies of the local cat population and did not have to fight much to keep it. He was a strong male cat, and fathered many litters of kittens.

In that place Hetty and he lived five happy years. She was trading well, for there were rich people close by to shed what the poor needed to buy cheaply. She was not lonely, for she made a quarrelling but satisfying friendship with a woman on the top floor, a widow like herself who did not see her children either. Hetty was sharp with the five children, complaining about their noise and mess, but she slipped them bits of money and sweets after telling their mother that "she was a fool to put herself out for them, because they wouldn't appreciate it." She was living well, even without her pension. She sold the television set and gave herself and her friend upstairs some day-trips to the coast, and bought a small radio. She never read books or magazines. The truth was that she could not write or read, or only so badly it was no pleasure to her. Her cat was all reward and no cost, for he fed himself, and continued to bring in pigeons for her to cook and eat, for which in return he claimed milk.

"Greedy Tibby, you greedy *thing*, don't think I don't know, oh yes I do, you'll get sick eating those old pigeons, I do keep telling you that, don't I?"

At last the street was being done up. No longer a uniform, long, disgraceful slum, houses were being bought by the middleclass people. While this meant more good warm clothes for trading—or begging, for she still could not resist the attraction of getting something for nothing by the use of her plaintive inventive tongue, her still-flashing handsome eyes—Hetty knew, like her neighbors, that soon this house with its cargo of poor people would be bought for improvement.

In the week Hetty was seventy years old came the notice that was the end of this little community. They had four weeks to find somewhere else to live.

Usually, the shortage of housing being what it is in London—and everywhere else in the world, of course—these people would have had to scatter, fending for themselves. But the fate of this particular street was attracting attention, because a municipal election was pending. Homelessness among the poor was finding a focus in this street which was a perfect symbol of the whole area, and indeed the whole city, half of it being fine converted tasteful houses, full of people who spent a lot of money, and half being dying houses tenanted by people like Hetty.

As a result of speeches by councillors and churchmen, local authorities found themselves unable to ignore the victims of this redevelopment. The people in the house Hetty was in were visited by a team consisting of an unemployment officer, a social worker, and a rehousing officer. Hetty, a strong gaunt old woman wearing a scarlet wool suit she had found among her cast offs that week, a black knitted teacosy on her head, and black buttoned Edwardian boots too big for her, so that she had to shuffle, invited them into her room. But although all were well used to the extremes of poverty, none wished to enter the place, but stood in the doorway and made her this offer: that she should be aided to get her pension—why had she not claimed it long ago?—and that she, together with the four other old ladies in the house, should move to a Home run by the Council out in the northern suburbs. All these women were used to, and enjoyed, lively London, and while they had no alternative but to agree, they fell into a saddened and sullen state. Hetty agreed too. The last two winters had set her bones aching badly, and a cough was never far away. And while perhaps she was more of an urban soul even than the others, since she had walked up and down so many streets with her old perambulator loaded with rags and laces, and since she knew so intimately London's texture and taste, she minded least of all the idea of a new home "among green fields." There were, in fact, no fields near the promised Home, but for some reason all the old ladies had chosen to bring out this old song of a phrase, as if it belonged to their situation, that of old women not far off death. "It will be nice to be near green fields again," they said to each other over cups of tea.

The housing officer came to make final arrangements. Hetty Pennefather was to move with the others in two weeks' time. The young man, sitting on the very edge of the only chair in the crammed room, because it was greasy and he suspected it had fleas or worse in it, breathed as lightly as he could because of the appalling stink: there was a lavatory in the house, but it had been out of order for three days, and it was just the other side of a thin wall. The whole house smelled.

The young man, who knew only too well the extent of the misery due to lack of housing, who knew how many old people abandoned by their children did not get the offer to spend their days being looked after by the authorities, could not help feeling that this wreck of a human being could count herself lucky to get a place in this "Home," even if it was—and he knew and deplored the fact—an institution in which the old were treated like naughty and dimwitted children until they had the good fortune to die.

But just as he was telling Hetty that a van would be coming to take her effects and those of the other four old ladies, and that she need not take anything more with her than her clothes "and perhaps a few photographs," he saw what he had thought was a heap of multicolored rags get up and put its ragged gingery-black paws on the old woman's skirt. Which today was a cretonne curtain covered with pink and red roses that Hetty had pinned around her because she liked the pattern.

"You can't take that cat with you," he said automatically. It was something he had to say often, and knowing what misery the statement caused, he usually softened it down. But he had been taken by surprise.

Tibby now looked like a mass of old wool that has been matting together in dust and rain. One eye was permanently half-closed, because a muscle had been ripped in a fight. One ear was vestigial. And down a flank was a hairless slope with a thick scar on it. A cat-hating man had treated Tibby as he treated all cats, to a pellet from his airgun. The resulting wound had taken two years to heal. And Tibby smelled.

No worse, however, than his mistress, who sat stiffly still, bright-eyed with suspicion, hostile, watching the well-brushed tidy young man from the Council.

"How old is that beast?"

"Ten years, no, only eight years, he's a young cat about five years old," said Hetty, desperate.

"It looks as if you'd do him a favor to put him out of his misery," said the young man.

When the official left, Hetty had agreed to everything. She was the only one of the old women with a cat. The others had budgerigars or nothing. Budgies were allowed in the Home.

She made her plans, confided in the others, and when the van came for them and their clothes and photographs and budgies, she was not there, and they told lies for her. "Oh we don't know where she can have gone, dear," the old women repeated again and again to the indifferent van driver. "She was here last night, but she did say something about going to her daughter in Manchester." And off they went to die in the Home.

Hetty knew that when houses have been emptied for redevelopment they may stay empty for months, even years. She intended to go on living in this one until the builders moved in.

It was a warm autumn. For the first time in her life she lived like her gypsy forebears, and did not go to bed in a room in a house like respectable people. She spent several nights, with Tibby, sitting crouched in a doorway of an empty house two doors from her own. She knew exactly when the police would come around, and where to hide herself in the bushes of the overgrown shrubby garden.

As she had expected, nothing happened in the house, and she moved back in. She smashed a back windowpane so that Tibby could move in and out without her having to unlock the front door for him, and without leaving a window suspiciously open. She moved to the top back room and left it every morning early, to spend the day in the streets with her pram and her rags. At night she kept a candle glimmering low down on the floor. The lavatory was still out of order, so she used a pail on the first floor, instead, and secretly emptied it at night into the canal, which in the day was full of pleasure boats and people fishing.

Tibby brought her several pigeons during that time.

''Oh you are a clever puss, Tibby, Tibby! Oh you're clever, you are. You know how things are, don't you, you know how to get around and about.''

The weather turned very cold; Christmas came and went. Hetty's cough came back, and she spent most of her time under piles of blankets and old clothes, dozing. At night she watched the shadows of the candle flame on floor and ceiling—the windowframes fitted badly, and there was a draught. Twice tramps spent the night in the bottom of the house and she heard them being moved on by the police. She had to go down to make sure the police had not blocked up the broken window the cat used, but they had not. A blackbird had flown in and had battered itself to death trying to get out. She plucked it, and roasted it over a fire made with bits of floorboard in a baking pan: the gas of course had been cut off. She had never eaten very much, and was not frightened that some dry bread and a bit of cheese was all that she had eaten during her sojourn under the heap of clothes. She was cold, but did not think about that much. Outside there was slushy brown snow everywhere. She went back to her nest thinking that soon the cold spell would be over and she could get back to her trading. Tibby sometimes got into the pile with her, and she clutched the warmth of him to her. ''Oh you clever cat, you clever old thing, looking after yourself, aren't you? That's right my ducky, that's right my lovely.''

And then, just as she was moving about again, with snow gone off the ground for a time but winter only just begun, in January, she saw a builder's van draw up outside, a couple of men unloading their gear. They did not come into the house: they were to start work next day. By then Hetty, her cat, her pram piled with clothes and her two blankets, were gone. She also took a box of matches, a candle, an old saucepan and a fork and spoon, a tinopener, and a rat-trap. She had a horror of rats.

About two miles away, among the homes and gardens of amiable Hampstead, where live so many of the rich, the intelligent and the famous, stood three empty, very large houses. She had seen them on an occasion, a couple of years before, when she had taken a bus. This was a rare thing for her, because of the remarks and curious looks provoked by her mad clothes, and by her being able to appear at the same time such a tough battling old thing and a naughty child. For the older she got, this disreputable tramp, the more there strengthened in her a quality of fierce, demanding childishness. It was all too much of a mixture; she was uncomfortable to have near.

She was afraid that "they" might have rebuilt the houses, but there they still stood, too tumbledown and dangerous to be of much use to tramps, let alone the armies of London's homeless. There was no glass left anywhere. The flooring at ground level was mostly gone, leaving small platforms and juts of planking over basements full of water. The ceilings were crumbling. The roofs were going. The houses were like bombed buildings.

But on the cold dark of a late afternoon she pulled the pram up the broken stairs and moved cautiously around the frail boards of a second-floor room that had a great hole in it right down to the bottom of the house. Looking into it was like looking into a well. She held a candle to examine the state of the walls, here more or less whole, and saw that rain and wind blowing in from the window would leave one corner dry. Here she made her home. A sycamore tree screened the gaping window from the main road twenty yards away. Tibby, who was cramped after making the journey under the clothes piled in the pram, bounded down and out and vanished into neglected undergrowth to catch his supper. He returned fed and pleased, and seemed happy to stay clutched in her hard thin old arms. She had come to watch for his return after hunting trips, because the warm purring bundle of bones and fur did seem to allay, for a while, the permanent ache of cold in her bones.

Next day she sold her Edwardian boots for a few shillings—they were fashionable again—and bought a loaf and some bacon scraps. In a corner of the ruins well away from the one she had made her own, she pulled up some floorboards, built a fire, and toasted bread and the bacon scraps. Tibby had brought in a pigeon, and she roasted that, but not very efficiently. She was afraid of the fire catching and the whole mass going up in flames; she was afraid too of the smoke showing and attracting the police. She had to keep damping down the fire, and so the bird was bloody and unappetising, and in the end Tibby got most of it. She felt confused, and discouraged, but thought it was because of the long stretch of winter still ahead of her before spring could come. In fact, she was ill. She made a couple of attempts to trade and earn money to feed herself before she acknowledged she was ill. She knew she was not yet dangerously ill, for she had been that in her life, and would have been able to recognize the cold listless indifference of a real last-ditch illness. But all her bones ached, and her head ached, and she coughed more than she ever had. Yet she still did not think of herself as suffering particularly from the cold, even in that sleety January weather. She had never, in all her life, lived in a properly heated place, had never known a really warm home, not even when she lived in the Council flats. Those flats had electric fires, and the family had never used them, for the sake of economy, except in very bad spells of cold. They piled clothes onto themselves, or went to bed early. But she did know that to keep herself from dying now she could not treat the cold with her usual indifference. She knew she must eat. In the comparatively dry corner of the windy room, away from the gaping window through which snow and sleet were drifting, she made another nest—her last. She had found a piece of plastic sheeting in the rubble, and she laid that down first, so that the damp would not strike up. Then she spread her two blankets over that. Over them were heaped the mass of old clothes. She wished she had another piece of plastic to put on top, but she used sheets of newspaper instead. She heaved herself into the middle of this, with a loaf of bread near to her hand. She dozed, and waited, and nibbled bits of bread, and watched the snow drifting softly in. Tibby sat close to the old blue face that poked out of the pile and put up a paw to touch it. He miaowed and was restless, and then went out into the frosty morning and brought in a pigeon. This the cat put, still struggling and fluttering a little, close to the old woman. But she was afraid to get out of the pile in which the heat was being made and kept with such difficulty. She really could not climb out long enough to pull up more splinters of plank from the floors, to make a fire, to pluck the pigeon, to roast it. She put out a cold hand to stroke the cat.

"Tibby, you old thing, you brought it for me then, did you? You did, did you? Come here, come in here. . . ." But he did not want to get in with her. He miaowed again, pushed the bird closer to her. It was now limp and dead.

"You have it then. You eat it. I'm not hungry, thank you Tibby."

But the carcass did not interest him. He had eaten a pigeon before bringing this one up to Hetty. He fed himself well. In spite of his matted fur, and his scars and his half-closed yellow eye, he was a strong healthy cat.

At about four the next morning there were steps and voices downstairs. Hetty shot out of the pile and crouched behind a fallen heap of plaster and beams, now covered with snow, at the end of the room near the window. She could see through the hole in the floorboards down to the first floor, which had collapsed entirely, and through it to the ground floor. She saw a man in a thick overcoat and muffler and leather gloves holding a strong torch to illuminate a thin bundle of clothes lying on the floor. She saw that this bundle was a sleeping man or woman. She was indignant—*her* home was being trespassed upon. And she was afraid because she had not been aware of this other tenant of the ruin. Had he, or she, heard her talking to the cat? And where was the cat? If he wasn't careful he would be caught, and that would be the end of him. The man with a torch went off and came back with a second man. In the thick dark far below Hetty was a small cave of strong light, which was the torchlight. In this space of light two men bent to lift the bundle, carried it out across the dangertraps of fallen and rotting boards that made gangplanks over the water-filled basements. One man was holding the torch in the hand that supported the dead person's feet, and the light jogged and lurched over trees and grasses: the corpse was being taken through the shrubberies to a car.

There are men in London who, between the hours of two and five in the morning—when the real citizens are asleep, who should not be disturbed by such unpleasantness as the corpses of the poor—make the rounds of all the empty, rotting houses they know about, to collect the dead, and to warn the living that they ought not to be there at all, inviting them to one of the official Homes or lodgings for the homeless.

Hetty was too frightened to get back into her warm heap. She sat with the blankets pulled around her, and looked through gaps in the fabric of the house, making out shapes and boundaries and holes and puddles and mounds of rubble, as her eyes, like her cat's, became accustomed to the dark.

She heard scuffling sounds and knew they were rats. She had meant to set the trap, but the thought of her friend Tibby, who might catch his paw, had stopped her. She sat up until the morning light came in grey and cold, after nine. Now she did know herself to be very ill and in danger, for she had lost all the warmth she had huddled into her bones under the rags. She shivered violently. She was shaking herself apart with shivering. In between spasms she drooped limp and exhausted. Through the ceiling above her—but it was not a ceiling, only a cobweb of slats and planks—she could see into a dark cave which had been a garret, and through the roof above that, the grey sky, teeming with incipient rain. The cat came back from where he had been hiding, and sat crouched on her knees, keeping her stomach warm, while she thought out her position. These were her last clear thoughts. She told herself that she would not last out until spring unless she allowed "them" to find her, and take her to hospital. After that, she would be taken to a Home.

But what would happen to Tibby, her poor cat? She rubbed the old beast's scruffy head with the ball of her thumb and muttered: "Tibby, Tibby, they won't get you, no, you'll be all right, yes, I'll look after you."

Towards midday, the sun oozed yellow through miles of greasy grey cloud, and she staggered down the rotting stairs, to the shops. Even in those London streets, where the extraordinary has become usual, people turned to stare at a tall gaunt woman, with a white face that had flaming red patches on it, and blue compressed lips, and restless black eyes. She wore a tightly buttoned man's overcoat, torn brown woollen mittens, and an old fur hood. She pushed a pram loaded with old dresses and scraps of embroidery and torn jerseys and shoes, all stirred into a tight tangle, and she kept pushing this pram up against people as they stood in queues, or gossiped, or stared into windows, and she muttered: "Give me your old clothes darling, give me your old pretties, give Hetty something, poor Hetty's hungry." A woman gave her a handful of small change, and Hetty bought a roll filled with tomato and lettuce. She did not dare go into a cafe, for even in her confused state she knew she would offend, and would probably be asked to leave. But she begged a cup of tea at a street stall, and when the hot sweet liquid flooded through her she felt she might survive the winter. She bought a carton of milk and pushed the pram back through the slushy snowy street to the ruins.

Tibby was not there. She urinated down through the gap in the boards, muttering, "A nuisance, that old tea," and wrapped herself in a blanket and waited for the dark to come.

Tibby came in later. He had blood on his foreleg. She had heard scuffling and she knew that he had fought a rat, or several, and had been bitten. She poured the milk into the tilted saucepan and Tibby drank it all.

She spent the night with the animal held against her chilly bosom. They did not sleep, but dozed off and on. Tibby would normally be hunting, the night was his time, but he had stayed with the old woman now for three nights.

Early next morning they again heard the corpse removers among the rubble on the ground floor, and saw the beams of the torch moving on wet walls and collapsed beams. For a moment the torchlight was almost straight on Hetty, but no one came up: who could believe that a person could be desperate enough to climb those dangerous stairs, to trust those crumbling splintery floors, and in the middle of winter?

Hetty had now stopped thinking of herself as ill, of the degrees of her illness, of her danger—of the impossibility of her surviving. She had cancelled out in her mind the presence of winter and its lethal weather, and it was as if spring were nearly here. She knew that if it had been spring when she had had to leave the other house, she and the cat could have lived here for months and months, quite safely and comfortably. Because it seemed to her an impossible and even a silly thing that her life, or, rather, her death, could depend on something so arbitrary as builders starting work on a house in January rather than in April, she could not believe it: the fact would not stay in her mind. The day before she had been quite clearheaded. But today her thoughts were cloudy, and she talked and laughed aloud. Once she scrambled up and rummaged in her rags for an old Christmas card she had got four years before from her good daughter.

In a hard harsh angry grumbling voice she said to her four children that she needed a room of her own now that she was getting on. "I've been a good mother to you," she shouted to them before invisible witnesses—former neighbors, welfare workers, a doctor. "I never let you want for anything, never! When you were little you always had the best of everything! You can ask anybody; go on, ask them, then!"

She was restless and made such a noise that Tibby left her and bounded on to the pram and crouched watching her. He was limping, and his foreleg was rusty with blood. The rat had bitten deep. When the daylight came, he left Hetty in a kind of sleep, and went down into the garden where he saw a pigeon feeding on the edge of the pavement. The cat pounced on the bird, dragged it into the bushes, and ate it all, without taking it up to his mistress. After he had finished eating, he stayed hidden, watching the passing people. He stared at them intently with his blazing yellow eye, as if he were thinking, or planning. He did not go into the old ruin and up the crumbling wet stairs until late—it was as if he knew it was not worth going at all.

He found Hetty, apparently asleep, wrapped loosely in a blanket, propped sitting in a corner. Her head had fallen on her chest, and her quantities of white hair had escaped from a scarlet woollen cap, and concealed a face that was flushed a deceptive pink—the flush of coma from cold. She was not yet dead, but she died that night. The rats came up the walls and along the planks and the cat fled down and away from them, limping still, into the bushes.

Hetty was not found for a couple of weeks. The weather changed to warm, and the man whose job it was to look for corpses was led up the dangerous stairs by the smell. There was something left of her, but not much.

As for the cat, he lingered for two or three days in the thick shrubberies, watching the passing people and beyond them, the thundering traffic of the main road. Once a couple stopped to talk on the pavement, and the cat, seeing two pairs of legs, moved out and rubbed himself against one of the legs. A hand came down and he was stroked and patted for a little. Then the people went away.

The cat saw he would not find another home, and he moved off, nosing and feeling his way from one garden to another, through empty houses, finally into an old churchyard. This graveyard already had a couple of stray cats in it, and he joined them. It was the beginning of a community of stray cats going wild. They killed birds, and the field mice that lived among the grasses, and they drank from puddles. Before winter had ended the cats had

had a hard time of it from thirst, during the two long spells when the ground froze and there was snow and no puddles and the birds were hard to catch because the cats were so easy to see against the clean white. But on the whole they managed quite well. One of the cats was female, and soon there were a swarm of wild cats, as wild as if they did not live in the middle of a city surrounded by streets and houses. This was just one of half a dozen communities of wild cats living in that square mile of London.

Then an official came to trap the cats and take them away. Some of them escaped, hiding till it was safe to come back again. But Tibby was caught. He was not only getting old and stiff—he still limped from the rat's bite—but he was friendly, and did not run away from the man, who had only to pick him up in his arms.

"You're an old soldier, aren't you?" said the man. "A real tough one, a real old tramp."

It is possible that the cat even thought that he might be finding another human friend and a home.

But it was not so. The haul of wild cats that week numbered hundreds, and while if Tibby had been younger a home might have been found for him, since he was amiable, and wished to be liked by the human race, he was really too old, and smelly and battered. So they gave him an injection and, as we say, "put him to sleep."

ALICE MUNRO

Spelling

In the store, in the old days, Flo used to say she could tell when some woman was going off the track. Special headgear or footwear were often the first giveaways. Galoshes flopping open on a summer day. Rubber boots they slopped around in, or men's workboots. They might say it was on account of corns, but Flo knew better. It was deliberate, it was meant to tell. Next might come the old felt hat, the torn raincoat worn in all weathers, the trousers held up at the waist with twine, the dim shredded scarves, the layers of ravelling sweaters.

Mothers and daughters often the same way. It was always in them. Waves of craziness, always rising, irresistible as giggles, from some place deep inside, gradually getting the better of them.

They used to come telling Flo their stories. Flo would string them along. ''Is that so?'' she would say. ''Isn't that a shame?''

My vegetable grater is gone and I know who took it.

There is a man comes and looks at me when I take my clothes off at night. I pull the blind down and he looks through the crack.

Two hills of new potatoes stolen. A jar of whole peaches. Some nice ducks' eggs.

One of those women they took to the County Home at last. The first thing they did, Flo said, was give her a bath. The next thing they did was cut off her hair, which had grown out like a haystack. They expected to find anything in it, a dead bird or maybe a nest of baby mouse skeletons. They did find burrs and leaves and a bee that must have got caught and buzzed itself to death. When they had cut down far enough they found a cloth hat. It had rotted on her head and the hair had just pushed up through it, like grass through wire. Flo had got into the habit of keeping the table set for the next meal, to save trouble. The plastic cloth was gummy, the outline of the plate and saucer plain on it as the outline of pictures on a greasy wall. The refrigerator was full of sulfurous scraps, dark crusts, furry oddments. Rose got to work cleaning, scraping, scalding. Sometimes Flo came lumbering through on her two canes. She might ignore Rose's presence altogether, she might tip the jug of maple syrup up against her mouth and drink it like wine. She loved sweet things now, craved them. Brown sugar by the spoonful, maple syrup, tinned puddings, jelly, globs of sweetness to slide down her throat. She had given up smoking, probably for fear of fire.

Another time she said, "What are you doing in there behind the counter? You ask me what you want, and I'll get it." She thought the kitchen was the store.

"I'm *Rose,*" Rose said in a loud, slow voice, "We're in the *kitchen*. I'm cleaning up the *kitchen*."

The old arrangement of the kitchen: mysterious, personal, eccentric. Big pan in the oven, medium-sized pan under the potato pot on the corner shelf, little pan hanging on the nail by the sink. Colander under the sink. Dishrags, newspaper clippings, scissors, muffin tins, hanging on various nails. Piles of bills and letters on the sewing-machine, on the telephone shelf. You would think someone had set them down a day or two ago, but they were years old. Rose had come across some letters written by herself, in a forced and spritely style. False messengers; false connections, with a lost period of her life.

"Rose is away," Flo said. She had a habit now of sticking her bottom lip out, when she was displeased or perplexed. "Rose got married."

The second morning Rose got up and found that a gigantic stirring-up had occurred in the kitchen, as if someone had wielded a big shaky spoon. The big pan was lodged behind the refrigerator; the egg lifter was in with the towels, the breadknife was in the flour bin and the roasting pan wedged in the pipes under the sink. Rose made Flo's breakfast porridge and Flo said, "You're that woman they were sending to look after me."

"Yes."

"You aren't from around here?"

"No."

"I haven't got money to pay you. They sent you, they can pay you."

Flo spread brown sugar over her porridge until the porridge was entirely covered, then patted the sugar smooth with her spoon.

After breakfast she spied the cutting board, which Rose had been using when she cut bread for her own toast. "What is this thing doing here getting in our road?" said Flo authoritatively, picking it up and marching off—as well as anybody with two canes could march—to hide it somewhere, in the piano bench or under the back steps.

Years ago, Flo had had a little glassed-in side porch built on to the house. From there she could watch the road just as she used to watch from behind the counter of the store (the store window was now boarded up, the old advertising signs painted over). The road wasn't the main road out of Hanratty through West Hanratty to the Lake, any more; there was a highway bypass. And it was paved, now, with wide gutters, new mercury vapor street lights. The old bridge was gone and a new, wide bridge, much less emphatic, had taken its place. The change from Hanratty to West Hanratty was hardly noticeable. West Hanratty had got itself spruced up with paint and aluminum siding; Flo's place was about the only eyesore left.

What were the things Flo put up to look at, in her little porch, where she had been sitting for years now with her joints and arteries hardening?

A calendar with a picture of a puppy and a kitchen on it. Faces turned towards each other so that the noses touched, and the space between the two bodies made a heart.

A photograph, in color, of Princess Anne as a child.

A Blue Mountain pottery vase, gift from Brian and Phoebe, with three yellow plastic roses in it, vase and roses bearing several seasons' sifting of dust.

Six shells from the Pacific coast, sent home by Rose but not gathered by her, as Flo believed, or had once believed. Bought on a vacation in the State of Washington. They were an impulse item in a plastic bag by the cashier's desk in a tourist restaurant.

THE LORD IS MY SHEPHERD, in black cutout scroll with a sprinkling of glitter. Free gift from a dairy.

Newspaper photograph of seven coffins in a row. Two large and five small. Parents and children, all shot by the father in the middle of the night, for reasons nobody knew, in a farmhouse out in the country. That house was not easy to find but Flo had seen it. Neighbors took her, on a Sunday drive, in the days when she was using only one cane. They had to ask directions at a gas station on the highway, and again at a crossroads store. They were told that many people had asked the same questions, had been equally determined. Though Flo had to admit there was nothing much to see. A house like any other. The chimney, the windows, the shingles, the door. Something that could have been a dishtowel, or a diaper, that nobody had felt like taking in, left to rot on the line.

Rose had not been back to see Flo for nearly two years. She had been busy, she had been traveling with small companies, financed by grants, putting on plays or scenes from plays, or giving readings, in high school auditoriums and community halls, all over the country. It was part of her job to go on local television chatting about these productions, trying to drum up interest, telling amusing stories about things that had happened during the tour. There was nothing shameful about any of this, but sometimes Rose was deeply, unaccountably ashamed. She did not let her confusion show. When she talked in public she was frank and charming; she had a puzzled, diffident way of leading into her anecdotes, as if she was just now remembering, had not told them a hundred times already. Back in her hotel room, she often shivered and moaned, as if she were having an attack of fever. She blamed it on exhaustion, or her approaching menopause. She couldn't remember any of the people she had met, the charming, interesting people who had invited her to dinner and to whom, over drinks in various cities, she had told intimate things about her life.

Neglect in Flo's house had turned a final corner, since Rose saw it last. The rooms were plugged up with rags and papers and dirt. Pull a blind to let some light in, and the blind comes apart in your hand. Shake a curtain and the curtain falls to rags, letting loose a choking dust. Put a hand into a drawer and it sinks into something soft and dark and rubbishy.

We hate to write bad news but it looks like she has got past where she can look after herself. We try to look in on her but we are not so young ourselves any more so it looks like maybe the time has come.

The same letter, more or less, had been written to Rose and to her half-brother, Brian, who was an engineer, living in Toronto. Rose had just come back from her tour. She had assumed that Brian and his wife, Phoebe, whom she saw seldom, were keeping in touch with Flo. After all, Flo was Brian's mother, Rose's stepmother. And it turned out that they had been keeping in touch, or so they thought. Brian had recently been in South America but Phoebe had been phoning Flo every Sunday night. Flo had little to say but she had never talked to Phoebe anyway; she had said she was fine, everything was fine, she had offered some information about the weather. Rose had observed Flo on the telephone, since she came home and she saw how Phoebe could have been deceived. Flo spoke normally, she said hello, fine, that was a big storm we had last night, yes, the lights were out here for hours. If you didn't live in the neighborhood you wouldn't realize there hadn't been any storm.

It wasn't that Rose had entirely forgotten Flo in those two years. She had fits of worry about her. It was just that for some time now she had been between fits. One time the fit had come over her in the middle of a January storm, she had driven two hundred miles through blizzards, past ditched cars, and when she finally parked on Flo's street, finally tramped up the walk Flo had not been able to shovel, she was full of relief for herself and concern for Flo, a general turmoil of feelings both anxious and pleasurable. Flo opened the door and gave a bark of warning.

"You can't park there!"

"What?"

"Can't park there!"

Flo said there was a new bylaw; no parking on the streets during the winter months.

"You'll have to shovel out a place."

Of course Rose had an explosion.

"If you say one more word right now. I'll get in the car and drive back."

"Well you can't park—"

"One more word!"

"Why do you have to stand here and argue with the cold blasting into the house?"

Rose stepped inside. Home.

That was one of the stories she told about Flo. She did it well; her own exhaustion and sense of virtue; Flo's bark, her waving cane, her fierce unwillingness to be the object of anybody's rescue.

After she read the letter Rose had phoned Phoebe, and Phoebe had asked her to come to dinner, so they could talk. Rose resolved to behave well. She had an idea that Brian and Phoebe moved in a permanent cloud of disapproval of her. She thought that they disapproved of her success, limited and precarious and provincial though it might be, and that they disapproved of her even more when she failed. She knew it was not likely they would have her on their minds so much, or feel anything so definite.

She put on a plain skirt and an old blouse, but at the last minute changed into a long dress, made of thin red and gold cotton from India, the very thing that would justify their saying that Rose was always so theatrical.

Nevertheless she made up her mind as she usually did that she would speak in a low voice, stick to facts, not to get into any stale and silly arguments with Brian. And as usual most of the sense seemed to fly out her head as soon as she entered their house, was subjected to their calm routines, felt the flow of satisfaction, self-satisfaction, perfectly justified self-satisfaction, that emanated from the very bowls and draperies. She was nervous, when Phoebe asked her about her tour, and Phoebe was a bit nervous too, because Brian sat silent, not exactly frowning but indicating that the frivolity of the subject did not please him. In Rose's presence Brian had said more than once that he had no use for people in her line of work. But he had no use for a good many people. Actors, artists, journalists, rich people (he would never admit to being one himself), the entire Arts faculty of universities. Whole classes and categories, down the drain. Convicted of woolly-mindedness, and showy behavior; inaccurate talk, many excesses. Rose did not know if he spoke the truth or if this was something he had to say in front of her. He offered the bait of his low-voiced contempt; she rose to it; they had fights, she had left his house in tears. And underneath all this, Rose felt, they loved each other. But they could never stop the old, old competition; who is the better person, who has chosen the better work? What were they looking for? Each other's good opinion, which perhaps they meant to grant, in full, but not yet. Phoebe, who was a calm and dutiful woman with a great talent for normalizing things (the very opposite of their family talent for blowing things up), would serve food and pour coffee and regard them with a polite puzzlement; their contest, their vulnerability, their hurt, perhaps seemed as odd to her as the antics of comic-strip characters who stick their fingers into light sockets.

"I always wished Flo could have come back for another visit with us," Phoebe said. Flo had come once, and asked to be taken home after three days. But afterwards it seemed to be a pleasure to her, to sit and list the things Brian and Phoebe owned, the features of their house. Brian and Phoebe lived quite unostentatiously, in Don Mills, and the things Flo dwelt on—the door chimes, the automatic garage doors, the swimming pool—were among the ordinary suburban acquisitions. Rose had said as much to Flo who believed that she, Rose, was jealous.

"You wouldn't turn them down if you was offered."

"Yes I would."

That was true, Rose believed it was true, but how could she ever explain it to Flo or anybody in Hanratty? If you stay in Hanratty and do not get rich it is all right because you are living out your life as was intended, but if you go away and do not get rich, or, like Rose, do not remain rich, then what was the point?

After dinner Rose and Brian and Phoebe sat in the backyard beside the pool, where the youngest of Brian and Phoebe's four daughters was riding an inflated dragon. Everything had gone amicably, so far. It had been decided that Rose would go to Hanratty, that she would make the arrangements to get Flo into the Wawanash County Home. Brian had already made inquiries about it, or his secretary had, and he said that it seemed not only cheaper but better-run, with more facilities, than any private nursing home.

"She'll probably meet old friends there," Phoebe said.

Rose's docility, her good behavior, was partly based on a vision she had been building up all evening, and would never reveal to Brian and Phoebe. She pictured herself going to Hanratty and looking after Flo, living with her, taking care of her for as long as was necessary. She thought how she would clean and paint Flo's kitchen, patch the shingles over the leaky spots (that was one of the things the letter had mentioned), plant flowers in the pots, and make nourishing soup. She wasn't so far gone as to imagine Flo fitting comfortably into this picture, settling down to a life of gratitude. But the crankier Flo got, the milder and more patient Rose would become, and who, then, could accuse her of egotism and frivolity?

This vision did not survive the first two days of being home.

"Would you like a pudding?" Rose said.

"Oh, I don't care."

The elaborate carelessness some people will show, the gleam of hope, on being offered a drink.

Rose made a trifle. Berries, peaches, custard, cake, whipped cream and sweet sherry.

Flo ate half the bowlful. She dipped in greedily, not bothering to transfer a portion to a smaller bowl.

''That was lovely,'' she said. Rose had never heard such an admission of grateful pleasure from her. ''Lovely,'' said Flo and sat remembering, appreciating, belching a little. The suave dreamy custard, the nipping berries, robust peaches, luxury of sherry-soaked cake, munificence of whipped cream.

Rose thought that she had never done anything in her life that came near pleasing Flo as this did.

''I'll make another soon.''

Flo recovered herself. ''Oh well. You do what you like.''

Rose drove out to the County Home. She was conducted through it. She tried to tell Flo about it when she came back.

''Whose home?'' said Flo.

''No, the *County* Home.''

Rose mentioned some people she had seen there. Flo would not admit to knowing any of them. Rose spoke of the view and the pleasant rooms. Flo looked angry; her face darkened and she stuck out her lip. Rose handed her a mobile she had bought for fifty cents in the County Home Crafts Center. Cutout birds of blue and yellow paper were bobbing and dancing, on undetectable currents of air.

''Stick it up your arse,'' said Flo.

Rose put the mobile up in the porch and said she had seen the trays coming up, with supper on them.

''They go to the dining room if they're able, and if they're not they have trays in their rooms. I saw what they were having.

''Roast beef, well done, mashed potatoes and green beans, the frozen not the canned kind. Or an omelette. You could have a mushroom omelette or a chicken omelette or a plain omelette, if you liked.''

''What was for dessert?''

''Ice cream. You could have sauce on it.''

''What kind of sauce was there?''

"Chocolate. Butterscotch. Walnut."
"I can't eat walnuts."
"There was marshmallow too."

Out at the Home the old people were arranged in tiers. On the first floor were the bright and tidy ones. They walked around, usually with the help of canes. They visited each other, played cards. They had singsongs and hobbies. In the Crafts Center they painted pictures, hooked rugs, made quilts. If they were not able to do things like that they could make rag dolls, mobiles like the one Rose bought, poodles and snowmen which were constructed Styrofoam balls, with sequins for eyes; they also made silhouette pictures by placing thumbtacks on traced outlines; knights on horseback, battleships, airplanes, castles.

They organized concerts; they held dances; they had checker tournaments.

"Some of them say they are the happiest here they have ever been in their lives."

Up one floor there was more television watching, there were more wheelchairs. There were those whose heads drooped, whose tongues lolled, whose limbs shook uncontrollably. Nevertheless sociability was still flourishing, also rationality, with occasional blanks and absences.

On the third floor you might get some surprises.

Some of them up there had given up speaking.

Some had given up moving, except for odd jerks and tosses of the head, flailing of the arms, that seemed to be without purpose or control.

Nearly all had given up worrying about whether they were wet or dry.

Bodies were fed and wiped, taken up and tied in chairs, untied and put to bed. Taking in oxygen, giving out carbon dioxide, they continued to participate in the life of the world.

Crouched in her crib, diapered, dark as a nut, with three tufts of hair like dandelion floss sprouting from her head, an old woman was making loud shaky noises.

"Hello Aunty," the nurse said. "You're spelling today. It's lovely weather outside." She bent to the old woman's ear. "Can you spell weather?"

This nurse showed her gums when she smiled, which was all the time; she had an air of nearly demented hilarity.

"Weather," said the old woman. She strained forward, grunting, to get the word. Rose thought she might be going to have a bowel movement. "W-E-A-T-H-E-R."

That reminded her.

"Whether, W-H-E-T-H-E-R."

So far so good.

"Now you say something to her," the nurse said to Rose.

The words in Rose's mind were for a moment all obscene or despairing.

But without prompting came another.

"Forest. F-O-R-E-S-T."

"Celebrate," said Rose suddenly.

"C-E-L-E-B-R-A-T-E."

You had to listen very hard to make out what the old woman was saying, because she had lost much of the power to shape sounds. What she said seemed not to come from her mouth or her throat, but from deep in her lungs and belly.

"Isn't she a wonder," the nurse said. "She can't see and that's the only way we can tell she can hear. Like if you say, 'Here's your dinner,' she won't pay any attention to it, but she might start spelling *dinner*.

"Dinner," she said, to illustrate, and the old woman picked it up. "D-I-N-N . . ." Sometimes a long wait, a long wait between letters. It seemed she had only the thinnest thread to follow, meandering through that emptiness or confusion that nobody on this side can do more than guess at. But she didn't lose it, she followed it through to the end, however tricky the word might be, or cumbersome. Finished. Then she was sitting waiting; waiting, in the middle of her sightless eventless day, till up from somewhere popped another word. She would encompass it, bend all her energy to master it. Rose wondered what the words were like, when she held them in her mind. Did they carry their usual meaning, or any meaning at all? Were they like words in dreams or in the minds of young children, each one marvelous and distinct and alive as a new animal? This one limp and clear, like a jellyfish, that one hard and mean and secretive, like a horned snail. They could be austere and comical as top hats, or smooth and lively and flattering as ribbons. A parade of private visitors, not over yet.

Something woke Rose early the next morning. She was sleeping in the little porch, the only place in Flo's house where the smell was bearable. The sky was milky and brightening. The trees across the river—due to be cut down soon, to make room for a trailer park—were hunched against the dawn sky like shaggy dark animals, like buffalo. Rose had been dreaming. She had been having a dream obviously connected with her tour of the Home the day before.

Someone was taking her through a large building where there were people in cages. Everything was dim and cobwebby at first, and Rose was protesting that this seemed a poor arrangement. But as she went on the cages got larger and more elaborate, they were like enormous wicker birdcages, Victorian birdcages, fancifully shaped and decorated. Food was being offered to the people in the cages and Rose examined it, saw that it was choice; chocolate mousse, trifle, Black Forest Cake. Then in one of the cages Rose spotted Flo, who was handsomely seated on a throne-like chair, spelling out words in a clear authoritative voice (what the words were, Rose, wakening, could not remember) and looking pleased with herself, for showing powers she had kept secret till now.

Rose listened to hear Flo breathing, stirring, in her rubble-lined room. She heard nothing. What if Flo had died? Suppose she had died at the very moment she was making her radiant, satisfied appearance in Rose's dream? Rose hurried out of bed, ran barefoot to Flo's room. The bed there was empty. She went into the kitchen and found Flo sitting at the table, dressed to go out, wearing the navy blue summer coat and matching turban hat she had worn to Brian's and Pheobe's wedding. The coat was rumpled and in need of cleaning, the turban was crooked.

"Now I'm ready for to go," Flo said.

"Go where?"

"Out there," said Flo, jerking her head. "Out to the whattayacallit. The Poorhouse."

"The Home," said Rose, "You don't have to go today."

"They hired you to take me, now you get a move on and take me," Flo said.

"I'm not hired. I'm Rose. I'll make you a cup of tea."

"You can make it. I won't drink it."

She made Rose think of a woman who had started in labor. Such was her concentration, her determination, her urgency. Rose thought Flo felt her death moving in her like a child, getting ready to tear her. So she gave up arguing, she got dressed, hastily packed a bag for Flo, got her to the car and drove her out to the Home, but in the matter of Flo's quickly tearing and relieving death she was mistaken.

Some time before this, Rose had been in a play, on national television. *The Trojan Women*. She had no lines, and in fact she was in the play simply to do a favor for a friend, who had got a better part elsewhere. The director thought to liven all the weeping and mourning by having the Trojan women go bare-breasted. One breast apiece, they showed, the right in the case of the royal personages such as Hecuba and Helen; the left, in the case of ordinary virgins or wives, such as Rose. Rose didn't think herself enhanced by this exposure—she was getting on, after all, her bosom tended to flop—but she got used to the idea. She didn't count on the sensation they would create. She didn't think many people would be watching. She forgot about those parts of the country where people can't exercise their preference for quiz shows, police-car chases, American situation comedies, and are compelled to put up with talks on public affairs and tours of art galleries and ambitious offerings of drama. She did not think they would be so amazed, either, now that every magazine rack in every town was serving up slices and cutlets of bare flesh. How could such outrage fasten on the Trojan ladies' sad-eyed collection, puckered with cold then running with sweat under the lights, badly and chalkily made-up, all looking rather foolish without their mates, rather pitiful and unnatural, like tumors?

Flo took to pen and paper over that, forced her stiff swollen fingers, crippled almost out of use with arthritis, to write the word *Shame*. She wrote that if Rose's father had not been dead long ago he would now wish that he was. That was true. Rose read the letter, or part of it, out loud to some friends she was having for dinner. She read it for comic effect, and dramatic effect, to show the gulf that lay behind her, though she did realize, if she thought about it, that such a gulf was nothing special. Most of her friends, who seemed to her ordinarily hard-working, anxious, and hopeful, people, could lay claim to being disowned or prayed for, in some disappointed home.

Halfway through, she had to stop reading. It wasn't that she thought how shabby it was, to be exposing and making fun of Flo this way. She had done it often enough before; it was no news to her that it was shabby. What stopped her was, in fact, that gulf; she had a fresh and overwhelming realization of it, and it was nothing to laugh about. These reproaches of Flo's made as much sense as a protest about raising umbrellas, a warning against eating raisins. But they were painfully, truly, meant; they were all a hard life had to offer. Shame on a bare breast.

Another time, Rose was getting an award. So were several other people. A reception was being held, in a Toronto hotel. Flo had been sent an invitation, but Rose had never thought that she would come. She had thought she should give someone's name, when the organizers asked about relatives, and she could hardly name Brian and Phoebe. Of course it was possible that she did, secretly, want Flo to come, wanted to show Flo, intimidate her, finally remove herself from Flo's shade. That would be a natural thing to want to do.

Flo came down on the train, unannounced. She got to the hotel. She was arthritic then, but still moving without a cane. She had always been decently, soberly, cheaply, dressed, but now it seemed she had spent money and asked advice. She was wearing a mauve and purple checked pants suit, and beads like strings of white and yellow popcorn. Her hair was covered by a thick gray-blue wig, pulled low on her forehead like a woollen cap. From the vee of the jacket, and its too-short sleeves, her neck and wrists stuck out brown and warty as if covered with bark. When she saw Rose she stood still. She seemed to be waiting—not just for Rose to go over to her but for her feelings about the scene in front of her to crystallize.

Soon they did.

"Look at the Nigger!" said Flo in a loud voice, before Rose was anywhere near her. Her tone was one of simple, gratified astonishment, as if she had been peering down the Grand Canyon or seen oranges growing on a tree.

She meant George, who was getting one of the awards. He turned around, to see if someone was feeding him a comic line. And Flo did look like a comic character, except that her bewilderment, her authenticity, were quite daunting. Did she note the stir she had caused? Possibly. After that one outburst she clammed up, would not speak again except in the most grudging monosyllables, would not eat any food or drink any drink offered her, would not sit down, but stood astonished and unflinching in the middle of that gathering of the bearded and beaded, the unisexual and the unashamedly un-Anglo-Saxon, until it was time for her to be taken to her train and sent home.

Rose found that wig under the bed, during the horrifying clean-up that followed Flo's removal. She took it out to the Home, along with some clothes she had washed or had dry-cleaned, and some stockings, talcum powder, cologne, that she had bought. Sometimes Flo seemed to think Rose was a doctor, and she said, "I don't want no woman doctor, you can just clear out." But when she saw Rose carrying the wig she said, "Rose! What is that you got in your hand, is it a dead gray squirrel?"

"No," said Rose, "it's a wig."

"What?"

"A wig," said Rose, and Flo began to laugh. Rose laughed too. The wig did look like a dead cat or squirrel, even though she had washed and brushed it; it was a disturbing-looking object.

"My God, Rose, I thought what is she doing bringing me a dead squirrel! If I put it on somebody'd be sure to take a shot at me."

Rose stuck it on her own head, to continue the comedy, and Flo laughed so that she rocked back and forth in her crib.

When she got her breath Flo said, "What am I doing with these damn sides up on my bed? Are you and Brian behaving yourselves? Don't fight, it gets on your father's nerves. Do you know how many gallstones they took out of me? Fifteen! One as big as a pullet's egg. I got them somewhere. I'm going to take them home." She pulled at the sheets, searching. "They were in a bottle."

"I've got them already," said Rose. "I took them home."

"Did you? Did you show your father?"

"Yes."

"Oh, well, that's where they are then," said Flo, and she lay down and closed her eyes.

TILLIE OLSEN

Tell Me a Riddle

I

For forty-seven years they had been married. How deep back the stubborn, gnarled roots of the quarrel reached, no one could say—but only now, when tending to the needs of others no longer shackled them together, the roots swelled up visible, split the earth between them, and the tearing shook even to the children, long since grown.

Why, now, why now? wailed Hannah.

As if when we grew up weren't enough, said Paul.

Poor Ma. Poor Dad. It hurts so for both of them, said Vivi. They never had very much; at least in old age they should be happy.

Knock their heads together, insisted Sammy; tell 'em: you're too old for this kind of thing; no reason not to get along now.

Lennie wrote to Clara: They've lived over so much together; what could possibly tear them apart?

Something tangible enough.

Arthritic hands, and such work as he got, occasional. Poverty all his life, and there was little breath left for running. He could not, could not turn away from this desire: to have the troubling of responsibility, the fretting with money, over and done with; to be free, to be *care*free where success was not measured by accumulation, and there was use for the vitality still in him.

There was a way. They could sell the house, and with the money join his lodge's Haven, cooperative for the aged. Happy communal life, and was he not already an official; had he not helped organize it, raise funds, served as a trustee?

But she—would not consider it.

"What do we need all this for?" he would ask loudly, for her hearing aid was turned down and the vacuum was shrilling. "Five rooms" (pushing the sofa so she could get into the corner) "furniture" (smoothing down the rug) "floors and surfaces to make work. Tell me, why do we need it?" And he was glad he could ask in a scream.

"Because I'm use't."

"Because you're use't. This is a reason, Mrs. Word Miser? Used to can get unused!"

"Enough unused I have to get used to already. . . . Not enough words?" turning off the vacuum a moment to hear herself answer. "Because soon enough we'll need only a little closet, no windows, no furniture, nothing to make work, but for worms. Because now I want room. . . . Screech and blow like you're doing, you'll need that closet even sooner. . . . Ha, again!" for the vacuum bag wailed, puffed half up, hung stubbornly limp. "This time fix it so it stays; quick before the phone rings and you get too important-busy."

But while he struggled with the motor, it seethed in him. Why fix it? Why have to bother? And if it can't be fixed, have to wring the mind with how to pay the repair? At the Haven they come in with their own machines to clean your room or your cottage; you fish, or play cards, or make jokes in the sun, not with knotty fingers fight to mend vacuums.

Over the dishes, coaxingly: "For once in your life, to be free, to have everything done for you, like a queen."

"I never liked queens."

"No dishes, no garbage, no towel to sop, no worry what to buy, what to eat."

"And what else would I do with my empty hands? Better to eat at my own table when I want, and to cook and eat how I want."

"In the cottages they buy what you ask, and cook it how you like. *You* are the one who always used to say: better mankind born without mouths and stomachs than always to worry for money to buy, to shop, to fix, to cook, to wash, to clean."

"How cleverly you hid that you heard. I said it then because eighteen hours a day I ran. And you never scraped a carrot or knew a dish towel sops. Now—for you and me—who cares? A herring out of a jar is enough. But when *I* want, and nobody to bother." And she turned off her ear button, so she would not have to hear.

But as *he* had no peace, juggling and rejuggling the money to figure: how will I pay for this now?; prying out the storm windows (there they take care of this); jolting in the streetcar on errands (there I would not have to ride to take care of this or that); fending the patronizing relatives just back from Florida (at the Haven it matters what one is, not what one can afford), he gave *her* no peace.

"Look! In their bulletin. A reading circle. Twice a week it meets."

"Haumm," her answer of not listening.

"A reading circle. Chekhov they read that you like, and Peretz. Cultured people at the Haven that you would enjoy."

"Enjoy!" She tasted the word. "Now, when it pleases you, you find a reading circle for me. And forty years ago when the children were morsels and there was a Circle, did you stay home with them once so I could go? Even once? You trained me well. I do not need others to enjoy. Others!" Her voice trembled. "Because *you* want to be there with others. Already it makes me sick to think of you always around others. Clown, grimacer, floormat, yesman, entertainer, whatever they want of you."

And now it was he who turned on the television loud so he need not hear.

Old scar tissue ruptured and the wounds festered anew. Chekhov indeed. She thought without softness of that young wife, who in the deep night hours while she nursed the current baby, and perhaps held another in her lap, would try to stay awake for the only time there was to read. She would feel again the weather of the outside on his cheek when, coming late from a meeting, he would find her so, and stimulated and ardent, sniffing her skin, coax: "I'll put the baby to bed, and you—put the book away, don't read, don't read."

That had been the most beguiling of all the "don't read, put your book away" her life had been. Chekhov indeed!

"Money?" She shrugged him off. "Could we get poorer than once we were? And in America, who starves?"

But as still he pressed:

"Let me alone about money. Was there ever enough? Seven little ones—for every penny I had to ask—and sometimes, remember, there was nothing. But always *I* had to manage. Now *you* manage. Rub your nose in it good."

But from those years she had had to manage, old humiliations and terrors rose up, lived again, and forced her to relive them. The children's needings; that grocer's face or this merchant's wife she had had to beg credit from when credit was a disgrace; the scenery of the long blocks walked around when she could not pay; school coming, and the desperate going over the old to see what could yet be remade; the soups of meat bones begged "for-the-dog" one winter. . . .

Enough. Now they had no children. Let *him* wrack his head for how they would live. She would not exchange her solitude for anything. *Never again to be forced to move to the rhythms of others.*

For in this solitude she had won to a reconciled peace.

Tranquillity from having the empty house no longer an enemy, for it stayed clean—not as in the days when it was her family, the life in it, that had seemed the enemy: tracking, smudging, littering, dirtying, engaging her in endless defeating battle—and on whom her endless defeat had been spewed.

The few old books, memorized from rereading; the pictures to ponder (the magnifying glass superimposed on her heavy eyeglasses). Or if she wishes, when he is gone, the phonograph, that if she turns up very loud and strains, she can hear: the ordered sounds and the struggling.

Out in the garden, growing things to nurture. Birds to be kept out of the pear tree, and when the pears are heavy and ripe, the old fury of work, for all must be canned, nothing wasted.

And her one social duty (for she will not go to luncheons or meetings) the boxes of old clothes left with her, as with a life-practised eye for finding what is still wearable within the worn (again the magnifying glass superimposed on the heavy glasses) she scans and sorts—this for rag or rummage, that for mending and cleaning, and this for sending away.

Being able at last to live within, and not move to the rhythms of others, as life had forced her to: denying; removing; isolating; taking the children one by one; then deafening, half-blinding—and at last, presenting her solitude.

And in it she had won to a reconciled peace.

Now he was violating it with his constant campaigning: *Sell the house and move to the Haven.* (You sit, you sit—there too you could sit like a stone.) He was making of her a battleground where old grievances tore. (Turn on your ear button—I am talking.) And stubbornly she resisted—so that from wheedling, reasoning, manipulation, it was bitterness he now started with.

And it came to where every happening lashed up a quarrel.

"I will sell the house anyway," he flung at her one night. "I am putting it up for sale. There will be a way to make you sign."

The television blared, as always it did on the evenings he stayed home, and as always it reached her only as noise. She did not know if the tumult was in her or outside. Snap! she turned the sound off. "Shadows," she whispered to him, pointing to the screen, "look, it is only shadows." And in a scream: "Did you say that you will sell the house? Look at me, not at that. I am no shadow. You cannot sell without me."

"Leave on the television. I am watching."

"Like Paulie, like Jenny, a four-year-old. Staring at shadows. *You cannot sell the house.*"

"I will. We are going to the Haven. There you would not hear the television when you do not want it. I could sit in the social room and watch. You could lock yourself up to smell your unpleasantness in a room by yourself—for who would want to come near you?

"No, no selling." A whisper now.

"The television is shadows. Mrs. Enlightened! Mrs. Cultured! A world comes into your house—and it is shadows. People you would never meet in a thousand lifetimes. Wonders. When you were four years old, yes, like Paulie, like Jenny, did you know of Indian dances, alligators, how they use bamboo in Malaya? No, you scratched in your dirt with the chickens and thought Olshana was the world. Yes, Mrs. Unpleasant, I will sell the house, for there better can we be rid of each other than here."

She did not know if the tumult was outside, or in her. Always a ravening inside, a pull to the bed, to lie down, to succumb.

"Have you thought maybe Ma should let a doctor have a look at her?" asked their son Paul after Sunday dinner, regarding his mother crumpled on the couch, instead of, as was her custom, busying herself in Nancy's kitchen.

"Why not the President too?"

"Seriously, Dad. This is the third Sunday she's lain down like that after dinner. Is she that way at home?"

"A regular love affair with the bed. Every time I start to talk to her."

Good protective reaction, observed Nancy to herself. The workings of hos-til-ity.

"Nancy could take her. I just don't like how she looks. Let's have Nancy arrange an appointment."

"You think she'll go?" regarding his wife gloomily. "All right, we have to have doctor bills, we have to have doctor bills." Loudly: "Something hurts you?"

She startled, looked to his lips. He repeated: "Mrs. Take It Easy, something hurts?"

"Nothing. . . . Only you."

"A woman of honey. That's why you're lying down?"

"Soon I'll get up to do the dishes, Nancy."

"Leave them, Mother, I like it better this way."

"Mrs. Take It Easy, Paul says you should start ballet. You should go to see a doctor and ask: how soon can you start ballet?"

"A doctor?" she begged. "Ballet?"

"We were talking, Ma," explained Paul, "you don't seem any too well. It would be a good idea for you to see a doctor for a checkup."

"I get up now to do the kitchen. Doctors are bills and foolishness, my son, I need no doctors."

"At the Haven," he could not resist pointing out, "a doctor is *not* bills. He lives beside you. You start to sneeze, he is there before you open up a Kleenex. You can be sick there for free, all you want."

"Diarrhea of the mouth, is there a doctor to make you dumb?"

"Ma. Promise me you'll go. Nancy will arrange it."

"It's all of a piece when you think of it," said Nancy, "the way she attacks my kitchen, scrubbing under every cup hook, doing the inside of the oven so I can't enjoy Sunday dinner, knowing that half-blind or not, she's going to find every speck of dirt. . . ."

"Don't Nancy, I've told you—it's the only way she knows to be useful. What did the *doctor* say?"

"A real fatherly lecture. Sixty-nine is young these days. Go out, enjoy life, find interests. Get a new hearing aid, this one is antiquated. Old age is sickness only if one makes it so. Geriatrics, Inc.''

''So there was nothing physical.''

''Of course there was. How can you live to yourself like she does without there being? Evidence of a kidney disorder, and her blood count is low. He gave her a diet, and she's to come back for follow-up and lab work. . . . But he was clear enough: Number One prescription—start living like a human being. . . . When I think of your dad, who could really play the invalid with that arthritis of his, as active as a teenager, and twice as much fun. . . .''

''You didn't tell me the doctor says your sickness is in you, how you live.'' He pushed his advantage. ''Life and enjoyments you need better than medicine. And this diet, how can you keep it? To weigh each morsel and scrape away each bit of fat, to make this soup, that pudding. There, at the Haven, they have a dietician, they would do it for you.''

She is silent.

''You would feel better there, I know it,'' he says gently. ''There there is life and enjoyments all around.''

''What is the matter, Mr. Importantbusy, you have no card game or meeting you can go to?''—turning her face to the pillow.

For a while he cut his meetings and going out, fussed over her diet, tried to wheedle her into leaving the house, brought in visitors:

''I should come to a fashion tea. I should sit and look at pretty babies in clothes I cannot buy. This is pleasure?''

''Always you are better than everyone else. The doctor said you should go out. Mrs. Brem comes to you with goodness and you turn her away.''

''Because *you* asked her to, she asked me.''

''They won't come back. People you need, the doctor said. Your own cousins I asked; they were willing to come and make peace as if nothing had happened. . . .''

''No more crushers of people, pushers, hypocrites, around me. No more in *my* house. You go to them if you like.''

"Kind he is to visit. And you, like ice."
"A babbler. All my life around babblers. Enough!"

"She's even worse, Dad? Then let her stew a while," advised Nancy. "You can't let it destroy you; it's a psychological thing, maybe too far gone for any of us to help."

So he let her stew. More and more she lay silent in bed, and sometimes did not even get up to make the meals. No longer was the tongue-lashing inevitable if he left the coffee cup where it did not belong, or forgot to take out the garbage or mislaid the broom. The birds grew bold that summer and for once pocked the pears, undisturbed.

A bellyful of bitterness and every day the same quarrel in a new way and a different old grievance the quarrel forced her to enter and relive. And the new torment: I am not really sick, the doctor said it, then why do I feel so sick?

One night she asked him: "You have a meeting tonight? Do not go. Stay . . . with me."

He had planned to watch "This Is Your Life," but half sick himself from the heavy heat, and sickening therefore the more after the brooks and woods of the Haven, with satisfaction he grated:

"Hah, Mrs. Live Alone And Like It wants company all of a sudden. It doesn't seem so good the time of solitary when she was a girl exile in Siberia. 'Do not go. Stay with me.' A new song for Mrs. Free As A Bird. Yes, I am going out, and while I am gone chew this aloneness good, and think how you keep us both from where if you want people, you do not need to be alone."

"Go, go. All your life you have gone without me."

After him she sobbed curses he had not heard in years, old-country curses from their childhood: Grow, oh shall you grow like an onion, with your head in the ground. Like the hide of a drum shall you be, beaten in life, beaten in death. Oh shall you be like a chandelier, to hang, and to burn. . . .

She was not in their bed when he came back. She lay on the cot on the sun porch. All week she did not speak or come near him; nor did he try to make peace or care for her.

He slept badly, so used to her next to him. After all the years, old harmonies and dependencies deep in their bodies; she curled to him, or he coiled to her, each warmed, warming, turning as the other turned, the nights a long embrace.

It was not the empty bed or the storm that woke him, but a faint singing. *She* was singing. Shaking off the drops of rain, the lightning riving her lifted face, he saw her so; the cot covers on the floor.

"This is a private concert?" he asked. "Come in, you are wet."

"I can breathe now," she answered; "my lungs are rich." Though indeed the sound was hardly a breath.

"Come in, come in." Loosing the bamboo shades. "Look how wet you are." Half helping, half carrying her, still faint-breathing her song.

A Russian love song of fifty years ago.

He had found a buyer, but before he told her, he called together those children who were close enough to come. Paul, of course, Sammy from New Jersey, Hannah from Connecticut, Vivi from Ohio.

With a kindling of energy for her beloved visitors, she arrayed the house, cooked and baked. She was not prepared for the solemn after-dinner conclave, they too probing in and tearing. Her frightened eyes watched from mouth to mouth as each spoke.

His stories were eloquent and funny of her refusal to go back to the doctor; of the scorned invitations; of her stubborn silence or the bile "like a Niagara"; of her contrariness: "If I clean it's no good how I cleaned; if I don't clean, I'm still a master who thinks he has a slave."

(Vinegar he poured on me all his life; I am well marinated; how can I be honey now?)

Deftly he marched in the rightness for moving to the Haven; their money from social security free for visiting the children, not sucked into daily needs and into the house; the activities in the Haven for him; but mostly the Haven for *her:* her health, her need of care, distraction, amusement, friends who shared her interests.

"This does offer an outlet for Dad," said Paul; "he's always been an active person. And economic peace of mind isn't to be sneezed at, either. I could use a little of that myself."

But when they asked: "And you, Ma, how do you feel about it?" could only whisper:

"For him it is good. It is not for me. I can no longer live between people."

"You lived all your life *for* people," Vivi cried.

"Not with." Suffering doubly for the unhappiness on her children's faces.

"You have to find some compromise," Sammy insisted. "Maybe sell the house and buy a trailer. After forty-seven years there's surely some way you can find to live in peace."

"There is no help, my children. Different things we need."

"Then live alone!" He could control himself no longer. "I have a buyer for the house. Half the money for you, half for me. Either alone or with me to the Haven. You think I can live any longer as we are doing now?"

"Ma doesn't have to make a decision this minute, however you feel, Dad," Paul said quickly, "and you wouldn't want her to. Let's let it lay a few months, and then talk some more."

"I think I can work it out to take Mother home with me for a while," Hannah said. "You both look terrible, but especially you, Mother. I'm going to ask Phil to have a look at you."

"Sure," cracked Sammy. "What's the use of a doctor husband if you can't get free service out of him once in a while for the family? And absence might make the heart . . . you know."

"There was something after all," Paul told Nancy in a colorless voice. "That was Hannah's Phil calling. Her gall bladder. . . . Surgery."

"Her *gall* bladder. If that isn't classic. 'Bitter as gall'—talk of psychosom—"

He stepped closer, put his hand over her mouth, and said in the same colorless, plodding voice. "We have to get Dad. They operated at once. The cancer was everywhere, surrounding the liver, everywhere. They did what they could . . . at best she has a year. Dad . . . we have to tell him."

II

Honest in his weakness when they told him, and that she was not to know. "I'm not an actor. She'll know right away by how I am. Oh that poor woman. I am old too, it will break me into pieces. Oh that poor woman. She will spit on me: 'So my sickness was how I live.' Oh Paulie, how she will be, that poor woman. Only she should not suffer. . . . I can't stand sickness, Paulie, I can't go with you."

But went. And play-acted.

"A grand opening and you did not even wait for me. . . . A good thing Hannah took you with her."

"Fashion teas I needed. They cut out what tore in me; just in my throat something hurts yet. . . . Look! so many flowers, like a funeral. Vivi called, did Hannah tell you? And Lennie from San Francisco, and Clara; and Sammy is coming." Her gnome's face pressed happily into the flowers.

It is impossible to predict in these cases, but once over the immediate effects of the operation, she should have several months of comparative well-being.

The money, where will come the money?

Travel with her, Dad. Don't take her home to the old associations. The other children will want to see her.

The money, where will I wring the money?

Whatever happens, she is not to know. No, you can't ask her to sign papers to sell the house; nothing to upset her. Borrow instead, then after. . . .

I had wanted to leave you each a few dollars to make life easier, as other fathers do. There will be nothing left now. (Failure! you and your "business is exploitation." Why didn't you make it when it could be made?—Is that what you're thinking, Sammy?)

Sure she's unreasonable, Dad—but you have to stay with her; if there's to be any happiness in what's left of her life, it depends on you.

Prop me up, children, think of me, too. Shuffled, chained with her, bitter woman. No Haven, and the little money going . . . How happy she looks, poor creature.

The look of excitement. The straining to hear everything (the new hearing aid turned full). Why are you so happy, dying woman?

How the petals are, fold on fold, and the gladioli color. The autumn air.

Stranger grandsons, tall above the little gnome grandmother, the little spry grandfather. Paul in a frenzy of picture-taking before going.

She, wandering the great house. Feeling the books; laughing at the maple shoemaker's bench of a hundred years ago used as a table. The ear turned to music.

"Let us go home. See how good I walk now." "One step from the hospital," he answers, "and she wants to fly. Wait till Doctor Phil says."

"Look—the birds too are flying home. Very good Phil is and will not show it, but he is sick of sickness by the time he comes home."

"Mrs. Telepathy, to read minds," he answers; "read mine what it says: when the trunks of medicines become a suitcase, then we will go."

The grandboys, they do not know what to say to us. . . . Hannah, she runs around here, there, when is there time for herself?

Let us go home. Let us go home.

Musing; gentleness—*but for the incidents of the rabbi in the hospital, and of the candles of benediction.*

Of the rabbi in the hospital:

Now tell me what happened, Mother.

From the sleep I awoke, Hannah's Phil, and he stands there like a devil in a dream and calls me by name. I cannot hear. I think he prays. Go away, please, I tell him, I am not a believer. Still he stands, while my heart knocks with fright.

You scared *him*, Mother. He thought you were delirious.

Who sent him? Why did he come to me?

It is a custom. The men of God come to visit those of their religion they might help. The hospital makes up the list for them—race, religion—and you are on the Jewish list.

Not for rabbis. At once go and make them change. Tell them to write: Race, human; Religion, none.

And of the candles of benediction:

Look how you have upset yourself, Mrs. Excited Over Nothing. Pleasant memories you should leave.

Go in, go back to Hannah and the lights. Two weeks I saw candles and said nothing. But she asked me.

So what was so terrible? She forgets you never did, she asks you to light the Friday candles and say the benediction like Phil's mother when she visits. If the candles give her pleasure, why shouldn't she have the pleasure?

Not for pleasure she does it. For emptiness. Because his family does. Because all around her do.

That is not a good reason too? But you did not hear her. For heritage, she told you. For the boys, from the past they should have tradition.

Superstition! From our ancestors, savages, afraid of the dark, of themselves: mumbo words and magic lights to scare away ghosts.

She told you: how it started does not take away the goodness. For centuries, peace in the house it means.

Swindler! does she look back on the dark centuries? Candles bought instead of bread and stuck into a potato for a candlestick? Religion that stifled and said: in Paradise, woman, you will be the footstool of your husband, and in life—poor chosen Jew—ground under, despised, trembling in cellars. And cremated. And cremated.

This is religion's fault? You think you are still an orator of the 1905 revolution? Where are the pills for quieting? Which are they?

Heritage. How have we come from our savage past, how no longer to be savages—this to teach. To look back and learn what humanizes—this to teach. To smash all ghettos that divide us—not to go back, not to go back—this to teach. Learned books in the house, will humankind live or die, and she gives to her boys—superstition.

Hannah that is so good to you. Take your pill, Mrs. Excited For Nothing, swallow.

Heritage! But when did I have time to teach? Of Hannah I asked only hands to help.

Swallow.

Otherwise—musing; gentleness.

Not to travel. To go home.

The children want to see you. We have to show them you are as thorny a flower as ever.

Not to travel.

Vivi wants you should see her new baby. She sent the tickets—airplane tickets—a Mrs. Roosevelt she wants to make of you. To Vivi's we have to go.

A new baby. How many warm, seductive babies. She holds him stiffly, *away* from her, so that he wails. And a long shudder begins, and the sweat beads on her forehead.

"Hush, shush," croons the grandfather, lifting him back. "You should forgive your grandmamma, little prince, she has never held a baby before, only seen them in glass cases. Hush, shush."

"You're tired, Ma," says Vivi. "The travel and the noisy dinner. I'll take you to lie down."

(*A long travel from, to, what the feel of a baby evokes.*)

In the airplane, cunningly designed to encase from motion (no wind, no feel of flight), she had sat severely and still, her face turned to the sky through which they cleaved and left no scar.

So this was how it looked, the determining, the crucial sky, and this was how man moved through it, remote above the dwindled earth, the concealed human life. Vulnerable life, that could scar.

There was a steerage ship of memory that shook across a great, circular sea: clustered, ill human beings; and through the thick-stained air, tiny fretting waters in a window round like the airplane's—sun round, moon round. (The round thatched roofs of Olshana.) Eye round—like the smaller window that framed distance the solitary year of exile when only her eyes could travel, and no voice spoke. And the polar winds hurled themselves across snows trackless and endless and white—like the clouds which had closed together below and hidden the earth.

Now they put a baby in her lap. Do not ask me, she would have liked to beg. Enough the worn face of Vivi, the remembered grandchildren. I cannot, cannot. . . .

Cannot what? Unnatural grandmother, not able to make herself embrace a baby.

She lay there in the bed of the two little girls, her new hearing aid turned full, listening to the sound of the children going to sleep, the baby's fretful crying and hushing, the clatter of dishes being washed and put away. They thought she slept. Still she rode on.

It was not that she had not loved her babies, her children. The love—the passion of tending—had risen with the need like a torrent; and like a torrent drowned and immolated all else. But when the need was done—oh the power that was lost in the painful damming back and drying up of what still surged, but had nowhere to go. Only the thin pulsing left that could not quiet, suffering over lives one felt, but could no longer hold nor help.

On that torrent she had borne them to their own lives, and the riverbed was desert long years now. Not there would she dwell, a memoried wraith. Surely, that was not all, surely there was more. Still the springs, the springs were in her seeking. Somewhere an older power that beat for life. Somewhere coherence, transport, meaning. If they would but leave her in the air now stilled of clamor, in the reconciled solitude, to journey on.

And they put a baby in her lap. Immediacy to embrace, and the breath of *that* past: warm flesh like this that had claims and nuzzled away all else and with lovely mouths devoured; hot-living like an animal—intensely and now; the turning maze; the long drunkenness; the drowning into needing and being needed. Severely she looked back—and the shudder seized her again, and the sweat. Not that way. Not there, not now could she, not yet. . . .

And all that visit, she could not touch the baby.

"Daddy, is it the . . . sickness she's like that?" asked Vivi. "I was so glad to be having the baby—for her. I told Tim, it'll give her more happiness than anything, being around a baby again. And she hasn't played with him once."

He was not listening. "Aahh little seed of life, little charmer," he crooned, "Hollywood should see you. A heart of ice you would melt. Kick, kick. The future you'll have for a ball. In 2050 still kick. Kick for your grandaddy then."

Attentive with the older children; sat through their performances (command performance; we command you to be the audience); helped Ann sort autumn leaves to find the best for a school program; listened gravely to Richard tell about his rock collection, while her lips mutely formed the words to remember: *igneous, sedimentary, metamorphic*; looked for missing socks, books, and bus tickets; watched the children whoop after their grandfather who knew how to tickle, chuck, lift, toss, do tricks, tell secrets, make jokes, match riddle for riddle. (Tell me a riddle, Grammy. I know no riddles, child.) Scrubbed sills and woodwork and furniture in every room; folded the laundry; straightened drawers; emptied the heaped baskets waiting for ironing (while he or Vivi or Tim nagged: You're supposed to rest here, you've been sick) but to none tended or gave food—and could not touch the baby.

After a week she said: "Let us go home. Today call about the tickets."

"You have important business, Mrs. Inahurry? The President waits to consult with you?" He shouted, for the fear of the future raced in him. "The clothes are still warm from the suitcase, your children cannot show enough how glad they are to see you, and you want home. There is plenty of time for home. We cannot be with the children at home."

"Blind to around you as always: the little ones sleep four in a room because we take their bed. We are two more people in a house with a new baby, and no help."

"Vivi is happy so. The children should have their grandparents a while, she told to me. I should have my mommy and daddy. . . ."

"Babbler and blind. Do you look at her so tired? How she starts to talk and she cries? I am not strong enough yet to help. Let us go home."

(To reconciled solitude.)

For it seemed to her the crowded noisy house was listening to her, listening for *her. She could feel it like a great ear pressed under her heart. And everything knocked: quick constant raps: let me in, let me in.*

How was it that soft reaching tendrils also became blows that knocked?

C'mon, Grandma, I want to show you . . .

Tell me a riddle, Grandma. (*I know no riddles.*)

Look, Grammy, he's so dumb he can't even find his hands. (Dody and the baby on a blanket over the fermenting autumn mould.)

I made them—for you. (Ann) (Flat paper dolls with aprons that lifted on scalloped skirts that lifted on flowered pants; hair of yarn and great ringed questioning eyes.)

Watch me, Grandma. (Richard snaking up the tree, hanging exultant, free, with one hand at the top. Below Dody hunching over in pretend-cooking.)

(*Climb too, Dody, climb and look.*)

Be my nap bed, Grammy. (The "No!" too late.)
Morty's abandoned heaviness, while his fingers ladder up and down her hearing-aid cord to his drowsy chant: eentsiebeentsie-spider. (*Children trust*.)
It's to start off your own rock collection, Grandma.
That's a trilobite fossil, 200 million years old (millions of years on a boy's mouth) and that one's obsidian, black glass.

Knocked and knocked.

Mother, I *told* you the teacher said we had to bring it back all filled out this morning. Didn't you even ask Daddy? Then tell *me* which plan and I'll check it: evacuate or stay in the city or wait for you to come and take me away. (Seeing the look of straining to hear.) It's for Disaster, Grandma. (*Children trust*.)

Vivi in the maze of the long, the lovely drunkenness. The old old noises: baby sounds; screaming of a mother flayed to exasperation; children quarreling; children playing; singing; laughter.

And Vivi's tears and memories, spilling so fast, half the words not understood.

She had started remembering out loud deliberately, so her mother would know the past was cherished, still lived in her.

Nursing the baby: My friends marvel, and I tell them, oh it's easy to be such a cow. I remember how beautiful my mother seemed nursing my brother, and the milk just flows. . . . Was that Davy? It must have been Davy. . . .

Lowering a hem: How did you ever . . . when I think how you made everything we wore . . . Tim, just think, seven kids and Mommy sewed everything . . . do I remember you sang while you sewed? That white dress with the red apples on the skirt you fixed over for me, was it Hannah's or Clara's before it was mine?

Washing sweaters: Ma, I'll never forget, one of those days so nice you washed clothes outside; one of the first spring days it must have been. The bubbles just danced while you scrubbed, and we chased after, and you stopped to show us how to blow our own bubbles with green onion stalks . . . you always. . . .

"Strong onion, to still make you cry after so many years," her father said, to turn the tears into laughter.

While Richard bent over his homework: Where is it now, do we still have it, the Book of the Martyrs? It always seemed so, well—exalted, when you'd put it on the round table and we'd all look at it together; there was even a halo from the lamp. The lamp with the beaded fringe you could move up and down; they're in style again, pulley lamps like that, but without the fringe. You know the book I'm talking about, Daddy, the Book of the Martyrs, the first picture was a bust of Spartacus . . . Socrates? I wish there was something like that for the children, Mommy, to give them what you . . . (And the tears splashed again.)

(What I intended and did not? Stop it, daughter, stop it, leave that time. And he, the hypocrite, sitting there with tears in his eyes—it was nothing to you then, nothing.)

. . . The time you came to school and I almost died of shame because of your accent and because I knew you knew I was ashamed; how could I? . . . Sammy's harmonica and you danced to it once, yes you did, you and Davy squealing in your arms. . . . That time you bundled us up and walked us down to the railway station to stay the night 'cause it was heated and we didn't have any coal, that winter of the strike, you didn't think I remembered that, did you, Mommy? . . . How you'd call us out to see the sunsets. . . .

Day after day, the spilling memories. Worse now, questions, too. Even the grandchildren: Grandma, in the olden days, when you were little. . . .

It was the afternoons that saved.

While they thought she napped, she would leave the mosaic on the wall (of children's drawings, maps, calendars, pictures, Ann's cardboard dolls with their great ringed questioning eyes) and hunch in the girls' closet on the low shelf where the shoes stood, and the girls' dresses covered.

For that while she would painfully sheathe against the listening house, the tendrils and noises that knocked, and Vivi's spilling memories. Sometimes it helped to braid and unbraid the sashes that dangled, or to trace the pattern on the hoop slips.

Today she had jacks and children under jet trails to forget. Last night, Ann and Dody silhouetted in the window against a sunset of flaming man-made clouds of jet trail, their jacks ball accenting the peaceful noise of dinner being made. Had she told them, yes she had told them of how they played jacks in her village though there was no ball, no jacks. Six stones, round and flat, toss them out, the seventh on the back of the hand, toss, catch and swoop up as many as possible, toss again. . . .

Of stones (repeating Richard) there are three kinds: earth's fire jetting; rock of layered centuries; crucibled new out of the old (*igneous, sedimentary, metamorphic*). But there was that other—frozen to black glass, never to transform or hold the fossil memory . . . (let not my seed fall on stone). There was an ancient man who fought to heights a great rock that crashed back down eternally—eternal labor, freedom, labor . . . (stone will perish, but the word remain). And you, David, who with a stone slew, screaming: Lord, take my heart of stone and give me flesh.

Who was screaming? Why was she back in the common room of the prison, the sun motes dancing in the shafts of light, and the informer being brought in, a prisoner now, like themselves. And Lisa leaping, yes, Lisa, the gentle and tender, biting at the betrayer's jugular. Screaming and screaming.

No, it is the children screaming. Another of Paul and Sammy's terrible fights?

In Vivi's house. Severely: you are in Vivi's house.

Blows, screams, a call: "Grandma!" For her? Oh please not for her. Hide, hunch behind the dresses deeper. But a trembling little body hurls itself beside her—surprised, smothered laughter, arms surround her neck, tears rub dry on her cheek, and words too soft to understand whisper into her ear (Is this where you hide too, Grammy? It's my secret place, we have a secret now).

And the sweat beads, and the long shudder seizes.

It seemed the great ear pressed inside now, and the knocking. "We have to go home," she told him, "I grow ill here."

"It's your own fault, Mrs. Bodybusy, you do not rest, you do too much." He raged, but the fear was in his eyes. "It was a serious operation, they told you to take care. . . . All right, we will go to where you can rest."

But where? Not home to death, not yet. He had thought to Lennie's, to Clara's; beautiful visits with each of the children. She would have to rest first, be stronger. If they could but go to Florida—it glittered before him, the never-realized promise of Florida. California: of course. (The money, the money, dwindling!) Los Angeles first for sun and rest, then to Lennie's in San Francisco.

He told her the next day. "You saw what Nancy wrote: snow

and wind back home, a terrible winter. And look at you—all bones and a swollen belly. I called Phil: he said, 'A prescription, Los Angeles sun and rest.' "

She watched the words on his lips. "You have sold the house," she cried, "that is why we do not go home. That is why you talk no more of the Haven, why there is money for travel. After the children you will drag me to the Haven."

"The Haven! Who thinks of the Haven any more? Tell her, Vivi, tell Mrs. Suspicious: a prescription, sun and rest, to make you healthy. . . . And how could I sell the house without *you?*"

At the place of farewells and greetings, of winds of coming and winds of going, they say their good-byes.

They look back at her with the eyes of others before them: Richard with her own blue blaze; Ann with the nordic eyes of Tim; Morty's dreaming brown of a great-grandmother he will never know; Dody with the laughing eyes of him who had been her springtide love (who stands beside her now); Vivi's, all tears.

The baby's eyes are closed in sleep.

Good-bye, my children.

III

It is to the back of the great city he brought her, to the dwelling places of the cast-off old. Bounded by two lines of amusement piers to the north and to the south, and between a long straight paving rimmed with black benches facing the sand—sands so wide the ocean is only a far fluting.

In the brief vacation season, some of the boarded stores fronting the sands open, and families, young people and children, may be seen. A little tasselled tram shuttles between the piers, and the lights of roller coasters prink and tweak over those who come to have sensation made in them.

The rest of the year it is abandoned to the old, all else boarded up and still; seemingly empty, except the occasional days and hours when the sun, like a tide, sucks them out of the low rooming houses, casts them onto the benches and sandy rim of the walk—and sweeps them into decaying enclosures once again.

A few newer apartments glint among the low bleached squares.

It is in one of these Lennie's Jeannie has arranged their rooms. "Only a few miles north and south people pay hundreds of dollars a month for just this gorgeous air, Grandaddy, just this ocean closeness."

She had been ill on the plane, lay ill for days in the unfamiliar room. Several times the doctor came by—left medicine she would not take. Several times Jeannie drove in the twenty miles from work, still in her Visiting Nurse uniform, the lightness and brightness of her like a healing.

"Who can believe it is winter?" he asked one morning. "Beautiful it is outside like an ad. Come, Mrs. Invalid, come to taste it. You are well enough to sit in here, you are well enough to sit outside. The doctor said it too."

But the benches were encrusted with people, and the sands at the sidewalk's edge. Besides, she had seen the far ruffle of the sea: "there take me," and though she leaned against him, it was she who led.

Plodding and plodding, sitting often to rest, he grumbling. Patting the sand so warm. Once she scooped up a handful, cradling it close to her better eye; peered, and flung it back. And as they came almost to the brink and she could see the glistening wet, she sat down, pulled off her shoes and stockings, left him and began to run. "You'll catch cold," he screamed, but the sand in his shoes weighed him down—he who had always been the agile one—and already the white spray creamed her feet.

He pulled her back, took a handkerchief to wipe off the wet and the sand. "Oh no," she said, "the sun will dry," seized the square and smoothed it flat, dropped on it a mound of sand, knotted the kerchief corners and tied it to a bag—"to look at with the strong glass" (for the first time in years explaining an action of hers)—and lay down with the little bag against her cheek, looking toward the shore that nurtured life as it first crawled toward consciousness the millions of years ago.

He took her one Sunday in the evil-smelling bus, past flat miles of blister houses, to the home of relatives. Oh what is this? she cried as the light began to smoke and the houses to dim and recede. Smog, he said, everyone knows but you. . . . Outside he kept his arms about her, but she walked with hands pushing the heavy air as if to open it, whispered: who has done this? sat down suddenly to vomit at the curb and for a long while refused to rise.

One's age as seen on the altered face of those known in youth. Is this they he has come to visit? This Max and Rose, smooth and pleasant, introducing them to polite children, disinterested grandchildren, "the whole family, once a month on Sundays. And why not? We have the room, the help, the food."

Talk of cars, of houses, of success: this son that, that daughter this. And *your* children? Hastily skimped over, the intermarriages, the obscure work—"my doctor son-in-law, Phil"—all he has to offer. She silent in a corner. (Car-sick like a baby, he explains.) Years since he has taken her to visit anyone but the children, and old apprehensions prickle: "no incidents," he silently begs, "no incidents." He itched to tell them. "A very sick woman," significantly, indicating her with his eyes, "a very sick woman." Their restricted faces did not react. "Have you thought maybe she'd do better at Palm Springs?" Rose asked. "Or at least a nicer section of the beach, nicer people, a pool." Not to have to say "money" he said instead: "would she have sand to look at through a magnifying glass?" and went on, detail after detail, the old habit betraying of parading the queerness of her for laughter.

After dinner—the others into the living room in men- or women-clusters, or into the den to watch TV—the four of them alone. She sat close to him, and did not speak. Jokes, stories, people they had known, beginning of reminiscence, Russia fifty-sixty years ago. Strange words across the Duncan Phyfe table: *hunger; secret meetings; human rights; spies; betrayals; prison; escape*—interrupted by one of the grandchildren: "Commercial's on; any Coke left? Gee, you're missing a real hair-raiser." And then a granddaughter (Max proudly: "look at her, an American queen") drove them home on her way back to U.C.L.A. No incident—except that there had been no incidents.

The first few mornings she had taken with her the magnifying glass, but he would sit only on the benches, so she rested at the foot, where slatted bench shadows fell, and unless she turned her hearing aid down, other voices invaded.

Now on the days when the sun shone and she felt well enough, he took her on the tram to where the benches ranged in oblongs, some with tables for checkers or cards. Again the blanket on the sand in the striped shadows, but she no longer brought the magnifying glass. He played cards, and she lay in the sun and looked towards the waters; or they walked—two blocks down to the scaling hotel, two blocks back—past chili-hamburger stands, open-doored bars, Next-to-New and perpetual rummage-sale stores.

Once, out of the aimless walkers, slow and shuffling like themselves, someone ran unevenly towards them, embraced, kissed, wept: "dear friends, old friends." A friend of *hers*, not his: Mrs. Mays who had lived next door to them in Denver when the children were small.

Thirty years are compressed into a dozen sentences; and the present, not even in three. All is told: the children scattered; the husband dead; she lives in a room two blocks up from the sing hall—and points to the domed auditorium jutting before the pier. The leg? phlebitis; the heavy breathing? that, one does not ask. She, too, comes to the benches each day to sit. And tomorrow, tomorrow, are they going to the community sing? Of course he would have heard of it, everybody goes—the big doings they wait for all week. They have never been? She will come to them for dinner tomorrow and they will all go together.

So it is that she sits in the wind of the singing, among the thousand various faces of age.

She had turned off her hearing aid at once they came into the auditorium—as she would have wished to turn off sight.

One by one they streamed by and imprinted on her—and though the savage zest of their singing came voicelessly soft and distant, the faces still roared—the faces densened the air—chorded into

children-chants, mother-croons, singing of the chained love serenades, Beethoven storms, mad Lucia's scream drunken joy-songs, keens for the dead, work-singing

while from floor to balcony to dome a bare-footed sore-covered little girl threaded the sound-thronged tumult, danced her ecstasy of grimace to flutes that scratched at a cross-roads village wedding

Yes, faces became sound, and the sound became faces; and faces and sound became weight—pushed, pressed

"Air"—her hands claw his.

"Whenever I enjoy myself. . . ." Then he saw the gray sweat on her face. "Here. Up. Help me, Mrs. Mays," and they support her out to where she can gulp the air in sob after sob.

"A doctor, we should get for her a doctor."

"Tch, it's nothing," says Ellen Mays, "I get it all the time. You've missed the tram; come to my place. Fix your hearing aid, honey . . . close . . . tea. My view. See, she *wants* to come. Steady now, that's how." Adding mysteriously: "Remember your advice, easy to keep your head above water, empty things float. Float."

The singing a fading march for them, tall woman with a swollen leg, weaving little man, and the swollen thinness they help between.

The stench in the hall: mildew? decay? "We sit and rest then climb. My gorgeous view. We help each other and here we are."

The stench along into the slab of room. A washstand for a sink, a box with oilcloth tacked around for a cupboard, a three-burner gas plate. Artificial flowers, colorless with dust. Everywhere pictures foaming: wedding, baby, party, vacation, graduation, family pictures. From the narrow couch under a slit of window, sure enough the view: lurching rooftops and a scallop of ocean heaving, preening, twitching under the moon.

"While the water heats. Excuse me . . . down the hall." Ellen Mays has gone.

"You'll live?" he asks mechanically, sat down to feel his fright; tried to pull her alongside.

She pushed him away. "For air," she said; stood clinging to the dresser. Then, in a terrible voice:

After a lifetime of room. Of many rooms.

Shhh.

You remember how she lived. Eight children. And now one room like a coffin.

She pays rent!

Shrinking the life of her into one room like a coffin Rooms and rooms like this I lie on the quilt and hear them talk

Please, Mrs. Orator-without-Breath.

Once you went for coffee I walked I saw A Balzac a Chekhov to write it Rummage Alone On scraps

Better old here than in the old country!

On scraps Yet they sang like like Wondrous! *Humankind one has to believe* So strong for what? To rot not grow?

Your poor lungs beg you. They sob between each word.

Singing. Unused the life in them. She in this poor room

with her pictures Max You The children Everywhere unused the life And who has meaning? Century after century still all in us not to grow?

Coffins, rummage, plants: sick woman. Oh lay down. We will get for you the doctor.

"And when will it end. Oh, *the end*." *That* nightmare thought, and this time she writhed, crumpled against him, seized his hand (for a moment again the weight, the soft distant roaring of humanity) and on the strangled-for breath, begged: "Man . . . we'll destroy ourselves?"

And looking for answer—in the helpless pity and fear for her (for *her*) that distorted his face—she understood the last months, and knew that she was dying.

IV

"Let us go home," she said after several days.

"You are in training for a cross-country run? That is why you do not even walk across the room? Here, like a prescription Phil said, till you are stronger from the operation. You want to break doctor's orders?"

She saw the fiction was necessary to him, was silent; then: "At home I will get better. If the doctor here says?"

"And winter? And the visits to Lennie and to Clara? All right," for he saw the tears in her eyes, "I will write Phil, and talk to the doctor."

Days passed. He reported nothing. Jeannie came and took her out for air, past the boarded concessions, the hooded and tented amusement rides, to the end of the pier. They watched the spent waves feeding the new, the gulls in the clouded sky; even up where they sat, the wind-blown sand stung.

She did not ask to go down the crooked steps to the sea.

Back in her bed, while he was gone to the store, she said: "Jeannie, this doctor, he is not one I can ask questions. Ask him for me, can I go home?"

Jeannie looked at her, said quickly: "Of course, poor Granny. You want your own things around you, don't you? I'll call him tonight. . . . Look, I've something to show you," and from her purse unwrapped a large cookie, intricately shaped like a little girl. "Look at the curls—can you hear me well, Granny—and the darling eyelashes. I just came from a house where they were baking them."

"The dimples, there in the knees," she marveled, holding it to the better light, turning, studying, "like art. Each singly they cut, or a mold?"

"Singly," said Jeannie, "and if it is a child only the mother can make them. Oh Granny, it's the likeness of a real little girl who died yesterday—Rosita. She was three years old. *Pan del Muerto*, the Bread of the Dead. It was the custom in the part of Mexico they came from."

Still she turned and inspected. "Look, the hollow in the throat, the little cross necklace. . . . I think for the mother it is a good thing to be busy with such bread. You know the family?"

Jeannie nodded. "On my rounds. I nursed. . . . Oh Granny, it is like a party; they play songs she liked to dance to. The coffin is lined with pink velvet and she wears a white dress. There are candles. . . ."

"In the house?" Surprised, "They keep her in the house?"

"Yes," said Jeannie, "and it is against the health law. The father said it will be sad to bury her in this country; in Oaxaca they have a feast night with candles each year; everyone picnics on the graves of those they loved until dawn."

"Yes, Jeannie, the living must comfort themselves." And closed her eyes.

"You want to sleep, Granny?"

"Yes, tired from the pleasure of you. I may keep the Rosita? There stand it, on the dresser, where I can see; something of my own around me."

In the kitchenette, helping her grandfather unpack the groceries, Jeannie said in her light voice:

"I'm resigning my job, Grandaddy."

"Ah, the lucky young man. Which one is he?"

"Too late. You're spoken for." She made a pyramid of cans, unstacked, and built again.

"Something is wrong with the job?"

"With me. I can't be"—she searched for the word—"what they call professional enough. I let myself feel things. And tomorrow I have to report a family. . . ." The cans clicked again. "It's not that, either. I just don't know what I want to do, maybe go back to school, maybe go to art school. I thought if you went to San Francisco I'd come along and talk it over with Momma and Daddy. But I don't see how you can go. She wants to go home. She asked me to ask the doctor.''

The doctor told her himself. ''Next week you may travel, when you are a little stronger.'' But next week there was the fever of an infection, and by the time that was over, she could not leave the bed—a rented hospital bed that stood beside the double bed he slept in alone now.

Outwardly the days repeated themselves. Every other afternoon and evening he went out to his newfound cronies, to talk and play cards. Twice a week, Mrs. Mays came. And the rest of the time, Jeannie was there.

By the sickbed stood Jeannie's FM radio. Often into the room the shapes of music came. She would lie curled on her side, her knees drawn up, intense in listening (Jeannie sketched her so, coiled, convoluted like an ear), then thresh her hand out and abruptly snap the radio mute—still to lie in her attitude of listening, concealing tears.

Once Jeannie brought in a young Marine to visit, a friend from high-school days she had found wandering near the empty pier. Because Jeannie asked him to, gravely, without self-consciousness, he sat himself cross-legged on the floor and performed for them a dance of his native Samoa.

Long after they left, a tiny thrumming sound could be heard where, in her bed, she strove to repeat the beckon, flight, surrender of his hands, the fluttering footbeats, and his low plaintive calls.

Hannah and Phil sent flowers. To deepen her pleasure, he placed one in her hair. ''Like a girl,'' he said, and brought the hand mirror so she could see. She looked at the pulsing red flower, the yellow skull face; a desolate, excited laugh shuddered from her, and she pushed the mirror away—but let the flower burn.

The week Lennie and Helen came, the fever returned. With it the excited laugh, and incessant words. She, who in her life had spoken but seldom and then only when necessary (never having learned the easy, social uses of words), now in dying, spoke incessantly.

In a half-whisper: ''Like Lisa she is, your Jeannie. Have I told you of Lisa who taught me to read? Of the highborn she was, but noble in herself. I was sixteen; they beat me; my father beat me so I would not go to her. It was forbidden, she was a Tolstoyan. At night, past dogs that howled, terrible dogs, my son, in the snows of winter to the road, I to ride in her carriage like a lady, to books. To her, life was holy, knowledge was holy, and she taught me to read. They hung her. Everything that happens one must try to understand why. She killed one who betrayed many. Because of betrayal, betrayed all she lived and believed. In one minute she killed, before my eyes (there is so much blood in a human being, my son), in prison with me. All that happens, one must try to understand.

''The name?'' Her lips would work. ''The name that was their pole star; the doors of the death houses fixed to open on it; I read of it my year of penal servitude. Thuban!'' very excited, ''Thuban, in ancient Egypt the pole star. Can you see, look out to see it, Jeannie, if it swings around *our* pole star that seems to *us* not to move.

''Yes, Jeannie, at your age my mother and grandmother had already buried children . . . yes, Jeannie, it is more than oceans between Olshana and you . . . yes, Jeannie, they danced, and for all the bodies they had they might as well be chickens, and indeed, they scratched and flapped their arms and hopped.

''And Andrei Yefimitch, who for twenty years had never known of it and never wanted to know, said as if he wanted to cry: but why my dear friend this malicious laughter?'' Telling to herself half-memorized phrases from her few books. ''Pain I answer with tears and cries, baseness with indignation, meanness with repulsion . . . for life may be hated or wearied of, but never despised.''

Delirious: ''Tell me, my neighbor, Mrs. Mays, the pictures never lived, but what of the flowers? Tell them who ask: no rabbis, no ministers, no priests, no speeches, no ceremonies: ah, false—let the living comfort themselves. Tell Sammy's boy, he who flies, tell him to go to Stuttgart and see where Davy has no grave. And what? . . . And what? where millions have no graves—save air.''

In delirium or not, wanting the radio on; not seeming to listen, the words still jetting, wanting the music on. Once, silencing it abruptly as of old, she began to cry, unconcealed tears this time. ''You have pain, Granny?'' Jeannie asked.

''The music,'' she said, ''still it is there and we do not hear;

knocks, and our poor human ears too weak. What else, what else we do not hear?"

Once she knocked his hand aside as he gave her a pill, swept the bottles from her bedside table: "no pills, let me feel what I feel," and laughed as on his hands and knees he groped to pick them up.

Nighttimes her hand reached across the bed to hold his.

A constant retching began. Her breath was too faint for sustained speech now, but still the lips moved:

When no longer necessary to injure others
Pick pick pick Blind chicken
As a human being responsibility

"David!" imperious, "Basin!" and she would vomit, rinse her mouth, the wasted throat working to swallow, and begin the chant again.

She will be better off in the hospital now, the doctor said.

He sent the telegrams to the children, was packing her suitcase, when her hoarse voice startled. She had roused, was pulling herself to sitting.

"Where now?" she asked. "Where now do you drag me?"

"You do not even have to have a baby to go this time," he soothed, looking for the brush to pack. "Remember, after Davy you told me—worthy to have a baby for the pleasure of the ten-day rest in the hospital?"

"Where now? Not home yet?" Her voice mourned. "Where *is* my home?"

He rose to ease her back. "The doctor, the hospital," he started to explain, but deftly, like a snake, she had slithered out of bed and stood swaying, propped behind the night table.

"Coward," she hissed, "runner."

"You stand," he said senselessly.

"To take me there and run. Afraid of a little vomit."

He reached her as she fell. She struggled against him, half slipped from his arms, pulled herself up again.

"Weakling," she taunted, "to leave me there and run. Betrayer. All your life you have run."

He sobbed, telling Jeannie. "A Marilyn Monroe to run for her virtue. Fifty-nine pounds she weighs, the doctor said, and she beats at me like a Dempsey. Betrayer, she cries, and I running like a dog when she calls; day and night, running to her, her vomit, the bedpan. . . ."

"She needs you, Grandaddy," said Jeannie. "Isn't that what they call love? I'll see if she sleeps, and if she does, poor worn-out darling, we'll have a party, you and I: I brought us rum babas."

They did not move her. By her bed now stood the tall hooked pillar that held the solutions—blood and dextrose—to feed her veins. Jeannie moved down the hall to take over the sickroom, her face so radiant, her grandfather asked her once: "you are in love?" (Shameful the joy, the pure overwhelming joy from being with her grandmother; the peace, the serenity that breathed.) "My darling escape," she answered incoherently, "my darling Granny"—as if that explained.

Now one by one the children came, those that were able. Hannah, Paul, Sammy. Too late to ask: and what did you learn with your living, Mother, and what do we need to know?

Clara, the eldest, clenched:

> *Pay me back, Mother, pay me back for all you took from me. Those others you crowded into your heart. The hands I needed to be for you, the heaviness, the responsibility.*
>
> *Is this she? Noises the dying make, the crablike hands crawling over the covers. The ethereal singing.*
>
> *She hears that music, that singing from childhood; forgotten sound—not heard since, since. . . . And the hardness breaks like a cry: Where did we lose each other, first mother, singing mother?*
>
> *Annulled: the quarrels, the gibing, the harshness between; the fall into silence and the withdrawal.*
>
> *I do not know you, Mother. Mother, I never knew you.*

Lennie, suffering not alone for her who was dying, but for that in her which never lived (for that which in him might never live). From him too, unspoken words: *good-bye Mother who taught me to mother myself.*

Not Vivi, who must stay with her children; not Davy, but he is already here, having to die again with *her* this time, for the living take their dead with them when they die.

Light she grew, like a bird, and, like a bird, sound bubbled in her throat while the body fluttered in agony. Night and day, asleep or awake (though indeed there was no difference now) the songs and the phrases leaping.

And he, who had once dreaded a long dying (from fear of himself, from horror of the dwindling money) now desired her quick death profoundly, for *her* sake. He no longer went out, except when Jeannie forced him; no longer laughed, except when, in the bright kitchenette, Jeannie coaxed his laughter (and she, who seemed to hear nothing else, would laugh too, conspiratorial wisps of laughter).

Light, like a bird, the fluttering body, the little claw hands, the beaked shadow on her face; and the throat, bubbling, straining.

He tried not to listen, as he tried not to look on the face in which only the forehead remained familiar, but trapped with her the long nights in that little room, the sounds worked themselves into his consciousness, with their punctuation of death swallows, whimpers, gurglings.

Even in reality (swallow) *life's lack of it*
Slaveships   deathtrains   clubs   eeenough
The bell   summon what enables
78,000 in one minute (whisper of a scream) *78,000 human beings   we'll destroy ourselves*?

"Aah, Mrs. Miserable," he said, as if she could hear, "all your life working, and now in bed you lie, servants to tend, you do not even need to call to be tended, and still you work. Such hard work it is to die? Such hard work?"

The body threshed, her hand clung in his. A melody, ghost-thin, hovered on her lips, and like a guilty ghost, the vision of her bent in listening to it, silencing the record instantly he was near. Now, heedless of his presence, she floated the melody on and on.

"Hid it from me," he complained, "how many times you listened to remember it so?" And tried to think when she had first played it, or first begun to silence her few records when he came near—but could reconstruct nothing. There was only this room with its tall hooked pillar and its swarm of sounds.

No man one except through others
Strong with the not yet in the now
Dogma dead war dead one country

"It helps, Mrs. Philosopher, words from books? It helps?" And it seemed to him that for seventy years she had hidden a tape recorder, infinitely microscopic, within her, that it had coiled infinite mile on mile, trapping every song, every melody, every word read, heard, and spoken—and that maliciously she was playing back only what said nothing of him, of the children, of their intimate life together.

"Left us indeed, Mrs. Babbler," he reproached, "you who called others babbler and cunningly saved your words. A lifetime you tended and loved, and now not a word of us, for us. Left us indeed? Left me."

And he took out his solitaire deck, shuffled the cards loudly, slapped them down.

Lift high banner of reason (tatter of an orator's voice) *justice freedom light*

Humankind life worthy capacities

Seeks (blur of shudder) *belong human being*

"Words, words," he accused, "and what human beings did *you* seek around you, Mrs. Live Alone, and what humankind think worthy?"

Though even as he spoke, he remembered she had not always been isolated, had not always wanted to be alone (as he knew there had been a voice before this gossamer one; before the hoarse voice that spoke from silence to lash, make incidents, shame him—a girl's voice of eloquence that spoke their holiest dreams). But again he could reconstruct, image, nothing of what had been before, or when, or how, it had changed.

Ace, queen, jack. The pillar shadow fell, so, in two tracks; in the mirror depths glistened a moonlike blob, the empty solution bottle. And it worked in him: *of reason and justice and freedom . . . Dogma dead*: he remembered the full quotation, laughed bitterly. "Hah, good you do not know what you say; good Victor Hugo died and did not see it, his twentieth century."

Deuce, ten, five. Dauntlessly she began a song of their youth of belief:

These things shall be, a loftier race
than e'er the world hath known shall rise

with flame of freedom in their souls
and light of knowledge in their eyes

King, four, jack "In the twentieth century, hah!"

They shall be gentle, brave and strong
to spill no drop of blood, but dare
all . . .
on earth and fire and sea and air

"To spill no drop of blood, hah! So, cadaver, and you too, cadaver Hugo, 'in the twentieth century ignorance will be dead, dogma will be dead, war will be dead, and for all mankind one country—of fulfilment?' Hah!"

And every life (long strangling cough) *shall*
be a song

The cards fell from his fingers. Without warning, the bereavement and betryal he had sheltered—compounded through the years—hidden even from himself—revealed itself,
uncoiled,
released,
sprung

and with it the monstrous shapes of what had actually happened in the century.

A ravening hunger or thirst seized him. He groped into the kitchenette, switched on all three lights, piled a tray—"you have finished your night snack, Mrs. Cadaver, now I will have mine." And he was shocked at the tears that splashed on the tray.

"Salt tears. For free. I forgot to shake on salt?"

Whispered: "Lost, how much I lost."

Escaped to the grandchildren whose childhoods were childish, who had never hungered, who lived unravaged by disease in warm houses of many rooms, had all the school for which they cared, could walk on any street, stood a head taller than their grandparents, towered above—beautiful skins, straight backs, clear straightforward eyes. "Yes, you in Olshana," he said to the town of sixty years ago, "they would be nobility to you."

And this was not the dream then, come true in ways undreamed? he asked.

And are there no other children in the world? he answered, as if in her harsh voice.

And the flame of freedom, the light of knowledge?

And the drop, to spill no drop of blood?

And he thought that at six Jeannie would get up and it would be his turn to go to her room and sleep, that he could press the buzzer and she would come now; that in the afternoon Ellen Mays was coming, and this time they would play cards and he could marvel at how rouge can stand half an inch on the cheek; that in the evening the doctor would come, and he could beg him to be merciful, to stop the feeding solutions, to let her die.

To let her die, and with her their youth of belief out of which her bright, betrayed words foamed; stained words, that on her working lips came stainless.

Hours yet before Jeannie's turn. He could press the buzzer and wake her to come now; he could take a pill, and with it sleep; he could pour more brandy into his milk glass, though what he had poured was not yet touched.

Instead he went back, checked her pulse, gently tended with his knotty fingers as Jeannie had taught.

She was whimpering; her hand crawled across the covers for his. Compassionately he enfolded it, and with his free hand gathered up the cards again. Still was there thirst or hunger ravening in him.

That world of their youth—dark, ignorant, terrible with hate and disease—how was it that living in it, in the midst of corruption, filth, treachery, degradation, they had not mistrusted man nor themselves; had believed so beautifully, so . . . falsely?

''Aaah, children,'' he said out loud, ''how we believed, how we belonged.'' And he yearned to package for each of the children, the grandchildren, for everyone, *that joyous certainty, that sense of mattering, of moving and being moved, of being one and indivisible with the great of the past, with all that freed, ennobled*. Package it, stand on corners, in front of stadiums and on crowded beaches, knock on doors, give it as a fabled gift.

''And why not in cereal boxes, in soap packages?'' he mocked himself. ''Aah. You have taken my senses, cadaver.''

Words foamed, died unsounded. Her body writhed; she made kissing motions with her mouth. (Her lips moving as she read, poring over the Book of the Martyrs, the magnifying glass superimposed over the heavy eyeglasses.) *Still she believed?* ''Eva!'' he whispered. "Still you believed? You lived by it? These Things Shall Be?"

"One pound soup meat," she answered distinctly, "one soup bone."

"My ears heard you. Ellen Mays was witness: 'Humankind . . . one has to believe.' " Imploringly: "Eva!"

"Bread, day-old." She was mumbling. "Please, in a wooden box . . . for kindling. The thread, hah, the thread breaks. Cheap thread"—and a gurgling, enormously loud, began in her throat.

"I ask for stone; she gives me bread—day-old." He pulled his hand away, shouted: "Who wanted questions? Everything you have to wake?" Then dully, "Ah, let me help you turn, poor creature."

Words jumbled, cleared. In a voice of crowded terror:

"Paul, Sammy, don't fight.

"Hannah, have I ten hands?

"How can I give it, Clara, how can I give it if I don't have?"

"You lie," he said sturdily, "there was joy too." Bitterly: "Ah how cheap you speak of us at the last."

As if to rebuke him, as if her voice had no relationship with her flailing body, she sang clearly, beautifully, a school song the children had taught her when they were little; begged:

"Not look   my hair   where they cut. . . ."

(The crown of braids shorn.) And instantly he left the mute old woman poring over the Book of the Martyrs; went past the mother treading at the sewing machine, singing with the children; past the girl in her wrinkled prison dress, hiding her hair with scarred hands, lifting to him her awkward, shamed, imploring eyes of love; and took her in his arms, dear, personal, fleshed, in all the heavy passion he had loved to rouse from her.

"Eva!"

Her little claw hand beat the covers. How much, how much can a man stand? He took up the cards, put them down, circled the beds, walked to the dresser, opened, shut drawers, brushed his hair, moved his hand bit by bit over the mirror to see what of the reflection he could blot out with each move, and felt that at any moment he would die of what was unendurable. Went to press the buzzer to wake Jeannie, looked down, saw on Jeannie's sketch pad the hospital bed, with *her*; the double bed alongside, with him; the tall pillar feeding into her veins, and their hands, his and hers, clasped, feeding each other. And as if he had been instructed he went to his bed, lay down, holding the sketch (as if it could shield against the monstrous shapes of loss, of betrayal, of death) and with his free hand took hers back into his.

So Jeannie found them in the morning.

That last day the agony was perpetual. Time after time it lifted her almost off the bed, so they had to fight to hold her down. He could not endure and left the room; wept as if there never would be tears enough.

Jeannie came to comfort him. In her light voice she said: Grandaddy, Grandaddy don't cry. She is not there, she promised me. On the last day, she said she would go back to when she first heard music, a little girl on the road of the village where she was born. She promised me. It is a wedding and they dance, while the flutes so joyous and vibrant tremble in the air. Leave her there, Grandaddy, it is all right. She promised me. Come back, come back and help her poor body to die.

For two of that generation
Seevya and Genya
Infinite, dauntless, incorruptible

Death deepens the wonder

MICHAEL ONDAATJE

The Passions of Lalla

My Grandmother died in the blue arms of a jacaranda tree. She could read thunder.

She claimed to have been born outdoors, abruptly, during a picnic, though there is little evidence for this. Her father—who came from a subdued line of Keyts—had thrown caution to the winds and married a Dickman. The bloodline was considered eccentric (one Dickman had set herself on fire) and rumors about the family often percolated across Colombo in hushed tones. "People who married the Dickmans were afraid."

There is no information about Lalla growing up. Perhaps she was a shy child, for those who are magical break from silent structures after years of chrysalis. By the time she was twenty she was living in Colombo and tentatively engaged to Shelton de Saram—a very good looking and utterly selfish man. He desired the good life, and when Frieda Donhorst arrived from England "with a thin English varnish and the Donhorst checkbook" he promptly married her. Lalla was heartbroken. She went into fits of rage, threw herself on and pounded various beds belonging to her immediate family, and quickly married Willie Gratiaen—a champion cricketer—on the rebound.

Willie was also a broker, and being one of the first Ceylonese to work for the English firm of E. John and Co. brought them most of their local business. The married couple bought a large house called "Palm Lodge" in the heart of Colombo and here, in the three acres that came with the house, they began a dairy. The dairy was Willie's second attempt at raising livestock. Fond of eggs, he had decided earlier to import and raise a breed of black chicken from Australia. At great expense the prize Australorp eggs arrived by ship, ready for hatching, but Lalla accidentally cooked them all while preparing for a dinner party.

Shortly after Willie began the dairy he fell seriously ill. Lalla, unable to cope, would run into neighbors' homes, pound on their beds, and promise to become a Catholic if Willie recovered. He never did and Lalla was left to bring up their two children.

She was not yet thirty, and for the next few years her closest friend was her neighbor, Rene de Saram, who also ran a dairy. Rene's husband disliked Lalla and disliked his wife's chickens. Lalla and the chickens would wake him before dawn every morning, especially Lalla with her loud laughter filtering across the garden as she organized the milkers. One morning Rene woke to silence and, stepping into the garden, discovered her husband tying the beaks of all the chickens with little pieces of string, or in some cases with rubber bands. She protested, but he prevailed and soon they saw their chickens perform a dance of death, dying of exhaustion and hunger, a few managing to escape along Inner Flower Road, some kidnapped by a furious Lalla in the folds of her large brown dress and taken to Palm Lodge where she had them cooked. A year later the husband lapsed into total silence and the only sounds which could be heard from his quarters were barkings and later on the cluck of hens. It is believed he was the victim of someone's charm. For several weeks he clucked, barked, and chirped, tearing his feather pillows into snowstorms, scratching at the expensive parquet floors, leaping from first-storey windows onto the lawn. After he shot himself, Rene was left at the age of thirty-two to bring up their children. So both Rene and Lalla, after years of excessive high living, were to have difficult times—surviving on their wits and character and beauty. Both widows became the focus of the attention of numerous bored husbands. Neither of them was to marry again.

Each had thirty-five cows. Milking began at four-thirty in the morning and by six their milkmen would be cycling all over town to deliver fresh milk to customers. Lalla and Rene took the law into their own hands whenever necessary. When one of their cows caught Rinderpest Fever—a disease which could make government officials close down a dairy for months—Rene took the army pistol which had already killed her husband and personally shot it dead. With Lalla's help she burnt it and buried it in her garden. The milk went out that morning as usual, the tin vessels clanking against the handlebars of several bicyles.

Lalla's head milkman at this time was named Brumphy, and when a Scot named McKay made a pass at a servant girl Brumphy stabbed him to death. By the time the police arrived Lalla had hidden him in one of her sheds, and when they came back a second time she had taken Brumphy over to a neighbor named Lillian Bevan. For some reason Mrs. Bevan approved of everything Lalla did. She was sick when Lalla stormed in to hide Brumphy under the bed whose counterpane had wide lace edges that came down to the floor. Lalla explained that it was only a minor crime; when the police came to the Bevan household and described the brutal stabbing in graphic detail Lillian was terrified as the murderer was just a few feet away from her. But she could never disappoint Lalla and kept quiet. The police watched the house for two days and Lillian dutifully halved her meals and passed a share under the bed. "I'm proud of you darling!" said Lalla when she eventually spirited Brumphy away to another location.

However, there was a hearing in court presided over by Judge E.W. Jayawardene—one of Lalla's favorite bridge partners. When she was called to give evidence she kept referring to him as "My Lord My God." E.W. was probably one of the ugliest men in Ceylon at the time. When he asked Lalla if Brumphy was good-looking—trying humorously to suggest some motive for her protecting him—she replied, "Good looking? Who can say, My Lord My God, some people may find *you* good looking." She was thrown out of court while the gallery hooted with laughter and gave her a standing ovation. This dialogue is still in the judicial records in the Buller's Road Court Museum. In any case she continued to play bridge with E.W. Jayawardene and their sons would remain close friends.

Apart from rare appearances in court (sometimes to watch other friends give evidence), Lalla's day was carefully planned. She would be up at four with the milkers, oversee the dairy, look after the books, and be finished by 9 A.M. The rest of the day would be given over to gallivanting—social calls, lunch parties, visits from admirers, and bridge. She also brought up her two children. It was in the garden at Palm Lodge that my mother and Dorothy Clementi-Smith would practise their dances, quite often surrounded by cattle.

For years Palm Lodge attracted a constant group—first as children, then teenagers, and then young adults. For most of her life children flocked to Lalla, for she was the most casual and irresponsible of chaperones, being far too busy with her own life to oversee them all. Behind Palm Lodge was a paddy field which separated her house from "Royden," where the Daniels lived. When there were complaints that hordes of children ran into Royden with muddy feet, Lalla bought ten pairs of stilts and taught them to walk across the paddy fields on these "borukakuls" or "lying legs." Lalla would say "yes" to any request if she was busy at bridge so they knew when to ask her for permission to do the most outrageous things. Every child had to be part of the group. She particularly objected to children being sent for extra tuition on Saturdays and would hire a Wallace Carriage and go searching for children like Peggy Peiris. She swept into the school at noon yelling "PEGGY!!!," fluttering down the halls in her long black clothes loose at the edges like a rooster dragging its tail, and Peggy's friends would lean over the bannisters and say "Look, look, your mad aunt has arrived."

As these children grew older they discovered that Lalla had very little money. She would take groups out for meals and be refused service as she hadn't paid her previous bills. Everyone went with her anyway, though they could never be sure of eating. It was the same with adults. During one of her grand dinner parties she asked Lionel Wendt who was very shy to carve the meat. A big pot was placed in front of him. As he removed the lid a baby goat jumped out and skittered down the table. Lalla had been so involved with the joke—buying the kid that morning and finding a big enough pot—that she had forgotten about the real dinner and there was nothing to eat once the shock and laughter had subsided.

In the early years her two children, Noel and Doris, could hardly move without being used as part of Lalla's daily theatre. She was constantly dreaming up costumes for my mother to wear to fancy dress parties, which were the rage at the time. Because of Lalla, my mother won every fancy dress competition for three years while in her late teens. Lalla tended to go in for animals or sea creatures. The crowning achievement was my mother's appearance at the Galle Face Dance as a lobster—the outfit bright red and covered with crustaceans and claws which grew out of her shoulder blades and seemed to move of their own accord. The problem was that she could not sit down for the whole evening but had to walk or waltz stiffly from side to side with her various beaux who, although respecting the imagination behind the outfit, found her beautiful frame almost unapproachable. Who knows, this may have been Lalla's ulterior motive. For years my mother tended to be admired from a distance. On the ballroom floor she stood out in her animal or shell fish beauty but claws and caterpillar bulges tended to deflect suitors from thoughts of seduction. When couples paired off to walk along Galle Face Green under the moonlight it would, after all, be embarrassing to be seen escorting a lobster.

When my mother eventually announced her engagement to my father, Lalla turned to friends and said, "What do you *think*, darling, she's going to marry an Ondaatje . . . she's going to marry a *Tamil!*" Years later, when I sent my mother my first book of poems, she met my sister at the door with a shocked face and in exactly the same tone and phrasing said, "What do you *think*, Janet" (her hand holding her cheek to emphasize the tragedy), "Michael has become a *poet!*" Lalla continued to stress the Tamil element in my father's background, which pleased him enormously. For the wedding ceremony she had two marriage chairs decorated in a Hindu style and laughed all through the ceremony. The incident was, however, the beginning of a war with my father.

Eccentrics can be the most irritating people to live with. My mother, for instance, strangely, *never* spoke of Lalla to me. Lalla was loved most by people who saw her arriving from the distance like a storm. She did love children, or at least loved company of any kind—cows, adults, babies, dogs. She always had to be surrounded. But being "grabbed" or "contained" by anyone drove her mad. She would be compassionate to the character of children but tended to avoid holding them on her lap. And she could not abide having grandchildren hold her hands when she took them for walks. She would quickly divert them into the entrance of the frightening maze in the Nuwara Eliya Park and leave them there, lost, while she went off to steal flowers. She was always determined to be physically selfish. Into her sixties she would still complain of how she used to be "pinned down" to breast feed her son before she could leave for dances.

With children grown up and out of the way, Lalla busied herself with her sisters and brothers. "Dickie" seemed to be marrying constantly; after David Grenier drowned she married a de Vos, a Wombeck, and then an Englishman. Lalla's brother Vere attempted to remain a bachelor all his life. When she was flirting with Catholicism she decided that Vere should marry her priest's sister—a woman who *had* planned on becoming a nun. The sister also had a dowry of thirty thousand rupees, and both Lalla and Vere were short of money at the time, for both enjoyed expensive drinking sessions. Lalla masterminded the marriage, even though the woman wasn't good-looking and Vere liked good-looking women. On the wedding night the bride prayed for half an hour beside the bed and then started singing hymns, so Vere departed, foregoing nuptial bliss, and for the rest of her life and poor woman had a sign above her door which read "Unloved. Unloved. Unloved." Lalla went to mass the following week, having eaten a huge meal. When refused mass she said, "Then I'll resign," and avoided the church for the rest of her life.

A good many of my relatives from this generation seem to have tormented the church sexually. Italian monks who became enamoured of certain aunts would return to Italy to discard their robes and return to find the women already married. Jesuit fathers too were falling out of the church and into love with the de Sarams with the regularity of mangoes thudding onto dry lawns during a drought. Vere also became the concern of various religious groups that tried to save him. And during the last months of his life he was "held captive" by a group of Roman Catholic nuns in Galle so that no one knew where he was until the announcement of his death.

Vere was known as "a sweet drunk" and he and Lalla always drank together. While Lalla grew loud and cheerful, Vere became excessively courteous. Drink was hazardous for him, however, as he came to believe he escaped the laws of gravity while under the influence. He kept trying to hang his hat on walls where there was no hook and often stepped out of boats to walk home. But drink quietened him except for these few excesses. His close friend, the lawyer Cox Sproule, was a different matter. Cox was charming when sober and brilliant when drunk. He would appear in court stumbling over chairs with a mind clear as a bell, winning cases under a judge who had pleaded with him just that morning not to appear in court in such a condition. He hated the English. Unlike Cox, Vere had no profession to focus whatever talents he had. He did try to become an auctioneer but being both shy and drunk he was a failure. The only job that came his way was supervising Italian prisoners during the war. Once a week he would ride to Colombo on his motorcyle, bringing as many bottles of alcohol as he could manage for his friends and his sister. He had encouraged the prisoners to set up a brewery, so that there was a distillery in every hut in the prison camp. He remained drunk with the prisoners for most of the war years. Even Cox Sproule joined him for six months when he was jailed for helping three German spies escape from the country.

What happened to Lalla's other brother, Evan, no one knows. But all through her life, when the children sent her money, Lalla would immediately forward it on to Evan. He was supposedly a thief and Lalla loved him. "Jesus died to save sinners," she said, "and I will die for Evan." Evan manages to escape family memory, appearing only now and then to offer blocs of votes to any friend running for public office by bringing along all his illegitimate children.

By the mid-thirties both Lalla's and Rene's dairies had been wiped out by Rinderpest. Both were drinking heavily and both were broke.

We now enter the phase when Lalla is best remembered. Her children were married and out of the way. Most of her social life had been based at Palm Lodge but now she had to sell the house, and she burst loose on the country and her friends like an ancient monarch who had lost all her possessions. She was free to move wherever she wished, to do whatever she wanted. She took thorough advantage of everyone and had bases all over the country. Her schemes for organizing parties and bridge games exaggerated themselves. She was full of the "passions," whether drunk or not. She had always loved flowers but in her last decade couldn't be bothered to grow them. Still, whenever she arrived on a visit she would be carrying an armful of flowers and announce, "Darling, I've just been to church and I've stolen some flowers for you. These are from Mrs. Abeysekare's, the lilies are from Mrs. Ratnayake's, the agapanthus is from Violet Meedeniya, and the rest are from *your* garden." She stole flowers compulsively, even in the owner's presence. As she spoke with someone her straying left hand would pull up a prize rose along with the roots, all so that she could appreciate it for that one moment, gaze into it with complete pleasure, swallow its qualities whole, and then hand the flower, discarding it, to the owner. She ravaged some of the best gardens in Colombo and Nuwara Eliya. For some years she was barred from the Hakgalle Public Gardens.

Property was there to be taken or given away. When she was

rich she had given parties for all the poor children in the neighborhood and handed out gifts. When she was poor she still organized them but now would go out to the Pettah market on the morning of the party and steal toys. All her life she had given away everything she owned to whoever wanted it and so now felt free to take whatever she wanted. She was a lyrical socialist. Having no home in her last years, she breezed into houses for weekends or even weeks, cheated at bridge with her closest friends, calling them "damn thieves," "bloody rogues." She only played cards for money and if faced with a difficult contract would throw down her hand, gather the others up, and proclaim "the rest are mine." Everyone knew she was lying but it didn't matter. Once when my brother and two sisters who were very young were playing a game of "beggar-my-neighbor" on the porch, Lalla came to watch. She walked up and down beside them, seemingly very irritated. After ten minutes she could stand it no longer, opened her purse, gave them each two rupees, and said, "Never, *never* play cards for love."

She was in her prime. During the war she opened up a boarding house in Nuwara Eliya with Muriel Potger, a chain smoker who did all the work while Lalla breezed through the rooms saying, "Muriel, for godsake, we can't breathe in this place!"—being more of a pest than a help. If she had to go out she would say, "I'll just freshen up" and disappear into her room for a stiff drink. If there was none she took a quick swig of eau de cologne to snap her awake. Old flames visited her constantly throughout her life. She refused to lose friends; even her first beau, Shelton de Saram, would arrive after breakfast to escort her for walks. His unfortunate wife, Frieda, would always telephone Lalla first and would spend most afternoons riding in her trap through the Cinnamon Gardens or the park searching for them.

Lalla's great claim to fame was that she was the first woman in Ceylon to have a mastectomy. It turned out to be unnecessary but she always claimed to support modern science, throwing herself into new causes. (Even in death her generosity exceeded the physically possible for she had donated her body to six hospitals). The false breast would never be still for long. She was an energetic person. It would crawl over to join its twin on the right hand side or sometimes appear on her back, "for dancing" she smirked. She called it her Wandering Jew and would yell at the grandchildren in the middle of a formal dinner to fetch her tit as she had forgotten to put it on. She kept losing the contraption to servants who were mystified by it as well as to the dog, Chindit, who would be found gnawing at the foam as if it were tender chicken. She went through four breasts in her lifetime. One she left on a branch of a tree in Hakgalle Gardens to dry out after a rainstorm, one flew off when she was riding behind Vere on his motorbike, and the third she was very mysterious about, almost embarrassed though Lalla was never embarrassed. Most believed it had been forgotten after a romantic assignation in Trincomalee with a man who may or may not have been in the Cabinet.

Children tell little more than animals, said Kipling. When Lalla came to Bishop's College Girls School on Parents' Day and pissed behind bushes—or when in Nuwara Eliya she simply stood with her legs apart and urinated—my sisters were so embarrassed and ashamed they did not admit or speak of this to each other for over fifteen years. Lalla's son Noel was most appalled by her. She, however, was immensely proud of his success, and my Aunt Nedra recalls seeing Lalla sitting on a sack of rice in the fish market surrounded by workers and fishermen, with whom she was having one of her long daily chats, pointing to a picture of a bewigged judge in *The Daily News* and saying in Sinhalese that *this* was *her* son. But Lalla could never be just a mother; that seemed to be only one muscle in her chameleon nature, which had too many other things to reflect. And I am not sure what my mother's relationship was to her. Maybe they were too similar to even recognize much of a problem, both having huge compassionate hearts that never even considered revenge or small-mindedness, both howling and wheezing with laughter over the frailest joke, both carrying their own theatre on their backs. Lalla remained the center of the world she moved through. She had been beautiful when young but most free after her husband died and her children grew up. There was some sense of divine right she felt she and everyone else had, even if she had to beg for it or steal it. This overbearing charmed flower.

In her last years she was searching for the great death. She never found, looking under leaves, the giant snake, the fang which would brush against the ankle like a whisper. A whole generation grew old or died around her. Prime Ministers fell off horses, a jellyfish slid down the throat of a famous swimmer. During the forties she moved with the rest of the country towards Independence and the 20th century. Her freedom accelerated. Her arms still flagged down strange cars for a lift to the Pettah market where she could trade gossip with her friends and place bets in the "bucket shops." She carried everything she really needed with her, and a friend meeting her once at a train station was appalled to be given as a gift a huge fish that Lalla had carried doubled up in her handbag.

She could be silent as a snake or flower. She loved the thunder; it spoke to her like a king. As if her mild dead husband had been transformed into a cosmic umpire, given the megaphone of nature. Sky noises and the abrupt light told her details of careers, incidental wisdom, allowing her to risk everything because the thunder would warn her along with the snake of lightning. She would stop the car and swim in the Mahaveli, serene among currents, still wearing her hat. Would step out of the river, dry in the sun for five minutes and climb back into the car among the shocked eyeballs of her companions, her huge handbag once more on her lap carrying four packs of cards, possibly a fish.

In August 1947, she received a small inheritance, called her brother Vere, and they drove off to Nuwara Eliya on his motorcycle. She was 68 years old. These were to be her last days. The boarding house she had looked after during the war was empty and so they bought food and booze and moved in to play "Ajoutha"—a card game that normally takes at least eight hours. It was a game the Portuguese had taught the Sinhalese in the 15th century to keep them quiet and preoccupied while they invaded the country. Lalla opened the bottles of Rocklands Gin (the same brand that was destroying her son-in-law) and Vere prepared the Italian menus, which he had learned from his prisoners of war. In her earlier days in Nuwara Eliya, Lalla would have been up at dawn to walk through the park—inhabited at that hour only by nuns and monkeys—walk round the golf-course where gardeners would stagger under the weight of giant python-like hoses as they watered the greens. But now she slept till noon, and in the early evening rode up to Moon Plains, her arms spread out like a crucifix behind Vere.

Moon Plains. Drowned in blue and gold flowers whose names she had never bothered to learn, tugged by the wind, leaning in angles for miles and miles against the hills 5000 feet above sea level. They watched the exit of the sun and the sudden appearance of the moon half way up the sky. Those lovely accidental moons—a horn a chalice a thumbnail—and then they would climb onto the motorcycle, the 60-year-old brother and the 68-year-old sister, who was his best friend forever.

Riding back on August 13, 1947, they heard the wild thunder and she knew someone was going to die. Death, however, not to be read out there. She gazed and listened but there seemed to be no victim or parabola end beyond her. It rained hard during the last mile to the house and they went indoors to drink for the rest of the evening. The next day the rains continued and she refused Vere's offer of a ride knowing there would be death soon. "Cannot wreck this perfect body, Vere. The police will spend hours searching for my breast thinking it was lost in the crash." So they played two-handed Ajoutha and drank. But now she could not sleep at all, and they talked as they never had about husbands, lovers, his various possible marriages. She did not mention her readings of the thunder to Vere, who was now almost comatose on the bluebird print sofa. But she could not keep her eyes closed like him and at 5 A.M. on August 15, 1947, she wanted fresh air, needed to walk, a walk to Moon Plains, no motorcycle, no danger, and she stepped out towards the still dark night of almost dawn and straight into the floods.

For two days and nights they had been oblivious to the amount of destruction outside their home. The whole country was mauled by the rains that year. Ratmalana, Bentota, Chilaw, Anuradhapura, were all under water. The forty-foot-high Peredeniya Bridge had been swept away. In Nuwara Eliya, Galways's Land Bird Sanctuary and the Golf Course were ten feet under water. Snakes and fish from the lake swam into the windows of the Golf Club, into the bar, and around the indoor badminton court. Fish were found captured in the badminton nets when the flood receded a week later. Lalla took one step off the front porch and was immediately hauled away by an arm of water, her handbag bursting open. 208 cards moved ahead of her like a disturbed nest as she was thrown downhill still comfortable and drunk, snagged for a few moments on the railings of the Good Shepherd Convent and then lifted away towards the town of Nuwara Eliya.

It was her last perfect journey. The new river in the street moved her right across the race course and park towards the bus station.

As the light came up slowly she was being swirled fast, ''floating'' (as ever confident of surviving this too) alongside branches and leaves, the dawn starting to hit flamboyant trees as she slipped past them like a dark log, shoes lost, false breast lost. She was free as a fish, travelling faster than she had in years, fast as Vere's motorcycle, only now there was this *roar* around her. She overtook Jesus lizards that swam and ran in bursts over the water, she was surrounded by tired half-drowned fly-catchers screaming *tack tack tack tack*, frogmouths, nightjars forced to keep awake, brain-fever birds and their irritating ascending scales, snake eagles, scimitar-babblers, they rode the air around Lalla wishing to perch on her unable to alight on anything except what was moving.

What was moving was rushing flood. In the park she floated over the intricate fir tree hedges of the maze—which would always continue to terrify her grandchildren—its secret spread out naked as a skeleton for her. The symmetrical flower beds also began to receive the day's light and Lalla gazed down at them with wonder, moving as lazily as that long dark scarf which trailed off her neck brushing the branches and never catching. She would always wear silk, as she showed us, her grandchildren, would pull the scarf like a fluid through the ring removed from her finger, pulled sleepily through, as she moved now, awake to the new angle of her favorite trees, the Syzygium, the Araucaria Pine, over the now unnecessary iron gates of the park, and through the town of Nuwara Eliya itself and its shops and stalls where she had haggled for guavas, now six feet under water, windows smashed in by the weight of all this collected rain.

Drifting slower she tried to hold onto things. A bicyle hit her across the knees. She saw the dead body of a human. She began to see the drowned dogs of the town. Cattle. She saw men on roofs fighting with each other, looting, almost surprised by the quick dawn in the mountains revealing them, not even watching her magic ride, the alcohol still in her—serene and relaxed.

Below the main street of Nuwara Eliya the land drops suddenly and Lalla fell into deeper waters, past the houses of ''Cranleigh'' and ''Ferncliff.'' They were homes she knew well, where she had played and argued over cards. The water here was rougher and she went under for longer and longer moments coming up with a gasp and then pulled down like bait, pulled under by something not comfortable any more, and then there was the great blue ahead of her, like a sheaf of blue wheat, like a large eye that peered towards her, and she hit it and was dead.

ISAAC BASHEVIS SINGER

Old Love

Harry Bendiner awoke at five with the feeling that as far as he was concerned the night was finished and he wouldn't get any more sleep. Actually, he woke up a dozen times every night. He had undergone an operation for his prostate years before, but this hadn't relieved the constant pressure on his bladder. He would sleep an hour or less, then wake up with the need to void. Even his dreams centered around this urge. He got out of bed and padded to the bathroom on shaky legs. On the way back he stepped out onto the balcony of his eleventh-story condominium. To the left he could see the skycrapers of Miami, to the right the rumbling sea. The air had turned a bit cooler during the night, but it was still tropically tepid. It smelled of dead fish, oil, and perhaps of oranges as well. Harry stood there for a long while enjoying the breeze from the ocean on his moist forehead. Even though Miami Beach had become a bit city, he imagined that he could feel the nearness of the Everglades, the smells and vapors of its vegetation and swamps. Sometimes a seagull would awake in the night, screeching. It happened that the waves threw onto the beach the carcass of a barracuda or even that of a baby whale. Harry Bendiner looked off in the direction of Hollywood. How long was it since the whole area had been undeveloped? Within a few years a wasteland had been transformed into a settlement crowded with hotels, condominiums, restaurants, supermarkets, and banks. The street lights and neon signs dimmed the stars in the sky. Cars raced along even in the middle of the night. Where were all these people hurrying to before dawn? Didn't they ever sleep? What kind of force drove them on? ''Well, it's no longer my world. Once you pass eighty, you're as good as a corpse.''

He leaned his hand on the railing and tried to reconstruct the dream he had been having. He recalled only that all those who had appeared in the dream were now dead—the men and the women both. Dreams obviously didn't acknowledge death. In his dreams, his three wives were still alive, and so was his son, Bill, and his daughter, Sylvia. New York, his hometown in Poland, and Miami Beach merged into one. He, Harry or Hershel, was both an adult and a cheder boy.

He closed his eyes for a moment. Why was it impossible to remember dreams? He could recall every detail of events that had happened seventy and even seventy-five years ago, but tonight's dreams dissolved like foam. Some force made sure that not a trace of them remained. A third of a person's life died before he went to his grave.

After a while Harry sat down on the plastic chaise that stood on the balcony. He looked toward the sea, to the east, where day would soon be dawning. There was a time when he went swimming the first thing in the morning, particularly during the summer months, but he no longer had the desire to do such things. The newspapers occasionally printed accounts of sharks attacking swimmers, and there were other sea creatures whose bites caused serious complications. For him it now sufficed to take a warm bath.

His thoughts turned to matters of business. He knew full well that money couldn't help him; still, one couldn't constantly brood about the fact that everything was vanity of vanities. It was easier to think about practical matters. Stocks and bonds rose or fell. Dividends and other earnings had to be deposited in the bank and marked down in an account book for tax purposes. Telephone and electric bills and the maintenance of the apartment had to be paid. One day a week a woman came to do his cleaning and press his shirts and underwear. Occasionally he had to have a suit dry-cleaned and shoes repaired. He received letters that he had to answer. He wasn't involved with a synagogue all year, but on Rosh Hashanah and Yom Kippur he had to have a place to worship, and because of this he received appeals to help Israel, yeshivas, Talmud Torahs, old-age homes, and hospitals. Each day he got a pile of "junk mail," and before he discarded it, he had to open and glance at it, at least.

Since he had resolved to live out his years without a wife or even a housekeeper, he had to arrange for his meals, and every other day he went shopping at the local supermarket. Pushing his cart through the aisles, he selected such items as milk, cottage cheese, fruit, canned vegetables, chopped meat, occasionally some mushrooms, a jar of borscht or gefilte fish. He certainly could have permitted himself the luxury of a maid, but some of the maids were thieves. And what would he do with himself if other people waited on him? He remembered a saying from the Gemara that slothfulness led to madness. Fussing over the electric stove in the kitchen, going to the bank, reading the newspaper—particularly the financial section—and spending an hour or two at the office of Merrill Lynch watching the quotations from the New York Exchange flash by on the board lifted his spirits. Recently he had had a television set installed, but he rarely watched it.

His neighbors in the condominium often inquired maliciously why he did things himself that others could do for him. It was known that he was rich. They offered him advice and asked him questions: Why didn't he settle in Israel? Why didn't he go to a hotel in the mountains during the summer? Why didn't he get married? Why didn't he hire a secretary? He had acquired the reputation of a miser. They constantly reminded him that "you can't take it with you"—as if this were some startling revelation. For this reason he stopped attending the tenants' meetings and their parties. Everyone tried in one way or another to get something out of him, but no one would have given him a penny if he needed it. A few years ago, he boarded a bus from Miami Beach to Miami and found he was two cents short of the fare. All he had with him was twenty-dollar bills. No one volunteered either to give him the two cents or to change one of his bank notes, and the driver made him get off.

The truth was, in no hotel could he feel as comfortable as he did in his own home. The meals served in hotels were too plentiful for him and not of the kind that he needed. He alone could see to it that his diet excluded salt, cholesterol, spices. Besides, plane and train rides were too taxing for a man of his delicate health. Nor did it make any sense to remarry at his age. Younger women demanded sex, and he hadn't the slightest interest in an old woman. Being what he was, he was condemned to live alone and to die alone.

A reddish glow had begun to tinge the eastern sky, and Harry went to the bathroom. He stood for a moment studying his image in the mirror—sunken cheeks, a bare skull with a few tufts of white hair, a pointed Adam's apple, a nose whose tip turned down like a parrot's beak. The pale-blue eyes were set somewhat off-center, one higher than the other, and expressed both weariness and traces of youthful ardor. He had once been a virile man. He had had wives and love affairs. He had a stack of love letters and photographs lying about somewhere.

Harry Bendiner hadn't come to America penniless and uneducated like the other immigrants. He had attended the study house in his hometown until the age of nineteen; he knew Hebrew and had secretly read newspapers and worldly books. He had taken lessons in Russian, Polish, and even German. Here in America he had attended Cooper Union for two years in the hope of becoming an engineer, but he had fallen in love with an American girl, Rosalie Stein, and married her, and her father, Sam Stein, had taken him into the construction business. Rosalie died of cancer at the age of thirty, leaving him with two small children. Even as the money came in to him so did death take from him. His son, Bill, a surgeon, died at forty-six, of a heart attack, leaving two children, neither of whom wanted to be Jewish. Their mother, a Christian, lived somewhere in Canada with another man. Harry's daughter, Sylvia, got the very same type of cancer as her mother, and at exactly the same age. Sylvia left no children. Harry refused to sire any more generations, even though his second wife, Edna, pleaded that he have a child or two with her.

Yes, the Angel of Death had taken everything from him. At first his grandchildren had called him occasionally from Canada and sent him a card for the New Year. But now he never heard from them, and he had cut them out of his will.

Harry shaved and hummed a melody—where it had come from he didn't know. Was it something he had heard on television, or a tune from Poland revived in his memory? He had no ear for music and sang everything off-key, but he had retained the habit of singing in the bathroom. His toilet took a long time. For years the pills he took to relieve constipation had had no effect, and every other day he gave himself an enema—a long and arduous process for a man in his eighties. He tried to do calisthenics in the bathtub, raising his skinny legs and splashing his hands in the water as if they were paddles. These were all measures to lengthen life, but even as Harry performed them he asked himself, "Why go on living?" What flavor did his existence possess? No, his life made no sense whatsoever—but did that of his neighbors make more sense? The condominium was full of old people, all well off, many rich. Some of the men couldn't walk, or dragged their feet; some of the women leaned on crutches. A number suffered from arthritis and Parkinson's disease. This wasn't a building but a hospital. People died, and he didn't find out about it until weeks or months afterward. Although he had been among the first tenants in the condominium, he seldom recognized anybody. He didn't go to the pool and he didn't play cards. Men and women greeted him in the elevator and at the supermarket, but he didn't know who any of them were. From time to time someone asked him, "How are you, Mr. Bendiner?" And he usually replied, "How *can* you be at my age? Each day is a gift."

This summer day began like all the others. Harry prepared his breakfast in the kitchen—Rice Krispies with skimmed milk and Sanka sweetened with saccharin. At about nine-thirty he took the elevator down to get the mail. A day didn't go by that he didn't receive a number of checks, but this day brought a bounty. The stocks had fallen, but the companies kept paying the dividends as usual. Harry got money from buildings on which he held mortgages, from rents, bonds, and all kinds of business ventures that he barely remembered. An insurance company paid him an annuity. For years he had been getting a monthly check from Social Security. This morning's yield came to over eleven thousand dollars. True, he would have to withhold a great part of this for taxes, but it still left him with some five thousand dollars for himself. While he totaled up the figures, he deliberated: Should he go to the office of Merrill Lynch and see what was happening on the Exchange? No, there was no point to it. Even if the stocks rose early in the morning, the day would end in losses. "The market is completely crazy," he mumbled to himself. He had considered it an iron rule that inflation always went along with a bullish market, not with a bearish market. But now both the dollar *and* the stocks were collapsing. Well, you could never be sure about anything except death.

Around eleven o'clock he went down to deposit the checks. The bank was a small one; all the employees knew him and said good morning. He had a safe-deposit box there, where he kept his valuables and jewelry. It so happened that all three of his wives had left him everything; none of them had made out a will. He didn't know himself exactly how much he was worth, but it couldn't be less than five million dollars. Still, he walked down the street in a shirt and trousers that any pauper could afford and a cap and shoes he had worn for years. He poked with his cane and took tiny steps. Once in a while he cast a glance backward. Maybe someone was following him. Maybe some crook had found out how rich he was and was scheming to kidnap him. Although the day was bright and the street full of people, no one would interfere if he was grabbed, forced into a car, and dragged off to some ruin or cave. No one would pay ransom for him.

After he had concluded his business at the bank, he turned back toward home. The sun was high in the sky and poured down a blazing fire. Women stood in the shade of canopies looking at dresses, shoes, stockings, brassières, and bathing suits in the store windows. Their faces expressed indecision—to buy or not to buy? Harry glanced at the windows. What could he buy there? There wasn't anything he could desire. From now until five, when he would prepare his dinner, he needed absolutely nothing. He knew precisely what he would do when he got home—take a nap on the sofa.

Thank God, no one had kidnapped him, no one had held him up, no one had broken into his apartment. The air conditioner was working, and so was the plumbing in the bathroom. He took off his shoes and stretched out on the sofa.

Strange, he still daydreamed; he fantasized about unexpected successes, restored powers, masculine adventures. The brain wouldn't accept old age. It teemed with the same passions it had in his youth. Harry often said to his brain, "Don't be stupid. It's too late for everything. You have nothing to hope for any more." But the brain was so constituted that it went on hoping nonetheless. Who was it who said, A man takes his hopes into the grave?

He had dozed off and was awakened by a jangling at the door. He became alarmed. No one ever came to see him. "It must be the exterminator," he decided. He opened the door the length of the chain and saw a small woman with reddish cheeks, yellow eyes, and a high pompadour of blond hair the color of straw. She wore a white blouse.

Harry opened the door, and the woman said in a foreign-accented English, "I hope I haven't awakened you. I'm your new neighbor on the left. I wanted to introduce myself to you. My name is Mrs. Ethel Brokeles. A funny name, eh? That was my late husband's name. My maiden name is Goldman."

Harry gazed at her in astonishment. His neighbor on the left had been an old woman living alone. He remembered her name—Mrs. Halpert. He asked, "What happened to Mrs. Halpert?"

"The same as happens to everybody," the woman replied smugly.

"When did it happen? I didn't know anything about it."

"It's more than five months already."

"Come in, come in. People die and you don't even know," Harry said. "She was a nice woman . . . kept herself at a distance."

"I didn't know her. I bought the apartment from her daughter."

"Please have a seat. I don't even have anything to offer you. I have a bottle of liqueur somewhere, but . . ."

"I don't need any refreshments and I don't drink liqueur. Not in the middle of the day. May I smoke?"

"Certainly, certainly."

The woman sat down on the sofa. She snapped a fancy lighter expertly and lit her cigarette. She wore red nail polish and Harry noticed a huge diamond on one of her fingers.

The woman asked, "You live here alone?"

"Yes, alone."

"I'm alone, too. What can you do? I lived with my husband twenty-five years, and we didn't have a bad day. Our life together was all sunshine without a single cloud. Suddenly he passed away and left me alone and miserable. The New York climate is unhealthy for me. I suffer from rheumatism. I'll have to live out my years here."

"Did you buy the apartment furnished?" Harry asked in businesslike fashion.

"Everything. The daughter wanted nothing for herself besides the dresses and linens. She turned it all over to me for a song. I wouldn't have had the patience to go out and buy furniture and dishes. Have you lived here a long time already?"

The woman posed one question after another, and Harry answered them willingly. She looked comparatively young—no more than fifty or possibly even younger. He brought her an ashtray and put a glass of lemonade and a plate of cookies on the coffee table before her. Two hours went by, but he hardly noticed. Ethel Brokeles crossed her legs, and Harry cast glances at her round knees. She had switched to a Polish-accented Yiddish. She exuded the intimate air of a relative. Something within Harry exulted. It could be nothing else but that heaven had acceded to his secret desires. Only now, as he listened to her, did he realize how lonely he had been all these years, how oppressed by the fact that he seldom exchanged a word with anyone. Even having her for a neighbor was better than nothing. He grew youthful in her presence, and loquacious. He told her about his three wives, the tragedies that had befallen his children. He even mentioned that, following the death of his first wife, he had had a sweetheart.

The woman said, "You don't have to make excuses. A man is a man."

"I've grown old."

"A man is never old. I had an uncle in Wloclawek who was eighty when he married a twenty-year-old girl, and she bore him three children."

"Wloclawek? That's near Kowal, my hometown."

"I know. I've been to Kowal. I had an aunt there."

The woman glanced at her wristwatch. "It's one o'clock. Where are you having lunch?"

"Nowhere. I only eat breakfast and dinner."

"Are you on a diet?"

"No, but at my age—"

"Stop talking about your age!" the woman scolded him. "You know what? Come over to my place and we'll have lunch together. I don't like to eat by myself. For me, eating alone is even worse than sleeping alone."

"Really, I don't know what to say. What did I do to deserve this?"

"Come, come; don't talk nonsense. This is America, not Poland. My refrigerator is stuffed with goodies. I throw out more than I eat, may I be forgiven."

The woman used Yiddish expressions that Harry hadn't heard in at least sixty years. She took his arm and led him to the door. He didn't have to go more than a few steps. By the time he had locked his door she had opened hers. The apartment he went into was larger than his and brighter. There were pictures on the walls, fancy lamps, bric-a-brac. The windows looked out directly at the ocean. On the table stood a vase of flowers. The air in Harry's apartment smelled of dust, but here the air was fresh. "She wants something; she has some ulterior motive," Harry told himself. He recalled what he had read in the newspapers about female cheats who swindled fortunes out of men and out of other women, too. The main thing was to promise nothing, to sign nothing, not to hand over even a single penny.

She seated him at a table, and from the kitchen soon issued the bubbling sound of a percolator and the smell of fresh rolls, fruit, cheese, and coffee. For the first time in years Harry felt an appetite in the middle of the day. After a while they both sat down to lunch.

Between one bite and the next, the woman took a drag from a cigarette. She complained, "Men run after me, but when it comes down to brass tacks they're all interested only in how much money I have. As soon as they start talking about money I break up with them. I'm not poor; I'm even—knock wood—wealthy. But I don't want anyone to take me for my money."

"Thank God I don't need anyone's money," Harry said. "I've got enough even if I live a thousand years."

"That's good."

Gradually they began to discuss their finances, and the woman enumerated her possessions. She owned buildings in Brooklyn and on Staten Island; she had stocks and bonds. Based on what she said and the names she mentioned, Harry decided that she was telling the truth. She had, here in Miami, a checking account and a safe-deposit box in the very same bank as Harry. Harry estimated that she was worth at least a million or maybe more. She served him food with the devotion of a daughter or wife. She talked of what he should and shouldn't eat. Such miracles had occurred to him in his younger years. Women had met him, grown instantly intimate, and stuck with him, never to leave again. But that such a thing should happen to him at his age seemed like a dream. He asked abruptly, "Do you have children?"

"I have a daughter, Sylvia. She lives all alone in a tent in British Columbia."

"Why in a tent? My daughter's name was Sylvia, too. You yourself could be my daughter," he added, not knowing why he had said such a thing.

"Nonsense. What are years? I always liked a man to be a lot older than me. My husband, may he rest in peace, was twenty years older, and the life we had together I would wish for every Jewish daughter."

"I've surely got forty years on you," Harry said.

The woman put down her spoon. "How old do you take me for?"

"Around forty-five," Harry said, knowing she was older.

"Add another twelve years and you've got it."

"You don't look it."

"I have a good life with my husband. I could get anything out of him—the moon, the stars, nothing was too good for his Ethel. That's why after he died I became melancholy. Also, my daughter was making me sick. I spent a fortune on psychiatrists, but they couldn't help me. Just as you see me now, I stayed seven months in an institution, a clinic for nervous disorders. I had a breakdown and I didn't want to live any more. They had to watch me day and night. He was calling me from his grave. I want to tell you something, but don't misunderstand me."

"What is it?"

"You remind me of my husband. That's why—"

"I'm eighty-two," Harry said and instantly regretted it. He could have easily subtracted five years. He waited a moment, then added, "If I were ten years younger, I'd make you a proposition."

Again he regretted his words. They had issued from his mouth as if of their own volition. He was still bothered by the fear of falling into the hands of a gold digger.

The woman looked at him inquisitively and cocked an eyebrow. "Since I decided to live, I'll take you just as you are."

"How is this possible? How can it be?" Harry asked himself again and again. They spoke of getting married and of breaking through the wall that divided their two apartments to make them into one. His bedroom was next to hers. She revealed the details of her financial situation to him. She was worth about a million and a half. Harry had already told her how much he had. He asked, "What will we do with so much money?"

"I wouldn't know what to do with money myself," the woman replied, "but together, we'll take a trip around the world. We'll buy an apartment in Tel Aviv or Tiberias. The hot springs there are good for rheumatism. With me beside you, you'll live a long time. I guarantee you a hundred years, if not more."

"It's all in God's hands," Harry said, amazed at his own words. He wasn't religious. His doubts about God and His providence had intensified over the years. He often said that, after what had happened to the Jews in Europe, one had to be a fool to believe in God.

Ethel stood up and so did he. They hugged and kissed. He pressed her close and youthful urges came throbbing back within him.

She said, "Wait till we've stood under the wedding canopy."

It struck Harry that he had heard these words before, spoken in the same voice. But when? And from whom? All three of his wives had been American-born and wouldn't have used this expression. Had he dreamed it? Could a person foresee the future in a dream? He bowed his head and pondered. When he looked up he was astounded. Within those few seconds the woman's appearance had undergone a startling transformation. She had moved away from him and he hadn't noticed it. Her face had grown pale, shrunken, and aged. Her hair seemed to him to have become suddenly disheveled. She gazed at him sidelong with a dull, sad, even stern expression. Did I insult her or what? he wondered. He heard himself ask, "Is something wrong? Don't you feel well?"

"No, but you'd better go back to your own place now," she said in a voice which seemed alien, harsh, and impatient. He wanted to ask her the reason for the sudden change that had come over her, but a long-forgotten (or a never-forgotten) pride asserted itself. With women, you never knew where you stood anyhow. Still, he asked, "When will we see each other?"

"Not today any more. Maybe tomorrow," she said after some hestiation.

"Goodbye. Thanks for the lunch."

She didn't even bother to escort him to the door. Inside his own apartment again, he thought, Well, she changed her mind. He was overcome with a feeling of shame—for himself and for her, too. Had she been playing a game with him? Had malicious neighbors arranged to make a fool of him? His apartment struck him as half empty. I won't eat dinner, he decided. He felt a pressure in his stomach. "At my age one shouldn't make a fool of oneself," he murmured. He lay down on the sofa and dozed off, and when he opened his eyes again it was dark outside. Maybe she'll ring my doorbell again. Maybe I should call her? She had given him her phone number. Though he had slept, he woke up exhausted. He had letters to answer, but he put it off until morning. He went out onto the balcony. One side of his balcony faced a part of hers. They could see each other here and even converse, if she should still be interested in him. The sea splashed and foamed. There was a freighter far in the distance. A jet roared in the sky. A single star that no street lights or neon signs could dim appeared above. It's a good thing one can see at least one star. Otherwise one might forget that the sky exists altogether.

He sat on the balcony waiting for her to possibly show up. What could she be thinking? Why had her mood changed so abruptly? One minute she was as tender and talkative as a bride in love; a moment later she was a stranger.

Harry dozed off again, and when he awoke it was late in the evening. He wasn't sleepy, and he wanted to go downstairs for the evening edition of the morning paper, with the reports of the New York Exchange; instead he went to lie down on his bed. He had drunk a glass of tomato juice before and swallowed a pill. Only a thin wall separated him from Ethel, but walls possessed a power of their own. Perhaps this is the reason some people prefer to live in a tent, he thought. He assumed that his broodings would keep him from sleeping, but he quickly nodded off. He awoke with pressure on his chest. What time was it? The luminous dial on his wristwatch showed that he had slept two hours and a quarter. He had dreamed, but he couldn't remember what. He retained only the impression of nocturnal horrors. He raised his head. Was she asleep or awake? He couldn't hear even a rustle from her apartment.

He slept again and was awakened this time by the sound of many people talking, doors slamming, footsteps in the corridor, and running. He had always been afraid of a fire. He read newspaper accounts of old people burning to death in old-age homes, hospitals, hotels. He got out of bed, put on his slippers and robe, and opened the door to the hall. There was no one there. Had he imagined it? He closed the door and went out onto the balcony. No, not a trace of firemen below. Only people coming home late, going out to nightclubs, making drunken noise. Some of the condominium tenants sublet their apartments in the summer to South Americans. Harry went back to bed. It was quiet for a few minutes; then he again heard a din in the corridor and the sound of men's and women's voices. Something had happened, but what? He had an urge to get up and take another look, but he didn't. He lay there tense. Suddenly he heard a buzzing from the house phone in the kitchen. When he lifted the receiver, a man's voice said, "Wrong number." Harry had turned on the fluorescent light in the kitchen and the glare dazzled him. He opened the refrigerator, took out a jug of sweetened tea, and poured himself half a glass, not knowing whether he did this because he was thirsty or to buoy his spirits. Soon afterward he had to urinate, and he went to the bathroom.

At that moment, his doorbell rang, and the sound curtailed his urge. Maybe robbers had broken into the building? The night watchman was an old man and hardly a match for intruders. Harry couldn't decide whether to go to the door or not. He stood over the toilet bowl trembling. *These might be my final moments on earth* flashed through his mind. ''God Almighty, take pity on me,'' he murmured. Only now did he remember that he had a peephole in the door through which he could see the hall outside. How could I have forgotten about it? he wondered. I must be getting senile.

He walked silently to the door, raised the cover of the peephole, and looked out. He saw a white-haired woman in a robe. He recognized her; it was his neighbor on the right. In a second everything became clear to him. She had a paralyzed husband and something had happened to him. He opened the door. The old woman held out an unstamped envelope.

''Excuse me, Mr. Bendiner, the woman next door left this envelope by your door. Your name is on it.''

''What woman?''

''On the left. She committed suicide.''

Harry Bendiner felt his guts constrict, and within seconds his belly grew as tight as a drum.

''The blond woman?''

''Yes.''

''What did she do?''

''Threw herself out the window.''

Harry held out his hand and the old woman gave him the envelope.

''Where is she?'' he asked.

''They took her away.''

''Dead?''

''Yes, dead.''

''My God!''

''It's already the third such incident here. People lose their minds in America.''

Harry's hand shook, and the envelope fluttered as if caught in a wind. He thanked the woman and closed the door. He went to look for his glasses, which he had put on his night table. ''I dare not fall,'' he cautioned himself. ''All I need now is a broken hip.'' He staggered over to his bed and lit the night lamp. Yes, the eyeglasses were lying where he had left them. He felt dizzy. The walls, the curtains, the dresser, the envelope all jerked and whirled like a blurry image on television. Am I going blind or what? he wondered. He sat and waited for the dizziness to pass. He barely had the strength to open the envelope. The note was written in pencil, the lines were crooked, and the Yiddish words badly spelled. It read:

Dear Harry, forgive me. I must go where my husband is. If it's not too much trouble, say Kaddish for me. I'll intercede for you where I'm going.

Ethel

He put the sheet of paper and his glasses down on the night table and switched off the lamp. He lay belching and hiccuping. His body twitched, and the bedsprings vibrated. Well, from now on I won't hope for anything, he decided with the solemnity of a man taking an oath. He felt cold, and he covered himself with the blanket.

It was ten past eight in the morning when he came out of his daze. A dream? No, the letter lay on the table. That day Harry Bendiner did not go down for his mail. He did not prepare breakfast for himself, nor did he bother to bathe and dress. He kept on dozing on the plastic chaise on the balcony and thinking about that other Sylvia—Ethel's daughter—who was living in a tent in British Columbia. Why had she run away so far? he asked himself. Did her father's death drive her into despair? Could she not stand her mother? Or did she already at her age realize the futility of all human efforts and decide to become a hermit? Is she endeavoring to discover herself, or God? An adventurous idea came into the old man's mind: to fly to British Columbia, find the young woman in the wilderness, comfort her, be a father to her, and perhaps try to meditate together with her on why a man is born and why he must die.

ELIZABETH TAYLOR

Mice and Birds and Boy

''Was this when you were pretty?'' William asked, holding the photograph in both hands and raising his eyes to the old lady's with a look of near certainty.

''I was thought to be beautiful,'' she said; and she wondered: How long ago was that? Who had been the last person to comment upon her beauty, and how many years ago? She thought that it might have been her husband, from loyalty or from still seeing what was no longer there. He had been dead for over twenty years and her beauty had not, by any means, been the burden of his dying words.

The photograph had faded to a pale coffee-color, but William could distinguish a cloud of fair hair, a rounded face with lace to the chin, and the drooping, sad expression so many beautiful women have. Poor Mrs. May, he thought.

The photographs were all jumbled up in a carved sandalwood box lined with dusty felt. There was a large one, mounted on stiff cardboard, of the big house where Mrs. May had lived as a child. It had been pulled down between the wars and in its grounds was built a housing estate, a row of small shops by the bus stop and a children's playground, with swings and slides. William could look out of the narrow window of the old gardener's lodge where Mrs. May lived now and watch the shrieking toddlers climbing the frames, swinging on the swings. He never went to the playground himself now that he was six.

''It was all fields,'' Mrs. May would often say, following his glance. ''All fields and parkland. I used to ride my pony over it. It was a different world. We had two grooms and seven indoor servants and four gardeners. Yet we were just ordinary people. Everybody had such things in those days.''

''Did every child have a pony?'' William asked.

"All *country* children had one," she said firmly.

His curiosity endeared him to her. It was so long since anyone had asked her a question and been interested in the answer. His curiosity had been the beginning of their friendship. Going out into her overgrown little garden one afternoon, she had found him leaning against the rickety fence staring at her house, which was round in shape and had attracted his attention. It was made of dark flint and had narrow, arched windows and an arched door studded with big square-headed nails. A high twisted chimney-stack rose from the center of the roof. Surrounded by the looped and tangled growth of the garden—rusty, black-leaved briers and crooked apple trees—the place reminded the boy of a menacing-looking illustration by Arthur Rackham in a book he had at home. Then the door had opened and the witch herself had come out, leaning on a stick. She had untidy white hair and a face cross-hatched with wrinkles; but her eyes weren't witch-like, not black and beady and evil, but large and milky blue and kind, though crows had trodden about them.

"How can your house be round inside?" William asked, in his high, clear voice. She looked about her and then saw his red jersey through the fence and, above it, his bright face with its straight fringe of hair. "How can rooms be round?" he asked. He came up to the broken gate and stood there.

Beyond a row of old elm trees which hid the lodge from the main road, a double-decker bus went by, taking the women from the estate to Market Swanford for their afternoon's shopping. When it had gone, William turned back to the old lady and said: "Or are they like this shape?" He made a wedge with his hands.

"You had better come and see," she said. He opened the gate at once and went in. "She might pop me into the oven," he thought.

One room was half a circle, the other two were quarters. All three were dark and crammed with furniture. A mouse streaked across the kitchen floor. The sink was stacked with dirty china, the table littered with odds and ends of food in torn paper wrappings.

"Do you live here alone?" he asked.

"Except for the mice; but I should prefer to be alone."

"You are more like a hermit than a witch."

"And would rather be," she said.

He examined a dish of stewed fruit which had a greenish-grey mantling of mold.

"Pooh! It smells like beer," he said.

"I meant to throw it away, but it seemed such a criminal waste when the natives are starving everywhere."

In the sitting-room, with frail and shaking hands, she offered him a chocolate box; there was one chocolate left in it. It was stale and had a bloom on it, and might be poisoned, he thought; but he took it politely and turned it about in his mouth. It was very hard and tasted musty. "Curiosity killed the cat," his mother would say, when his body was discovered.

Mrs. May began then to tell him about the fields and park and her pony. He felt drowsy and wondered if the poison were taking effect. She had such a beautiful voice—wavering, floating—that he could not believe in his heart that she would do him any harm. The room was airless and he sat in a little spoon-shaped velvet chair and stared up at her, listening to a little of her story, here and there. Living alone, except for the mice, she had no one to blame her when she spilt egg and tea down her front, he supposed; and she had taken full advantage of her freedom. She was really very dirty, he decided dispassionately. But smelt nice. She had the cosy smell that he liked so much about his guinea-pigs—a warm, stuffy, old smell.

"I'd better go," he said suddenly. "I might come back again tomorrow."

She seemed to understand at once, but like all grown-up people was compelled to prolong the leave-taking a little. He answered her questions briefly, anxious to be off once he had made up his mind to go.

"There," he said, pointing up the hill. "My house is there." The gilt weather-vane, veering round, glittered in the sun above the slate roofs.

"Our old stables," Mrs. May said quite excitedly. "Oh, the memories."

He shut the gate and sauntered off, between piles of bricks and tiles on the site where more houses were being built. Trees had been left standing here and there, looking strange upon the scarred, untidy landscape. William walked round the foundations of a little house, stood in the middle of a rectangle and tried to imagine a family sitting at a table in the middle of it, but it seemed far too small. The walls were only three bricks high. He walked round them, one foot before the other, his arms lifted to keep his balance. Some workmen shouted at him. They were tiling the roof of a nearby house. He took no notice, made a completed round of the walls and then walked off across the rough grass, where Mrs. May had ridden her pony when she was a little girl.

"Do you *hear* me?" his mother said again, her voice shrill, with anxiety and vexation. She even took William's shoulder and shook him. "You are *not* to talk to strangers."

His sister, Jennifer, who was ballet-mad, practised an arabesque, and watched the scene without interest, her mind on her own schemes.

William looked gravely at his mother, rubbing his shoulder.

"Do you understand?"

He nodded.

"That's right, remember what your mother told you," his father said, for the sake of peace.

The next morning, William took a piece of cheese from the larder and a pen-knife and went to the building-site. His mother was having an Italian lesson. Some of the workmen were sitting against a wall in the sun, drinking tea and eating bread and cheese, and William sat down amongst them, settling himself comfortably with his back against the wall. He cut pieces of cheese against his thumb as the others did and popped them neatly into his mouth. They drew him into solemn conversation, winking at one another above his head. He answered them politely, but knew that they were making fun of him. One wag, going too far, grimacing too obviously, asked: "And what is your considered opinion of the present emergency?"

"I don't know," William replied, and he got up and walked away—more in sorrow than in anger, he tried to convey.

He lingered for a while, watching a bulldozer going over the uneven ground, opening wounds in the fields where Mrs. May had ridden her pony; then he wandered on towards the main road. Mrs. May came out to her front doorstep and dropped an apronful of crumbs on to the path. Thrushes and starlings descended about her.

"So you're back again," she called. "I am shortly off to the shops. It will be nice to have a boy go with me." She went inside, untying her apron.

He tried to swing on the gate, but it was lopsided. When she came out after a long time, she was wearing a torn raincoat, although it was quite hot already. It had no buttons and hung open. Her dirty jersey was held to her flat chest with rows of jet beads.

William noted that they were much stared at as they passed the bus queue and, in the butcher's shop, Mrs. May was the subject of the same knowing looks and gravely-kept straight faces that he himself had suffered from the builders. He felt, uncomfortably, that this behavior was something that children came to expect, but that an older person should neither expect nor tolerate. He could not find words to explain his keen uneasiness on Mrs. May's account.

He watched the butcher unhook a drab piece of liver, slap it on the counter and cut off a slice.

"When I think of the saddles of mutton, the sucking pigs . . ." said Mrs. May vaguely, counting out coppers.

"Yes, I expect so," said the butcher's wife, with a straight face turned towards her husband.

Outside the shop, Mrs. May continued the list. "And ribs of beef, green goose at Michaelmas," she chattered on to herself, going past the dairy, the grocer's, the draper's, with quick, herringbone steps. William caught glimpses of themselves reflected in the shop windows, against a pyramid of syrup tins, then a bolt of sprigged cotton.

"And what are *you* going to tell *me*?" Mrs. May suddenly asked. "I can't do all the entertaining, you know. Are you quite warm up there in the stables? Have you beds and chairs and all you need?"

"We have even more beds than we need."

"Well, don't ask me to imagine it, because I can't. Shall we turn back? I'll buy an egg at the dairy and I might get some stale bread for the birds. 'My only friends,' I say to them, as they come to greet me."

"You have the mice as well."

"I can't make friends with mice. The mice get on my nerves, as a matter of fact."

"You could get a cat," he suggested.

"And seem more like a witch than ever?"

There appeared to be no stale bread at the baker's. At sight of Mrs. May, the woman behind the counter seemed to shutter her face; stood waiting with lowered eyes for them to go.

When they reached Mrs. May's broken gate—with only the slice of meat and the egg—William would not go in. He ran home as fast as he could over the uneven ground, his heart banging, his throat aching.

When he reached it, the house was quiet and a strange, spicy smell he could not identify came from the kitchen. His mother, as well as her Italian lessons, had taken up Japanese cooking. His sister, returning from ballet class, with her shoes hanging from her neck by their ribbons, found him lying on the floor pushing a toy car back and forth. Her suspicions were roused; for he was pretending to be playing, she was convinced, with an almost cross-eyed effort at concentration. He began to hum unconcernedly. Jennifer's nose wrinkled. "It smells as if we're going to have that horrid soup with stalks in it."

"I like it," he murmured.

"You would. What have you been doing, anyway?"

Still wearing her coat, she practised a few pliés.

Never waste a moment, he thought.

"Nothing."

But she was not interested in him; had been once—long ago, it seemed to her, when his birth she hoped would brighten up the house. The novelty of him had soon worn off.

"The death duties," Mrs. May explained. Because of them, she could not light a fire until the really chilly days and sometimes had only an egg to eat all day. These death duties William thought of as moral obligations upon which both her father and husband had insisted on discharging while dying—some charitable undertakings, plainly not approved of by Mrs. May. He was only puzzled by the varying effect of this upon her day-to-day life; sometimes she was miserably conscious of her poverty, but at other times she bought peppermint creams for herself and William and digestive biscuits for the birds.

Every time she opened or shut the garden gate, she explained how she would have had it mended if it were not for the death duties. *The* death duties made them sound a normal sort of procedure, a fairly usual change of heart brought about perhaps by the approach of death and clearly happening not only in Mrs. May's family.

The days were beginning to grow chilly, too chilly to be without a fire. The leaves on the great chestnut trees about the building site turned yellow and fell. William went back to school and called on

Mrs. May only on Saturday mornings. He did not miss her. His life was suddenly very full and some weeks he did not go at all and she fretted for him, watching from a window like a love-sick girl, postponing her visit to the shops. She missed not only him, but her glimpses—from his conversation—of the strange life going on up in the old stables. His descriptions—in answer to her questions—and what she read into them formed a bewildering picture. She imagined the family sitting round the bench in the old harness room, drinking a thin soup with blades of grass in it—the brisk mother, the gentle, dreamy father and an objectionable little girl who kept getting down from the frugal meal to practise pas-de-chats across the old, broken brick floor. She had built the scene from his phrases—"My mother will be cross if I'm late" (more polite, he thought, than, "My mother will be cross if she knows I came to see you"), and "My father wouldn't mind." His sister, it seemed, complained about the soup; apart from this, she only talked of Margot Fonteyn. But confusions came into it—in William's helping to clean silver for a dinner-party and having been sent to bed early for spilling ink on a carpet. Silver and carpets were hard to imagine as part of the old stables.

She had forgotten what a family was like, and had never had much chance of learning—only child and childless wife. William was too young to be a satisfactory informant. He was haphazardly selective, interested too much in his own separate affairs, unobservant and forgetful of the adult world; yet she managed to piece something together and it had slowly grown—a continuous story, without direction or catharsis—but could no longer grow if he were not to visit her.

Holding the curtains, her frail hands shook. When he did come, he was enticed to return. On those mornings now, there were always sweets. But her questions tired him, as they tire and antagonize all children, who begin to feel uneasily in the wrong role. He had by now satisfied his curiosity about her and was content to let what he did not understand—the death duties, for instance—lie at peace.

"You shall have this when I'm gone," she began to say, closing the lid of the sandalwood box in which she kept the old photographs. Also promised was her father's sword and scabbard, in which William was more interested, and a stuffed parrot called Bertha—once a childhood pet and still talked to as if no change had taken place.

One morning, she saw him playing on the building-site and went out to the gate and called to him, lured him into the garden and then the house with witch-like tactics, sat him down on the spoon-shaped chair and gave him a bag of sweets.

"And how is your mother?" she enquired. She had a feeling that she detested the woman. William nodded absentmindedly, poking about in the sweet bag. His hair was like gold silk, she thought.

"People have always lost patience with me," she said, feeling his attention wandering from her. "I only had my beauty."

She was going on to describe how her husband's attention had also wandered, then thought it perhaps an unsuitable subject to discuss with a child. She had never discussed it with anyone else. Such a vague marriage, and her memories of it were vague, too—seemed farther away than her childhood.

A mouse gnawed with a delicate sound in the wainscot and William turned his gaze towards it, waiting for the minutes to pass until the time when he could rise politely from the dusty chair and say good-bye.

If only he would tell me! Mrs. May thought in despair. Tell me what there was for breakfast, for instance, and who said what and who went where, so that I could have something to think about in the evening.

"Oh, well, the winter will come if it means to," she said aloud. Rain had swept in a gust upon the window, as if cast upon the little panes in spite. "Nothing we can do can stop it. Only dig in and make ourselves comfortable—roast chestnuts on my little coal shovel." William glanced from the wainscot to the empty grate, but Mrs. May seemed not to see its emptiness. "Once, when I had a *nice* governess, we roasted some over the school-room fire. But the next governess would never let me do anything that pleased me. Want must be your master," she said. She had many low phrases of that kind. "Yes, want must be your master," she said again, and sighed.

The visit was running down and her visitor simply sitting there until he could go. Courageously, when he had refused another peppermint cream and showed that he did not want to see again the photograph of her home, she released him, she even urged him to go, speeding him on his way, and watched him from the open door, her hands clasped close to her flat chest. He was like a most beloved caged bird that she had set at liberty. She felt regret and yet a sense of triumph, seeing him go.

She returned to the room and looked dully at the stuffed parrot, feeling a little like crying, but she had been brought up not to do so. "Yes, want must be your master, Bertha," she said, in a soft but serene voice.

"I can't see harm in it," William's father told his wife. Jennifer had seen William leaving Mrs. May's and hurried to tell her mother, who began complaining the moment her husband returned for lunch.

"She's stark, staring mad and the place is filthy, everybody says so."

"Children sometimes see what we can't."

"I don't know what you mean by that. I forbade him to go there and he repeatedly disobeyed me. You should speak to him."

So his father spoke to William—rather off-handedly, over his shoulder, while hanging his coat up in the hall, as William passed through.

To be reprimanded for what he had not wanted to do, for what he looked on as a duty, did not vex William. It was the kind of thing that happened to him a great deal and he let it go, rather than tie himself up in explanations.

"You did hear what I said?" his father asked.

"Yes, I heard."

"Your mother has her reasons. You can leave it at that."

It happened that he obeyed his parents. His father one day passing Mrs. May's garden came on her feeding her birds there. He raised his hat and saw, as she glanced up, her ruined face, bewildered eyes, and was stirred by pity as he walked on.

As the nights grew colder, Mrs. May was forced to light a fire and she wandered about the building site collecting sawn off pieces of batten and wood-shavings. She met William there once, playing with another boy. He returned her greeting, answered her questions unwillingly, knowing that his companion had ducked his head, trying to hide a smile. When she had wandered on at last, there were more questions from his friend. "Oh, she's only an old witch I know," he replied.

The truth was that he could hardly remember how once he had liked to go to see her. Then he had tired of her stories about her childhood, grew bored with her photographs, became embarrassed by her and realized, in an adult way, that the little house was filthy. One afternoon, on his way home from school, he had seen her coming out of the butcher's shop ahead of him and had slackened his pace, almost walked backwards not to overtake her.

She was alone again, except for the birds in the daytime, the mice at night. The deep winter came and the birds grew fewer and the mice increased. The cold weather birds, double their summer size, hopped dottily about the crisp, rimed grass, jabbing their beaks into frozen puddles, bewildered as refugees. Out she hurried, first thing in the mornings, to break the ice and scatter crumbs. She found a dead thrush and grieved over it. "Oh, Bertha, one of ours," she mourned.

Deep snow came and she was quite cut off—the garden was full of strange shapes, as if heaped with pillows and bolsters, and the birds made their dagger tracks across the drifts. She could not open her door.

Seeing the untrodden path, William's father, passing by, went to borrow a spade from the nearest house and cleared the snow from the gateway to the door. He saw her watching from a window and, when at last she could, she opened the door to thank him.

"I'm afraid I don't know who you are," she began.

"I live in the old stables up on the hill."

"Then I know your little boy. He used to visit me. It was very kind of you to come to my rescue."

William's father returned the spade and then walked home, feeling sad and ashamed. "Oh, dear, that house," he said to his wife. "It is quite filthy—what I glimpsed of it. You were perfectly right. Someone ought to do something to help her."

"She should help herself. She must have plenty of money—All this building land."

"I think she misses William."

"It was just a passing thing," said his wife, who was a great one herself for passing things. "He simply lost interest."

"Lost innocence, perhaps. The truth is, I suppose, that children grow up and begin to lose their simple vision."

"The truth is," she said tartly, "that if people don't wash themselves they go unloved." Her voice was cold and disdainful. She had summed up many other lives than Mrs. May's and knew the tone to use.

The thaw began, then froze in buds upon the red twigs of the dog-wood in Mrs. May's untidy hedge. The hardening snow was pitted with drips from the branches.

Mrs. May was afraid to venture on her frozen path beyond her doorway, and threw her remaining bits of bread from there. There was no one to run an errand for her. The cold drove her inside, but she kept going to the window to see if the ice were melting. Instead, the sky darkened. Both sky and earth were iron.

''It's my old bones,'' she said to Bertha. ''I'm afraid for my old bones.''

Then she saw William running and sliding on the ice, his red scarf flying, his cheeks bright. He fell, and scrambled up, laughing.

''It's falling I'm afraid of,'' Mrs. May whispered to the window pane. ''My old bones are too brittle.''

She went to the front door and opened it. Standing shivering on the step, she called to William. He seemed not to hear and she tried to raise her voice. He took a run and, with his arms flung up above his head, slithered across a patch of ice. He shouted to someone out of sight and dashed forward.

Mrs. May shut the door again. ''Someone will come,'' she told Bertha briskly. She straightened her father's sword suspended above the fireplace and bustled about, trying to tidy the room ready for an unknown visitor. ''There's no knowing what might happen. Anyone might call,'' she murmured.

GUY VANDERHAEGHE

Dancing Bear

The old man lay sleeping on the taut red rubber sheet as if he were some specimen mounted and pinned there to dry. His housekeeper, the widowed Mrs. Hax, paused in the doorway and then walked heavily to the bedside window, where she abruptly freed the blind and sent it up, whirring and clattering.

She studied the sky. Far away, to the east, and high above the bursting green of the elms that lined the street, greasy black clouds rolled languidly, their swollen underbellies lit by the occasional shudder of lightning that popped in the distance. After each flash she counted aloud to herself until she heard the faint, muttering accompaniment of thunder. Finally satisfied, she turned away from the window to find Dieter Bethge awake and watching her cautiously from his bed.

"It's going to rain," she said, moving about the room and grunting softly as she stooped to gather up his clothes and pile them on a chair.

"Oh?" he answered, feigning some kind of interest. He picked a flake of dried skin from his leg and lifted it tenderly to the light like a jeweller, intently examining its whorled grain and yellow translucence.

Sighing, Mrs. Hax smoothed the creases of his carelessly discarded trousers with a soft, fat palm and draped them over the back of a chair. The old bugger made more work than a whole tribe of kids.

She glanced over her shoulder and saw him fingering the bit of skin between thumb and forefinger. "Leave that be," she said curtly. "It's time we were up. Quit dawdling."

He looked up, his pale blue eyes surprised. "What?"

"Time to get up."

"No," he said. "Not yet."

"It's reveille. No malingering. Won't have it," she said, fixing an unconvincing smile on her broad face. "Come on now, up and at 'em. We've slept long enough."

"That rubber thing kept me awake last night," he said plaintively. "Every time I move it squeaks and pulls at my skin. There's no give to it."

"Complainers' noses fall off," Mrs. Hax said absent-mindedly as she held a shirt up to her own wrinkled nose. She sniffed. It wasn't exactly fresh but she decided it would do, and tossed it back on the chair.

The old man felt his face burn with humiliation, as it did whenever he was thwarted or ignored. "I want that damn thing off my bed!" he yelled. "This is my bed! This is my house! Get it off!"

Mrs. Hax truculently folded her arms across her large, loose breasts and stared down at him. For a moment he met her gaze defiantly, but then he averted his eyes and his trembling jaw confirmed his confusion.

"I am not moved by childish tempers," she announced. "You haven't learned that yet?" Mrs. Hax paused. "It's about time you did. One thing about Mrs. Hax," she declared in a piping falsetto that betrayed her anger, "is that when someone pushes her, she pushes back twice as hard. I am ruthless." She assumed a stance that she imagined to be an illustration of ruthlessness, her flaccid arms akimbo. A burlesque of violence. "So let me make this perfectly, crystal clear. That rubber sheet is staying on that bed until you forget your lazy, dirty habits and stop them accidents. A grown man," she said disparagingly, shaking her head. "I just got sick and tired of hauling one mattress off the bed to dry and hauling another one on. Just remember I'm not getting any younger either. I'm not up to heavy work like that. So if you want that rubber thing off, you try and remember not to pee the bed."

The old man turned on his side and hid his face.

"No sulking allowed," she said sternly. "Breakfast is ready and I have plenty to do today. I can't keep it waiting forever."

Dieter turned on to his back and fixed his eyes on the ceiling. Mrs. Hax shook her head in exasperation. It was going to be one of those days. What went on in the old bastard's head, if anything? What made him so peculiar, so difficult at times like these?

She walked over to the bed and took him firmly by the wrist. "Upsy-daisy!" she cried brightly, planting her feet solidly apart and jerking him upright. She skidded him to the edge of the bed, the rubber sheet whining a muffled complaint, and his hands, in startled protest and ineffectual rebellion, pawing at the front of her dress. Mrs. Hax propped him upright while his head wobbled feebly from side to side and his tongue flickered angrily, darting and questing like a snake's.

"There," she said, patting his hand, "that's better. Now let's let bygones be bygones. A fresh start. I'll say, 'Good morning, Mr. Bethge!' and you answer. 'Good morning, Mrs. Hax!' "

He gave no sign of agreement. Mrs. Hax hopefully cocked her head to one side and, like some huge, querulous bird, chirped, "Good morning, Mr. Bethge!" The old man stubbornly disregarded her, smiling sweetly and vacantly into space.

"Well," she said, patting her dress down around her wide hips and heavy haunches, "it's no skin off my teeth, mister."

She stumped to the door, stopped, and looked back. The old man sat perched precariously on the edge of the bed, his white hair ruffled, tufted and crested like some angry heron. A pale shadow fell across the lower half of his face and threw his eyes into relief, so that they shone with the dull, glazed intensity of the most devout of worshippers.

Mrs. Hax often saw him like this, mute and still, lost in reverie; and she liked to suppose that, somehow, he was moved by a dim apprehension of mortality and loss. Perhaps he was even overcome with memories of his wife, and felt the same vast yearning she felt for her own dead Albert.

She mustered a smile and offered it. "Five minutes, dear," she said, and then closed the door softly behind her.

Bethge made no response. He was thinking—trying to pry those memories out of the soft beds into which they had so comfortably settled, sinking deeper and deeper under the weight of all the years, growing more somnolent and lazy, less easily stirred from sleep. He could no longer make his head crackle with the sudden, decisive leap of quick thought hurtling from synapse to synapse. Instead, memories had now to be pricked and prodded, and sometimes, if he was lucky, they came in revelatory flashes. Yet it was only old, old thoughts and things that came to him. Only they had any real clarity—and the sharpness to wound.

And now it was something about a bear. What?

Bethge, with a jerky, tremulous movement, swiped at the spittle on his chin with the back of his hand. In his agitation he crossed and recrossed his thin legs, the marbly, polished legs of a very old man.

Bear? He rubbed the bridge of his nose; somehow, it was important. He began to rock himself gently, his long, curving nose slicing like a scythe, back and forth, reaping the dim air of his stale little room. And as he swayed, it all began to come to him, and he began to run, swiftly, surely, silently back into time.

In the dark barn that smells of brittle straw, and sharply of horse dung, the knife is making little greedy, tearing noises. It is not sharp enough. Then he hears the hoarse, dragging whisper of steel on whetstone. Although he is afraid that the bear his father is skinning may suddenly rear to life, he climbs over the wall of the box stall and steps into the manger and crouches down. He is only five, so the manger is a nice, tight, comforting fit.

What a bear! A killer, a marauder who had left two sows tangled in their guts with single blows from his needle-sharp claws.

The smell of the bear makes him think of gun metal—oily, smoky. Each hair bristles like polished black wire, and when the sun catches the pelt it shines vividly, electrically blue.

The curved blade of the knife, now sharpened, slices through the bear's fat like butter, relentlessly peeling back the coat and exposing long, flat, pink muscles. As his father's busy, bloody hands work, Dieter feels a growing uneasiness. The strong hands tug and tear, wrestling with the heavy, inert body as if they are frantically searching for something. Like clay under a sculptor's hand, the bear begins to change. Each stroke of the knife renders him less bear-like and more like something else. Dieter senses this and crouches lower in the manger in anticipation.

His father begins to raise the skin off the back, his forearms hidden as the knife moles upward toward the neck. At last he grunts and stands. Reaches for the axe. In two sharp, snapping blows the head is severed from the trunk and the grinning mask flung into a corner. He gathers up the skin and carries it out to salt it and peg it down in the yard. Dieter hears the chickens clamouring to pick it clean.

He stares down into the pit of the shadowy stall. This is no bear. Stripped of its rich, glossy fur, naked, it is no bear. Two arms, two legs, a raw pink skin. A man. Under all that lank, black hair a man was hiding, lurking in disguise.

He feels the spiralling terror of an unwilling accomplice to murder. He begins to cry and call for his father, who suddenly appears in the doorway covered in grease and blood, a murderer.

From far away, he heard someone call him. "Mr. Bethge! Mr. Bethge!" The last syllable of his name was drawn out and held like a note, so that it quivered in the air and urged him on with its stridency.

He realized he had been crying, that his eyes were filled with those unexpected tears that came so suddenly they constantly surprised and embarrassed him.

For a bear? But this wasn't all of it. There had been another bear; he was sure of it. A bear who had lived in shame and impotence.

He edged himself off the bed and painfully on to his knobbed, arthritic feet. Breakfast.

At breakfast they quarrel in the dreary, passionless manner of master and charge. He wants what she has, bacon and eggs. He tells her he hates porridge.

"Look," Mrs. Hax said, "I can't give you bacon and eggs. Doctor's orders."

"What doctor?"

"The doctor we saw last month. You remember."

"No." It was true. He couldn't remember any doctor.

"Yes you do. Come on now. We took a ride downtown in a cab. Remember now?"

"No."

"And we stopped by Woolworth's and bought a big bag of that sticky candy you like so much. Remember?"

"No."

"That's fine," she said irritably. "You don't want to remember, there's nothing I can do. It doesn't matter, because you're not getting bacon and eggs."

"I don't want porridge," he said tiredly.

"Eat it."

"Give me some corn flakes."

"Look at my plate," she said, pointing with her knife. "I'm getting cold grease scum all over everything. Fight, fight. When do I get a moment's peace to eat?"

"I want corn flakes," he said with a little self-satisfied tuck to the corners of his mouth.

"You can't have corn flakes," she said. "Corn flakes bung you up. That's why you eat hot cereal—to keep you regular. Just like stewed prunes. Now, which you want,'' she asked slyly, ''Sunny Boy or stewed prunes?''

''I want corn flakes.'' He smiled up happily at the ceiling.

''Like a stuck record.'' She folded her hands on the table and leaned conspiratorially toward him. ''You don't even care if you eat or not, do you? You're just trying to get under my skin, aren't you?''

''I want corn flakes,'' he said definitely and happily.

''I could kill that man,'' she told her plate. ''Just kill him.'' Then, abruptly, she asked. ''Where's your glasses? No, not there, in the other pocket. Okay, put them on. Now take a good long look at that porridge.''

The old man peered down intently into his bowl.

''That's fine. Take it easy. It's not a goddamn wishing-well. You see them little brown specks?''

He nodded.

''That's what this whole fight's about? Something as tiny as that? You know what this is. It's flax. And flax keeps you regular. So eat it.''

''I'm not eating it. What do I want with flax?'' he asked quizzically.

''Sure you're crazy,'' she said. ''Crazy like a fox.''

''I want some coffee.''

Mrs. Hax slammed down her fork and knife, snatched up his cup, and marched to the kitchen counter. While she poured the coffee, Bethge's hand crept across the table and stole several strips of bacon from her plate. He crammed these clumsily into his mouth, leaving a grease shine on his chin.

Mrs. Hax set his cup down in front of him. ''Be careful,'' she said. ''Don't spill.''

Bethge giggled. In a glance, Mrs. Hax took in his grease-daubed chin and her plate. ''Well, well, look at the cat who swallowed the canary. Grinning from ear-lobe to ear-lobe with a pound of feathers bristling from his trap.''

''So?'' he said defiantly.

''You think I enjoy the idea of you pawing through my food?'' Mrs. Hax carried her plate to the garbage and scraped it with a flourish. ''Given all your dirty little habits, who's to know where your hands have been?'' she asked, smiling wickedly. ''But go ahead and laugh. Because he who laughs last, laughs best. Chew this around for a bit and see how she tastes. You're not getting one single, solitary cigarette today, my friend."

Startled, he demanded his cigarettes.

"We're singing a different tune now, aren't we?" She paused, "N-O spells no. Put that in your pipe and smoke it."

"You give them. They're mine."

"Not since you set the chesterfield on fire. Not since then. Your son told me I was to give them out one at a time so's I could watch you and avoid 'regrettable accidents'. Thank God, there's some sense in the family. How he came by it I'm sure I don't know."

The old man hoisted himself out of his chair. "Don't you dare talk to me like that. I want my cigarettes—and I want them now."

Mrs. Hax crossed her arms and set her jaw. "No."

"You're fired!" he shouted. "Get out!" He flapped his arms awkwardly in an attempt to startle her into motion.

"Oho!" she said, rubbing her large red hands together in delight, "fired am I? On whose say-so? Them that hires is them that fires. He who pays the piper calls the tune. And you don't do neither. Not a bit. Your son hired me, and your son pays me. I don't budge a step unless I get the word straight from the horse's mouth."

"Get out!"

"Save your breath."

He is beaten and he knows it. This large, stubborn woman cannot, will not, be moved.

"I want to talk to my son."

"If you got information you feel your son should have, write him a letter."

He knows this would never do. He would forget, she would steal the letter, conveniently forget to mail it. Justice demands immediate action. The iron is hot and fit for striking. He feels the ground beneath his feet is treacherous; he cannot become confused, or be led astray. One thing at a time. He must talk to his son.

"Get him on the telephone."

"Your son, if you remember," Mrs. Hax said, "got a little upset about all those long-distance phone calls—collect. And his words to me were, 'Mrs. Hax, I think it best if my father phone only on important matters, at your discretion.' At my discretion, mind you. And my discretion informs me that this isn't one of those times. I've got a responsibility to my employer."

"I'll phone him myself."

"That I've got to see."

"I will."

"Yes, like the last time. Half the time you can't remember the city John lives in, let alone his street. The last time you tried to phone him you got the operator so balled up you would have been talking to a Chinaman in Shanghai if I hadn't stepped in and saved your bacon."

"I'll phone. I can do it."

"Sure you will. Where does John live?"

"I know."

"Uh-huh, then tell me. Where does he live?"

"I know."

"Jesus, he could be living in the basement and you wouldn't realize it."

This makes him cry. He realizes she is right. But minutes ago he had known where his son lived. How could he have forgotten? In the sudden twistings and turnings of the conversation he has lost his way, and now he hears himself making a wretched, disgusting noise; but he cannot stop.

Mrs. Hax feels she has gone too far. She goes over to him and puts an arm around his shoulders. "Now see what's happened. You went and got yourself all upset over a silly old bowl of porridge. Doctor says you have to watch that with your blood pressure. It's no laughing matter." She boosts him out of his chair. "I think you better lie down on the chesterfield for a bit."

Mrs. Hax led him into the living-room and made him comfortable on the chesterfield. She wondered how an old bugger like him could make so much water: if he wasn't peeing, he was crying.

"You want a Kleenex?" she asked.

He shook his head and, ashamed, covered his face with his forearm.

"No harm in crying," she said bleakly. "We all do some time."

"Leave me be."

"I suppose it's best," she sighed. "I'll be in the kitchen clearing up if you need me."

Dieter lay on the chesterfield trying to stifle his tears. It was not an easy job because even the sound of Mrs. Hax unconcernedly clacking the breakfast dishes reminded him of her monstrous carelessness with everything. His plates, his feelings. He filled with anger at the notion that he would never be nimble enough to evade her commands, or even her wishes. That he cannot outwit her or even flee her.

The living-room gradually darkens as the low, scudding rain clouds blot out the sun. He wishes it were a fine sunny day. The kind of day which tricks you into believing you are young and carefree as you once were. Like in Rumania before his family emigrated. Market days almost always felt that way. People bathed in sun and noise, their wits honed to a fine edge for trading and bartering. Every kind of people. The Jews with their curling sidelocks, the timid Italian tenant farmers, the Rumanians, and people like himself, German colonists. Even a gypsy or two. Then you had a sense of life, of living. Every good thing the earth offers or man's hand fashions could be found there. Gaily painted wagons, piles of potatoes with the wet clay still clinging to them; chickens, ducks and geese; tethered pigs tugging their back legs and squealing; horses with hooves as black and shining as basalt, and eyes as large and liquid-purple as plums.

Nothing but a sheet of sky above and good smells below: pickled herring and leather, paprika and the faint scent of little, hard, sweet apples.

Innocence. Innocence. But then again, on the other hand—yes, well, sometimes cruelty too. Right in the market.

A stranger arrived with a dancing bear once. Yes, the other bear, the one he had forgotten. He led him by a ring through the nose. When a crowd gathered, the man unsnapped the chain from the bear's nose and began to play a violin. It was a sad, languorous tune. For a moment, the bear tossed his head from side to side and snuffled in the dirt. This, for him, was a kind of freedom.

But the man spoke to him sharply. The bear lifted his head and then mournfully raised himself up on to his hind legs. His arms opened in a wide, charitable manner, as if he were offering an embrace. His mouth grinned, exposing black-speckled gums and sharp teeth. He danced, slowly, ponderously, tiredly.

The music changed tempo. It became gay and lively. The bear began to prance unsteadily; the hot sun beat down on him. A long, glittering thread of saliva fell from his panting mouth on to the cinnamon-colored fur of his chest.

Dieter, fascinated, tugged and pushed himself through the crowd. The bear hopped heavily from leg to leg. It was pathetic and comic. The pink tip of his penis jiggled up and down in the long hair of his loins. There was a wave of confused sniggering.

The trainer played faster and faster. The bear pirouetted wildly.

He whirled and whirled, raising a small cloud of dust. The crowd began to clap. The bear spun and spun, his head lolling from side to side, his body tense with the effort of maintaining his human posture. And then he lost his balance and fell, blindly, with a bone-wrenching thump, onto his back.

The scraping of the violin bow stopped. The bear turned lazily on to his feet and bit savagely at his fleas.

"Up, Bruno!"

The bear whined and sat down. People began to laugh; some hooted and insulted the bear's master. He flourished the bear's nose lead and shouted, but the bear refused to budge. In the end, however, he could do nothing except attempt to save face; he bowed deeply, signifying an end to the performance. A few coins, a very few, bounced and bounded at his feet. He scooped them up quickly, as if he were afraid they might be reclaimed.

The audience began to disperse. Some hurried away to protect their wares. But Dieter had nothing to protect and nowhere to go, and so he stayed.

The sight of so many fleeing backs seemed to pique the bear. He got to his feet and began, once again, to dance. He mocked them. Or so it seemed. Of course, there was no music, but the bear danced much more daintily and elegantly than before, to a tune only he could perceive. And he grinned hugely, sardonically.

But the trainer reached up, caught his nose ring and yanked him down on all fours. He swore and cursed, and the bear breathed high, squeaking protests, feigning innocence.

This was unacceptable. This was rebellion. This was treason to the man who fed him, cared for him, taught him.

"Hairy bastard. Play the fool, will you," the stranger muttered, wrenching and twisting the nose ring while the bear squealed with pain. The man punched his head, kicked him in the belly, shook him by the ears. "Traitor. Ingrate."

Dieter held his breath. His mind's eye had seen the bear suddenly strike, revenge himself. Yet nothing happened. Nothing; except the bear was beaten and battered, humiliated, even spat upon.

What shame he felt witnessing such an indignity, such complete indifference to the rightful pride of the bear. Such flaunting of the respect owed him for his size and his power. Couldn't the man realize what he did? Dieter wanted to shout out the secret. To warn him that appearances deceive. That a bear is a man in masquerade. Perhaps even a judge, but at the very least a brother.

But he couldn't. He ran away instead.

The house is still. He hears her footsteps, knows that she is watching him from the doorway. As always, she is judging him, calculating her words and responses, planning. Her plots deny him even the illusion of freedom. He decides he will not turn to look at her. But perhaps she knows this will be his reaction? Petulant, childish.

"I want to be left in peace." He surprises himself. This giving voice to thought without weighing the consequences is dangerous.

But she doesn't catch it. "What?"

"I don't chew my words twice," he says.

She comes to the side of the chesterfield. "Feeling better now?"

"Yes."

"Truth?"

He nods.

"Now mind, you got to be sure. I'm going down to the store. You need the bathroom?"

"No."

"All right then. I'll just be a few minutes. That's all. You'll be okay?"

He is trying to think. All this talk, these interruptions, annoy him. He burns with impatience. "Fine. That's fine. Good." Suddenly, he feels happy. He can steal a little peace. He'll do it.

"I must be careful," he tells himself aloud. How do these things slip out?

But Mrs. Hax doesn't understand. "With your blood pressure, I should say so."

His luck, his good fortune, make him feel strong and cunning. Following her to the front door, he almost pities this fat woman. He watches her start down the street. It is lined with old and substantial homes, most of them painted modestly white, and their yards flourish tall, rough-barked elms. On this street, Mrs. Hax, in her fluorescent orange rain slicker, appears ridiculous and inappropriate. Like a bird of paradise in an English garden. He waits until he loses sight of her at the first turning of the street.

He hurries to his business. His hands fumble with the chain on the front door; at last it is fastened. His excitement leaves him breathless, but he shuffles to the back door and draws the bolt. Safe. Mrs. Hax is banished, exiled.

At first he thinks the noise is caused by the blood pulsing in his temples. But it fades to an insistent, whispering rush. Dieter goes to the window to look out. The rain is falling in a gleaming, thick curtain that obscures the outlines of the nearest house; striking the roadway, it throws up fine silvery plumes of spray. He decides to wait for Mrs. Hax at the front door. He stands there and smells the coco matting, the dust and rubber boots. Somehow, he has forgotten they smell this way, a scent that can be peculiarly comforting when you are dry and warm, with a cold rain slashing against the windows.

And here is Mrs. Hax trotting stiff-legged up the street with a shredding brown-paper bag huddled to her body. She flees up the walk, past the beaten and dripping caraganas, and around back to the kitchen door. He hears her bumping and rattling it.

Here she comes again, scurrying along, head bent purposefully, rain glancing off her plastic cap. But as she begins to climb the front steps he withdraws and hides himself in the coat closet. Her key rasps in the chamber, the spring lock snaps free. The door opens several inches but then meets the resistance of the chain, and sticks. She grumbles and curses; some fat, disembodied fingers curl through the gap and pluck at the chain. For a moment he is tempted to slam the door shut on those fingers, but he resists the impulse. The fingers are replaced by a slice of face, an eye and a mouth.

''Mr. Bethge! Mr. Bethge! Open up!''

Bethge stumbles out of the closet and lays his face along the door jamb, eye to eye with Mrs. Hax. They stare at each other. At last she breaks the spell.

''Well, open this door,'' she says irritably. ''I feel like a drowned cat.''

''Go away. You're not wanted here.''

''What!''

''Go away.''

Her one eye winks suspiciously. ''You do know who I am? This is Mrs. Hax, your housekeeper. Open up.''

''I know who you are. I don't want any part of you. So go away.''

She shows him the soggy paper bag. ''I brought you a Jersey Milk.''

''Pass it through.''

Her one eye opens wide in blue disbelief. "You open this door."

"No."

"It's the cigarettes, I suppose? All right, I give up. You can have your damn cigarettes."

"Go away."

"I'm losing my patience," she says, lowering her voice; "now open this door, you senile old fart."

"Old fart yourself. Old fat fart."

"You wait until I get in there. There'll be hell to pay."

He realizes his legs are tired from standing. There is a nagging pain in the small of his back. "I've go to go now," he says. "Goodbye," and he closes the door in her face.

He is suddenly very light-headed and tired, but nevertheless exultant. He decides he will have a nap. But the woman has begun to hammer at the door.

"Stop it," he shouts. He makes his way to his bedroom on unsteady legs; in fact, one is trailing and he must support himself by leaning against the wall. What is this?

The bedroom lies in half-light, but he can see the red rubber sheet. It must go. He tugs at it and it resists him like some living thing, like a limpet clinging to a rock. His leg crumples, his mouth falls open in surprise as he falls. He lands loosely like a bundle of sticks, his legs and arms splayed wide, but feels nothing but a prickling sensation in his bladder. No pain, nothing. There are shadows everywhere in the room, they seem to float, and hover, and quiver. He realizes the front of his pants is wet. He tries to get up, but the strength ebbs out of his limbs and is replaced by a sensation of dizzying heaviness. He decides he will rest a minute and then get up.

But he doesn't. He sleeps.

Mrs. Hax waited under the eaves for the rain to abate. It fell for an hour with sodden fury, and then began to slacken into a dispirited drizzle. When it did, she picked her way carefully through the puddles in the garden to where the hoe lay. With it, she broke a basement window and methodically trimmed the glass out of the frame. Then she settled herself onto her haunches and, gasping, wriggled into the opening. She closed her eyes, committed her injuries in advance to Bethge's head, and then let herself drop. She landed on one leg, which buckled, and sent her headlong against the gas furnace, which set every heat vent and duct in the building vibrating with a deep, atonal ringing. Uninjured, she picked herself up from the floor. Her dignity bruised, her authority wounded, she began to edge her way through the basement clutter toward the stairs.

Dieter Bethge woke with a start. Some noise had broken into his dream. It had been a good and happy dream. The dancing bear had been performing for him under no compulsion, a gift freely given. It had been a perfect, graceful dance, performed without a hint of the foppishness or studied concentration that mars the dance of humans. As the bear had danced he had seemed to grow, as if fed by the pure, clear notes of the music. He had grown larger and larger, but Dieter had watched this with a feeling of great peace rather than alarm.

The sun glinted on his cinnamon fur and burnished his coat with red, winking light. And when the music stopped, the bear had opened his arms very wide in a gesture of friendship and welcome. His mouth had opened as if he were about to speak. And that was exactly what Dieter had expected all along. That the bear would confide in him the truth, and prove that under the shagginess that belied it, there was something that only Dieter had recognized.

But then something had broken the spell of the dream.

He was confused. Where was he? His hand reached out and touched something smooth and hard and resisting. He gave a startled grunt. This was wrong. His mind slipped backward and forward, easily and smoothly, from dream to the sharp, troubling present.

He tried to get up. He rose, trembling, swayed, felt the floor shift, and fell, striking his head on a chest of drawers. His mouth filled with something warm and salty. He could hear something moving in the house, and then the sound was lost in the tumult of the blood singing in his veins. His pulse beat dimly in his eyelids, his ears, his neck and fingertips.

He managed to struggle to his feet and beat his way into the roar of the shadows which slipped by like surf, and out into the hallway.

And then he saw a form in the muted light, patiently waiting. It was the bear.

"Bear?" he asked, shuffling forward, trailing his leg.

The bear said something he did not understand. He was waiting.

Dieter lifted his arms for the expected embrace, the embrace that would fold him into the fragrant, brilliant fur; but, curiously, one arm would not rise. It dangled limply like a rag. Dieter felt something strike the side of his face—a numbing blow. His left eyelid fell like a shutter. He tried to speak but his tongue felt swollen and could only batter noiselessly against his teeth. He felt himself fall but the bear reached out and caught him in the warm embrace he desired above all.

And so, Dieter Bethge, dead of a stroke, fell gently, gently, like a leaf, into the waiting arms of Mrs. Hax.

EUDORA WELTY

A Worn Path

It was December—a bright frozen day in the early morning. Far out in the country there was an old Negro woman with her head tied in a red rag, coming along a path through the pinewoods. Her name was Phoenix Jackson. She was very old and small and she walked slowly in the dark pine shadows, moving a little from side to side in her steps, with the balanced heaviness and lightness of a pendulum in a grandfather clock. She carried a thin, small cane made from an umbrella, and with this she kept tapping the frozen earth in front of her. This made a grave and persistent noise in the still air, that seemed meditative like the chirping of a solitary little bird.

She wore a dark striped dress reaching down to her shoe tops, and an equally long apron of bleached sugar sacks, with a full pocket: all neat and tidy, but every time she took a step she might have fallen over her shoelaces, which dragged from her unlaced shoes. She looked straight ahead. Her eyes were blue with age. Her skin had a pattern all its own of numberless branching wrinkles and as though a whole little tree stood in the middle of her forehead, but a golden color ran underneath, and the two knobs of her cheeks were illumined by a yellow burning under the dark. Under the red rag her hair came down on her neck in the frailest of ringlets, still black, and with an odor like copper.

Now and then there was a quivering in the thicket. Old Phoenix said, "Out of my way, all you foxes, owls, beetles, jack rabbits, coons and wild animals! . . . Keep out from under these feet, little bob-whites. . . . Keep the big wild hogs out of my path. Don't let none of those come running my direction. I got a long way." Under her small black-freckled hand her cane, limber as a buggy whip, would switch at the brush as if to rouse up any hiding things.

On she went. The woods were deep and still. The sun made

the pine needles almost too bright to look at, up where the wind rocked. The cones dropped as light as feathers. Down in the hollow was the mourning dove—it was not too late for him.

The path ran up a hill. "Seem like there is chains about my feet, time I get this far," she said, in the voice of argument old people keep to use with themselves. "Something always take a hold of me on this hill—pleads I should stay."

After she got to the top she turned and gave a full, severe look behind her where she had come. "Up through pines," she said at length. "Now down through oaks."

Her eyes opened their widest, and she started down gently. But before she got to the bottom of the hill a bush caught her dress.

Her fingers were busy and intent, but her skirts were full and long, so that before she could pull them free in one place they were caught in another. It was not possible to allow the dress to tear. "I in the thorny bush," she said. "Thorns, you doing your appointed work. Never want to let folks pass, no sir. Old eyes thought you was a pretty little *green* bush."

Finally, trembling all over, she stood free, and after a moment dared to stoop for her cane.

"Sun so high!" she cried, leaning back and looking, while the thick tears went over her eyes. "The time getting all gone here."

At the foot of this hill was a place where a log was laid across the creek.

"Now comes the trial," said Phoenix.

Putting her right foot out, she mounted the log and shut her eyes. Lifting her skirt, leveling her cane fiercely before her, like a festival figure in some parade, she began to march across. Then she opened her eyes and she was safe on the other side.

"I wasn't as old as I thought," she said.

But she sat down to rest. She spread her skirts on the bank around her and folded her hands over her knees. Up above her was a tree in a pearly cloud of mistletoe. She did not dare to close her eyes, and when a little boy brought her a plate with a slice of marble-cake on it she spoke to him. "That would be acceptable," she said. But when she went to take it there was just her own hand in the air.

So she left that tree, and had to go through a barbed-wire fence. There she had to creep and crawl, spreading her knees and stretching her fingers like a baby trying to climb the steps. But she talked loudly to herself: she could not let her dress be torn now, so late in the day, and she could not pay for having her arm or her leg sawed off if she got caught fast where she was.

At last she was safe through the fence and risen up out in the clearing. Big dead trees, like black men with one arm, were standing in the purple stalks of the withered cotton field. There sat a buzzard.

''Who you watching?''

In the furrow she made her way along.

''Glad this not the season for bulls,'' she said, looking sideways, ''and the good Lord made his snakes to curl up and sleep in the winter. A pleasure I don't see no two-headed snake coming around that tree, where it come once. It took a while to get by him, back in the summer.''

She passed through the old cotton and went into a field of dead corn. It whispered and shook and was taller than her head. ''Through the maze now,'' she said, for there was no path.

Then there was something tall, black, and skinny there, moving before her.

At first she took it for a man. It could have been a man dancing in the field. But she stood still and listened, and it did not make a sound. It was as silent as a ghost.

''Ghost,'' she said sharply, ''who be you the ghost of? For I have heard of nary death close by.''

But there was no answer—only the ragged dancing in the wind.

She shut her eyes, reached out her hand, and touched a sleeve. She found a coat and inside that an emptiness, cold as ice.

''You scarecrow,'' she said. Her face lighted. ''I ought to be shut up for good,'' she said with laughter. ''My senses is gone. I too old. I the oldest people I ever know. Dance, old scarecrow,'' she said, ''while I dancing with you.''

She kicked her foot over the furrow, and with mouth drawn down, shook her head once or twice in a little strutting way. Some husks blew down and whirled in streamers about her skirts.

Then she went on, parting her way from side to side with the cane, through the whispering field. At last she came to the end, to a wagon track where the silver grass blew between the red ruts. The quail were walking around like pullets, seeming all dainty and unseen.

''Walk pretty,'' she said. ''This the easy place. This the easy going.''

She followed the track, swaying through the quiet bare fields, through the little strings of trees silver in their dead leaves, past cabins silver from weather, with the doors and windows boarded shut, all like old women under a spell sitting there. "I walking in their sleep," she said, nodding her head vigorously.

In a ravine she went where a spring was silently flowing through a hollow log. Old Phoenix bent and drank. "Sweet-gum makes the water sweet," she said, and drank more. "Nobody know who made this well, for it was here when I was born."

The track crossed a swampy part where the moss hung as white as lace from every limb. "Sleep on, alligators, and blow your bubbles." Then the track went into the road.

Deep, deep the road went down between the high green-colored banks. Overhead the live-oaks met, and it was as dark as a cave.

A black dog with a lolling tongue came up out of the weeds by the ditch. She was meditating, and not ready, and when he came at her she only hit him a little with her cane. Over she went in the ditch, like a little puff of milkweed.

Down there, her senses drifted away. A dream visited her, and she reached her hand up, but nothing reached down and gave her a pull. So she lay there and presently went to talking. "Old woman," she said to herself, "that black dog come up out of the weeds to stall you off, and now there he sitting on his fine tail, smiling at you."

A white man finally came along and found her—a hunter, a young man, with his dog on a chain.

"Well, Granny!" he laughed. "What are you doing there?"

"Lying on my back like a June-bug waiting to be turned over, mister," she said, reaching up her hand.

He lifted her up, gave her a swing in the air, and set her down. "Anything broken, Granny?"

"No sir, them old dead weeds is springy enough," said Phoenix, when she had got her breath. "I thank you for your trouble."

"Where do you live, Granny?" he asked, while the two dogs were growling at each other.

"Away back yonder, sir, behind the ridge. You can't even see it from here."

"On your way home?"

"No sir, I going to town."

"Why, that's too far! That's as far as I walk when I come out myself, and I get something for my trouble." He patted the stuffed bag he carried, and there hung down a little closed claw. It was one of the bob-whites, with its beak hooked bitterly to show it was dead. "Now you go on home, Granny!"

"I bound to go to town, mister," said Phoenix. "The time come around."

He gave another laugh, filling the whole landscape. "I know you old colored people! Wouldn't miss going to town to see Santa Claus!"

But something held old Phoenix very still. The deep lines in her face went into a fierce and different radiation. Without warning, she had seen with her own eyes a flashing nickel fall out of the man's pocket onto the ground.

"How old are you, Granny?" he was saying.

"There is no telling, mister," she said, "no telling."

Then she gave a little cry and clapped her hands and said, "Git on away from here, dog! Look! Look at that dog!" She laughed as if in admiration. "He ain't scared of nobody. He a big black dog." She whispered, "Sic him!"

"Watch me get rid of that cur," said the man. "Sic him, Pete! Sic him!"

Phoenix heard the dogs fighting, and heard the man running and throwing sticks. She even heard a gunshot. But she was slowly bending forward by that time, further and further forward, the lids stretched down over her eyes, as if she were doing this in her sleep. Her chin was lowered almost to her knees. The yellow palm of her hand came out from the fold of her apron. Her fingers slid down and along the ground under the piece of money with the grace and care they would have in lifting an egg from under a setting hen. Then she slowly straightened up, she stood erect, and the nickel was in her apron pocket. A bird flew by. Her lips moved. "God watching me the whole time. I come to stealing."

The man came back, and his own dog panted about them. "Well, I scared him off that time," he said, and then he laughed and lifted his gun and pointed it at Phoenix.

She stood straight and faced him.

"Doesn't the gun scare you?" he said, still pointing it.

"No, sir, I seen plenty go off closer by, in my day, and for less than what I done," she said, holding utterly still.

He smiled, and shouldered the gun. "Well, Granny," he said, "you must be a hundred years old, and scared of nothing. I'd give you a dime if I had any money with me. But you take my advice and stay home, and nothing will happen to you.''

''I bound to go on my way mister,'' said Phoenix. She inclined her head in the red rag. Then they went in different directions, but she could hear the gun shooting again and again over the hill.

She walked on. The shadows hung from the oak trees to the road like curtains. Then she smelled wood-smoke, and smelled the river, and she saw a steeple and the cabins on their steep steps. Dozens of little black children whirled around her. There ahead was Natchez shining. Bells were ringing. She walked on.

In the paved city it was Christmas time. There were red and green electric lights strung and criss-crossed everywhere, and all turned on in the daytime. Old Phoenix would have been lost if she had not distrusted her eyesight and depended on her feet to know where to take her.

She paused quietly on the sidewalk where people were passing by. A lady came along in the crowd, carrying an armful of red-, green- and silver-wrapped presents; she gave off perfume like the red roses in hot summer, and Phoenix stopped her.

''Please, missy, will you lace up my shoe?'' She held up her foot.

''What do you want, Grandma?''

''See my shoe,'' said Phoenix. ''Do all right for out in the country, but wouldn't look right to go in a big building.''

''Stand still then, Grandma,'' said the lady. She put her packages down on the sidewalk beside her and laced and tied both shoes tightly.

''Can't lace 'em with a cane,'' said Phoenix. ''Thank you, missy. I doesn't mind asking a nice lady to tie up my shoe, when I gets out on the street.''

Moving slowly and from side to side, she went into the big building, and into a tower of steps, where she walked up and around and around until her feet knew to stop.

She entered a door, and there she saw nailed up on the wall the document that had been stamped with the gold seal and framed in the gold frame, which matched the dream that was hung up in her head.

''Here I be,'' she said. There was a fixed and ceremonial stiffness over her body.

''A charity case, I suppose,'' said an attendant who sat at the desk before her.

But Phoenix only looked above her head. There was sweat on

her face, the wrinkles in her skin shone like a bright net.

"Speak up, Grandma," the woman said. "What's your name? We must have your history, you know. Have you been here before? What seems to be the trouble with you?"

Old Phoenix only gave a twitch to her face as if a fly were bothering her.

"Are you deaf?" cried the attendant.

But then the nurse came in.

"Oh, that's just old Aunt Phoenix," she said. "She doesn't come for herself—she has a little grandson. She makes these trips just as regular as clockwork. She lives away back off the Old Natchez Trace." She bent down. "Well, Aunt Phoenix, why don't you just take a seat? We won't keep you standing after your long trip." She pointed.

The old woman sat down, bolt upright in the chair.

"Now, how is the boy?" asked the nurse.

Old Phoenix did not speak.

"I said, how is the boy?"

But Phoenix only waited and stared straight ahead, her face very solemn and withdrawn into rigidity.

"Is his throat any better?" asked the nurse. "Aunt Phoenix, don't you hear me? Is your grandson's throat any better since the last time you came for the medicine?"

With her hands on her knees, the old woman waited, silent, erect and motionless, just as if she were in armor.

"You mustn't take up our time this way, Aunt Phoenix," the nurse said. "Tell us quickly about your grandson, and get it over. He isn't dead, is he?"

At last there came a flicker and then a flame of comprehension across her face, and she spoke.

"My grandson. It was my memory had left me. There I sat and forgot why I made my long trip."

"Forgot?" The nurse frowned. "After you came so far?"

Then Phoenix was like an old woman begging a dignified forgiveness for waking up frightened in the night. "I never did go to school, I was too old at the Surrender," she said in a soft voice. "I'm an old woman without an education. It was my memory fail me. My little grandson, he is just the same, and I forgot it in the coming."

"Throat never heals, does it?" said the nurse, speaking in a loud, sure voice to old Phoenix. By now she had a card with something written on it, a little list. "Yes. Swallowed lye. When was it?—January—two-three years ago—"

Phoenix spoke unasked now. "No, missy, he not dead, he just the same. Every little while his throat begin to close up again, and he not able to swallow. He not get his breath. He not able to help himself. So the time come around, and I go on another trip for the soothing medicine."

"All right. The doctor said as long as you came to get it, you could have it," said the nurse. "But it's an obstinate case."

"My little grandson, he sit up there in the house all wrapped up, waiting by himself," Phoenix went on. "We is the only two left in the world. He suffer and it don't seem to put him back at all. He got a sweet look. He going to last. He wear a little patch quilt and peep out holding his mouth open like a little bird. I remembers so plain now. I not going to forget him again, no, the whole enduring time. I could tell him from all the others in creation."

"All right." The nurse was trying to hush her now. She brought her a bottle of medicine. "Charity," she said, making a check mark in a book.

Old Phoenix held the bottle close to her eyes, and then carefully put it into her pocket.

"I thank you," she said.

"It's Christmas time, Grandma," said the attendant. "Could I give you a few pennies out of my purse?"

"Five pennies is a nickel," said Phoenix stiffly.

"Here's a nickel," said the attendant.

Phoenix rose carefully and held out her hand. She received the nickel and then fished the other nickel out of her pocket and laid it beside the new one. She stared at her palm closely, with her head on one side.

Then she gave a tap with her cane on the floor.

"This is what come to me to do," she said. "I going to the store and buy my child a little windmill they sells, made out of paper. He going to find it hard to believe there such a thing in the world. I'll march myself back where he waiting, holding it straight up in this hand."

She lifted her free hand, gave a little nod, turned around, and walked out of the doctor's office. Then her slow step began on the stairs, going down.

848019X012